WHEN I WAS A GIRL

ROS JONES

Fisher King Publishing

When I Was A Girl

Print ISBN 978-1-914560-36-1
Digital ISBN 978-1-914560-37-8

This is a work of fiction. Names, characters, businesses, places, events and incidents are either the products of the author's imagination or used in a fictitious manner. Any resemblance to actual persons, living or dead, or actual events is purely coincidental.

Thank you for respecting the author of this work.

Fisher King Publishing
fisherkingpublishing.co.uk

To my mother,

Mary Vivian Carter,

1941-2019

and to Lynn

with love from

Ros

Acknowledgements

I am grateful to Amber Dickinson for helping me reclaim my desire to write, to Dr Charlotte Booth for guidance and encouragement, to Rick Armstrong and Fisher King Publishing for your generous faith in me, to my great friend and first reader Katie McCaw, to the many friends who cheered me on, and to Chris Gray for endless love and patience.

Part One

1964 - 1968

She was tired but he insisted on his rights.

She said no, she had to see to the babies who were crying in the next room. He slapped her hard across her face, stunning her. Breathing heavily over her, he reached down and grasped his already erect penis. She said, "God no!" and screamed. He slapped her hard again.

"Shut up, you Bitch. This is your fault. You're asking for it!"

He forced her legs apart and rubbed his dick over her. She was still raw from the birth of her last baby just five weeks before. She bit into her thumb to stop herself shrieking with pain as he rammed himself hard into her body. Dear God, I'm pregnant again, she thought, filled with shame and sorrow at her situation.

***

And so, I, the fourth daughter, chose these parents. I was a Big Fat Baby there was no doubt. 8lbs 13oz and I couldn't get out! I was around the wrong way which didn't help. My mother had been in labour at home for thirty-six hours when the doctor, having given up with his forceps and with shirtsleeves rolled up his sweaty hairy arms, he drove us both (though Big Fat Baby was still inside of course so the two appeared as one to anyone looking) to the nearest hospital which was in the next county.

No husband allowed to enter in those days. Not that he would have come if he could. There was just my mother and the Fat Baby trying to get out – or rather resisting coming out. I was stubbornly content where I was, sloshing around these last 9 months and 2½ days, completely comfortable, growing fatter every day but with an intuition that all was not well outside – so I'd rather stay where I was.

I did everything I could to stay inside, to delay that awful shocking moment when I'd have to leave the warm safe womb and be delivered beneath the bright lights of the hospital theatre, to be slapped on the rump and made to open my lungs to breathe by myself.

So, I'd turned myself around, plump bum facing south. I had my feet pressed tightly against the wall of the uterus and smugly sucked my thumb.

Because of this my mother nearly died. She would never forgive me, Big Fat Baby. She had three other babies to look after, and I nearly killed her. What might have happened?

When I was finally pulled free from between my mother's legs, with a crack of bone and a pouring and sucking of fluids, my mother felt a moment of intense hatred for me – I sensed it. "You nearly killed us both," were the first words she said to her newborn daughter.

Later that evening, home again, the vicar from the village church, who had taken an interest in this young mother's soul, arrived with a bunch of the brightest daffodils. The kind, concerned district nurse was there and let him in.

"For you both," he said to my Mother. "Happy Mother's Day! Welcome to the world, little one," he said to me, the sleeping baby. "These are a symbol of rebirth and new beginnings."

But I didn't sleep well. It turned out I'd been born with inflamed tonsils and as months went by, I coughed and cried in place of sleeping and smiling. My angry father was even more angry than usual. My mother was pregnant again though she would lose this one shortly when my father, once again, pushed her down the stairs. "Can you take her to the doctor please, David? I have these babies to look after and you're not working today."

Amazingly, he agreed.

And so, I went for my first ride in a pram. I was lying so I could look at Daddy as he took me off to the doctor's surgery. Something wasn't right. He was angry. He walked quickly, cursing, as he struggled to push the pram across the field, over the lumpy grass, then across the wooden bridge that straddled the fast-flowing brook. Daddy's hair was red – ginger! His face was red too with pent up rage. I cried miserably on and on and on.

And he cursed on and on and on.

At the surgery, the doctor put me on a bed and took off all my clothes. I cried even louder, practically screaming. My curly dark brown hair stuck to my sweaty face. The doctor listened to my heart with his cold stethoscope, felt along the sides of my throat and peered into my mouth with a little torch.

"Tonsils", he said, "I'll give you some medicine for her."

Daddy dressed me back in my clothes and back in the pram I went. Exhausted with my crying, I slept soundly all the way home, protecting myself from his anger through deep slumber.

There were other times when I was left with Daddy, me and my four sisters - since another had arrived. These were the worst times. I was deeply afraid, though I couldn't yet express the feeling, that Mummy had abandoned us to our angry father. Maybe it wasn't for long – I had no concept of time back then.

One day I looked out of the window and saw Mummy walking towards the house dragging some branches from a tree. Another time, she was gone for so long, Daddy knew he had to feed us. He gave us leftovers from the fridge and told us angrily that we had to finish every scrap. We had to be good, he said, and eat everything. Or he would be very very angry.

I quickly learned that I had to be good to avoid Daddy flying into a sudden rage. So I ate all the food in my bowl. When my sisters struggled to finish their meals, I helped keep the peace and ate their food too. Mummy laughed and said, "You're such a Fat Baby," and tickled my baby fat. My sisters called me 'Dustbin'. I don't think I minded. If I ate up all the food, no-one would get hurt.

And then one day, Daddy was out. Somewhere. With my eldest sister. Mummy told us all to sit where we were and be good. She was excited. I could sense her excitement – and also fear too. She kept disappearing and coming back into the room with bags, clothes and toys.

A big black car arrived and Mummy hurried us all out of the house.

"Get in the taxi, get in the taxi." She picked us up one at a time and put us on the back seat. "We're going on an adventure," she said as the taxi drove off, leaving Daddy and my eldest sister behind.

The taxi stopped at a garage and Mummy got out. I watched as she went over to a lorry trailer and spoke to the nice-looking man who stood there. He was smiling and looked happy. I felt safe now and pleased to be away from our angry daddy.

***

The nice-looking man was called Jim and he came to live with us and Mummy – though my eldest sister was still missing.

"She'll be back soon," said Mummy whenever we asked, 'Where's Kim?' We didn't see her in real life for eight years.

We went to live with Mummy's pretty twin sister who was called Lizzie and a man called Tommy. They had a lovely old house next to a disused airfield.

Between them, Mummy and Lizzie worked out put-me-up beds for us all.

There were lots of animals living in the big garden – dogs and cats, sheep and goats, rabbits and guinea pigs and chickens and geese. The man called Tommy was always busy in the garden. He was angry too. The beautiful black dog was a Labrador called Bella. She was Lizzie's favourite pet. Lizzie loved Bella. But Bella killed the guinea pigs.

No-one knew why but Tommy had to shoot Bella. He buried her under the tree that had snowdrops all around it. "She tasted blood," Tommy said. "She'd kill again.

That's why I had to kill her first." Tommy was very angry. We were scared of Tommy and fought and bickered amongst ourselves, pulling each other's hair and pinching each other's bare skin.

"Will you stop it?!" Mummy demanded. "Just be good!"

I was in the garden one day. I could see Tommy talking angrily to Mummy. He was holding the handles of a wheelbarrow full of manure. Suddenly he tipped up the wheelbarrow and the manure went all over Mummy's bare feet.

1968 - 1971

We didn't live with Lizzie and Tommy for very long.

We all moved into a lovely white cottage that had lots of land and was surrounded by farmers' fields and tractor lanes.

Kim was still missing – I could still remember her though. She was much taller than I was and had bunches on the side of her head. Now there was just Mummy, Jim, Louise, Melanie, Carol and me. We had a black Labrador called Ruby and then Grandfather gave us a corgi puppy called Penny. Penny had her tail chopped off and Mummy kept it in a drawer wrapped in tissue paper. We had lots of animals too: chickens and geese and ducks, rabbits and pigs. Jim had lots of pigeons.

We were free to roam the surrounding fields and lanes, making up stories of exciting adventures. One day Melanie and I walked through a field of the brightest yellow hot mustard, off to the North Pole we told Carol the youngest who we forbade from following us. When we got home, Melanie was covered with a rash, an allergic reaction to the mustard.

There was a haystack immediately behind our house with a tunnel through the middle we crawled through on our hands and knees. We climbed up the stack and took it in turns to slide down. "There are rats in there," the farmer said. "Keep out!"

We found a donkey in a field and we coaxed it over to the gate and I felt that Kim was there and helped me climb up onto its back from on top of the gate. It immediately shrugged me off and I fell over its tail, landing on the hard earth.

The field of cows was littered with cow pats. We found sticks which we dipped into the cow pats and chased each other with them.

Then we would hear the sound of the old cow bell. It was Mummy standing at our back door shaking the old bell by its wooden handle summoning us home for mealtimes.

Mummy worked so hard to make sure we had enough to eat. But mealtimes were where we argued most. My sisters refused to eat all their food. Mummy spent a long time making meals for us but I watched as my sisters said they don't like this and they don't like that. They pushed their food around the plate until Mummy gets upset and then angry that the time and money spent on the food is wasted.

"Be good and eat everything up. I worked hard to prepare this meal. Please don't make me angry. Eat up!"

I never wanted to hurt my beautiful Mummy. We couldn't get down from the table until we'd eaten everything, so I was Dustbin again and ate all the things no-one else wanted to eat – even leeks and carrots that I didn't like.

One day, Mummy called out for help in the kitchen where she was preparing our meal. It turned out that when Mummy was adding pepper , the top came off the pepper pot and we had half a pot of pepper in our cabbage. We helped to scrape some of the pepper off but we still had to eat it even though there was still a lot of pepper in the cabbage. It was very hot.

"Where's Kim?" I used to ask. Mummy always said, 'She's being looked after. She'll be back soon.'

***

I loved being good. When I was good, I would stand in front of Mummy who I adored and stretch up my arms. "I've been good, Mummy. Pick me up." And she would pick me up and hug and rock me in her arms. I felt safe and loved, I was the special one.

One day, after eating all the food no-one else would eat, I went to stand by Mummy and stretched up my arms. "Pick me up, Mummy," I pleaded. And my beautiful Mummy obligingly bent down to pick me up.

"Oh," she cried, "you're too heavy now for me to pick you up."

I felt so ashamed. I had become fat and Mummy could no longer love me. I felt quite sick with shame. I was greedy and therefore unlovable.

***

I loved wandering around by myself, away from my sisters. And so, it happened one day that I wandered into the main bedroom that Mummy and Jim shared. Jim was standing at the window watching his racing pigeons flying about in the sky above the front garden.

"What are you doing?" I asked.

"I'm watching my pigeons," he said. "Do you want to see? Come here," he said.

He picked me up and held me very close in his strong arms, hugging me to him. I liked that. It felt good to be hugged so close by his strong arms. We both looked out the window together as the pigeons flew back and forth round and round the garden. They were homing pigeons so they wouldn't go astray or get lost. They knew where their home was.

"Good to get some exercise," Jim said. He pulled my face into the warm space between his head and his shoulder with one large hand. And with the other he slipped his fingers up inside one leg of my shorts, sliding beneath my pants until he found the smooth bit that I wee from. I heard him breath in sharply as he rubbed his big fingers between my legs. It wasn't uncomfortable but I didn't like it. But I did like being held in his arms, feeling like I was being good and pleasing him. I stayed obediently still.

After a while he took his hand away and put me back on the ground.

"I'd better go and get the pigeons back home," he said. The next time I found him watching his pigeons, he crouched down beside me and pulled me close, both hands working their way up the legs of my shorts. He was struggling to get his fingers inside my pants beneath my shorts.

"Tell you what," he said in my ear, "why don't you go and take off your knickers? Put your shorts back on and come back. That way I can get to it better."

I didn't want to do that. It wasn't nice. I didn't like it. I slid out from his arms and ran out of the room.

One day, I wandered into the empty pigsty. I found Jim chopping kindling for the fire with a small axe on a block of wood. He put down the axe when he saw me.

"Hello Bess," he smiled (that was another nickname I had).

He crouched down beside me and pulled me close, rummaging in my knickers in his usual way.

"Hold this," he said and wrapped my 4-year-old fingers around what I thought was his wrist. It was hard and bony like a wrist. He rubbed away at me and I looked down and saw his wrist was red and inflamed. I closed my eyes tight and pressed my face into his chest as he rubbed and rubbed.

***

There were times of great peace when my beautiful Mummy sat us around the blazing log fire and read to us from books: fairy tales and exciting adventures. I was entranced listening to Mummy's beautiful voice as she read the story of Rapunzel, changing her voice according to which character was speaking.

Then we ate crumpets toasted over the fire with the long collapsible toasting fork, spread thickly with butter that melted into the holes and were so delicious.

And then it was off upstairs to bed.

"One, two, three, one, two, three," Mummy said

laughing, climbing the stairs behind us pretending to nip at our bottoms to hurry us along.

My bed was under the window that overlooked the back yard. I was woken by thunder and I knelt on my pillow to look out of the window. A thunderstorm was raging with rain lashing down. I saw Mummy lit up by a flash of lightning as she crossed the yard to put the animals to bed, making sure the ducks and geese and chickens and rabbits were all locked in safe from the fox that used to visit.

I felt real terror fearing that Mummy would be killed in the storm and I would be left without her.

***

I adored Mummy.

One morning I had to get out of bed to go to the toilet before it was time to get up. On my way back to bed I went to look for Mummy in her bedroom. Her door was very slightly open and as I peeped in, I saw her standing completely naked in front of her mirror brushing her hair. I had never seen her hair down before as she always wore it pinned up in a bun on her head. Now it hung down to the top of her thighs so long just like Rapunzel's hair. I was mesmerised as I watched her and then crept shyly back to bed.

***

While we were eating our tea, I needed to go to the toilet which was upstairs. Afterwards, instead of going straight back to the table downstairs, I crept into Mummy's bedroom she shared with Jim. I touched Mummy's things on the dressing table. There was a lipstick which I opened and began painting my 4-year-old lips with.

Suddenly I heard Mummy calling me. I instinctively ran to the bathroom, grabbed my flannel to rub off the guilty colour.

"What are you doing, Bessie?" Mummy caught me by my shoulders and turned my face to her. "What… ?" she looked amused. She led me back to her bedroom.

"You should have asked if you wanted some lipstick on," she said and gently applied the gorgeous pink to my mouth before leading me back to the tea table.

My sisters looked at me but said nothing. I felt a mixture of pride and shame at being caught being sneaky.

***

I suddenly realised I was alone. Everyone had gone. Where had everyone gone? Why had they left me? The usual babble we made as a family of four noisy argumentative sisters was still.

I panicked.

I wandered from empty room to empty room searching for my family. Finally, I pushed open the door of Mummy's bedroom. There they were! I felt so relieved. They were all gathered around the small table in the corner passing a pen between them, Mummy and my three sisters.

All eyes turned to me standing in the doorway, hand

clutching the handle.

"Who asked you to come in?" Mummy snarled at me.

I could see that they had been taking it in turn to write in a card. I wasn't supposed to be there. I turned around and went back to my bedroom feeling guilty that I'd come across them all signing their names in a birthday card for me. They'd been keeping it as a surprise.

The next day was my fifth birthday and I was given the card Mummy, Jim and all my sisters had signed except Kim because she was somewhere else, being looked after. The picture was of a collection of toys with a lovely big teddy bear in a dark blue jumper.

I was also given a doll as a present. It had a plastic curl on its head and when I turned it over, she said "Mama". I liked turning her over to make her speak to me like that. I called her 'Fat Baby', my special doll.

***

One day the three of us were in the kitchen with Mummy. It was a long narrow room. Mummy was washing up at the sink while we scrabbled behind her, pushing and bickering.

Suddenly Mummy, who was so lovely and calm, turned around from the sink, her hands and forearms red from the hot water and covered in soapsuds.

"Stop that, or I'll bang your heads together," she snapped.

I pushed my sister and Mummy was true to her word: she got our heads in her hands and banged them together.

She'd never hit us before.

We were momentarily stunned into silence. And then the pain of bone on bone, skull on skull set in and we rubbed our heads instinctively as we left the room in shock.

***

We were invited to go and visit our grandfather. We were excited to be going on an adventure. Grandfather was Mummy's father. Mummy's mummy had died a few years earlier and Grandfather was now married to Auntie Megan. He lived in a really big old house with a huge garden.

We had to wash our faces and put on a dress and wear long white socks.

On the journey there in our Humber car, Jim told us that we had be good when we were at Grandfather's house – no bickering. No talking. We had to be on our best behaviour.

When we got to grandfather's house, Auntie Megan had made us jelly which she had mixed up so it looked like amber crystals. When we had jelly at home it was smooth. I liked Auntie Megan's jelly best.

We had to sit around a table in the huge hallway to eat our dinner. Grandfather, Auntie Megan, Mummy and Jim ate in the dining room.

Sometimes, Mummy or Jim would come and look at us to make sure we were eating our food and behaving. When they went back into the dining room, we took it in turns to chase around the table. It was funny. We all laughed because we hadn't been caught misbehaving.

The jelly was the thing I liked best.

I was really good and well behaved. Louise and Melanie started arguing when we were playing with the games that were in the big wooden chest in the hallway. The grown-ups were in the sitting room talking but Mummy must have heard them bickering and came out to tell us off and to be quiet and good. We all got into trouble even though I'd been trying to be good.

I found a thread hanging from my long white socks and showed it to Megan. She said she would cut it off. She found some scissors in the kitchen drawer and snipped off the loose thread. A big hole appeared in my sock.

"Oh dear," she said.

"It doesn't matter," I said although I knew I'd get into trouble for making a hole in my new socks.

It was really late when we left Grandfather's house. On our way home in the car, Jim was cross with us for not behaving nicely.

Mummy found the hole in my sock and sewed it up. She always had a huge basket of clothes that needed sewing. She gave me the sock back all mended and told me to be more careful with my best clothes. I promised her I would. I didn't tell her it was Auntie Megan who made the hole. Mummy didn't like tell-tales. I felt relieved I didn't get into trouble.

***

Mummy was knitting a blue and orange stripey thing.

"What are you making?" I asked shyly. "A little dress," she said, needles clicking.

"Who is it for?" I asked, snuggling into her.

"A little girl I know," she said.

"What's her name?"

She paused a moment and said, "Annabelle".

"Annabelle," I repeated. "That's a nice name."

And then Mummy presented me with Annabelle's new clothes: a dress, a cape and a hat, all blue and orange stripes. They were for my Fat Baby doll.

"Thank you, Mummy!"

I renamed my precious doll Annabelle as I dressed her in her new clothes. As I turned her over, she said, "Mama!"

***

I was very shy. Apart from Mummy, I didn't like to speak with adults in case I wasn't good and said something wrong.

I was allowed to go to school when I was just four. There were two classrooms, one for younger children where I was. Our teacher was Mrs Field. The other class was for older children where my two older sisters went. The teacher was Mr Watson. He was also the headteacher. My youngest sister, Carol, stayed at home with Mummy. I was very quick at learning and could read and write almost at once. When I wrote in my book, I did as Mrs Field said we should and put one finger between each word I wrote which made a pattern on the page. It felt nice to be told that I was good and clever and coming along nicely.

We were allowed to listen to 'Listen With Mother' on the big radio. I was allowed to put the plug of the radio into the wall socket. Once I pulled the cable by accident and the radio fell over. Mrs Field slapped my bare legs which stung a lot. After that I didn't want to put the plug into the socket in case I got slapped again.

One day we were playing in the playground and it was time to go back inside. I fell on the steps that went from the playground up to the school building and there was a lot of blood running down my face and over my hands. I started to scream. I saw Kim my eldest sister looking back at me as she was about to go inside even though I knew it wasn't really her. She was being looked after. I saw her start to cry. Her face went all red.

Mr Watson came running and scooped me up and took me inside and put me on the sick bed. Mummy came and I went to the doctor's surgery. I didn't tell Mummy that I'd seen Kim. The doctor put stitches in where I had split my head open. I had a bandage wound all around my head which looked silly.

When I went back to school everyone said I was a brave little soldier.

When it was my birthday, I had a present from Mrs Field. It was a beautiful book of fairy tales with pictures to colour in. The cover of the book was all shiny and white. It was a lovely present. Mummy said Mrs Field had given it to me because she liked me very much and I had to be sure to say thank you to her.

When it was home time, I went up to Mrs Field's desk to say thank you as Mummy had told me. There were lots of other children in front of me as we queued up to speak with her. I saw Mrs Field see me in the queue. I waited and waited and got more afraid of what I was going to say to her. After a while I just went home. Then I felt really bad for not saying thank you to Mrs Field for her kind present.

***

Kim taught me to ride a two-wheeled bicycle.

Even though I knew she wasn't really there, I could feel her pushing the bike for me along the lane leading to our house, then give it a great shove. I didn't know I had to turn the pedals and fell over into the ditch which was full of stinging nettles.

"I have to let go of you and then you're supposed to turn the pedals," Kim laughed.

I found some dock leaves to rub into the nettle stings on my bare legs. Then she was gone again.

We went to the dentist in a nearby town. The dentist was Mr Sharp and he whistled while he looked in our mouth at our teeth.

Kim didn't like the dentist. When it was her turn to go into the dentist's surgery, she wedged herself in the doorway with her hands and feet pressed into the edges of the open doorway making a cross with her body. I felt really sorry for her even though I knew she wasn't really there because she was being looked after somewhere else. I watched as Mummy had to prise her hands away.

When it was my turn, Mr Sharp said I had too many teeth and would have to have an extraction. I would have to come back for that.

I asked Mummy why Kim didn't like the dentist and Mummy had to prise her fingers off the door. She looked at me oddly. "You're a strange thing, Bessie, the stories you make up."

When the day came for my extraction, I was quite excited. The doctor was there too. He had to give me gas. I sat in the chair and the doctor put a black rubber mask over my mouth and nose. It smelled horrible. I went to sleep.

When I woke up I was lying on the back seat of our Humber car all by myself. I looked out of the window and could see a long brick wall with a maroon-coloured wooden gate. I lay looking at it for ages.

Then Mummy and Jim got into the car and told me we

were moving into this house in a place called the Fens.

It turned out that our Granny who I'd never met had left Mummy a lot of money in her Will. Auntie Megan had found the perfect home for us and Mummy could buy it with the money from Granny.

At last, we had our very own house.

***

Mummy took me to my new school. My teacher was Miss Taylor. Miss Taylor and Mummy talked for a while. And then Mummy went. Miss Taylor took me to a chair at a table where other children were painting. Mummy was gone.

I cried and cried and put my head into my arms and cried.

When I stopped crying, Miss Taylor came and asked me to read to her. I could see she was surprised at how many words I could read.

***

Our new house had three floors. I shared a bedroom with Melanie. When I was in my bed, I could see along the hallway to the attic stairway. We had two playrooms in the attic where we could play dressing up.

Miss Black lived in the house next door. She was a retired headteacher and lived alone in her huge house. We were friends with Miss Black. She let us play in her house. Her house was much more old-fashioned than ours. When you went to the toilet you had to pull a chain and there was a sack above your head.

Miss Black liked to eat peanut cracknel and always had a white paper bag of them that she bought from the sweetshop at the top of our road.

Miss Black loved us all, especially Mummy. She had been lonely for a long time and loved it when we all moved in next door to her. She used to tap on her kitchen wall and Mummy would tap back that meant yes, please come round and have a cup of tea. Miss Black would sit in the rocking chair in the corner and talk with Mummy while we sat at the table and ate sandwiches with Marmite or sandwich spread or jam.

Miss Black said Mummy was like the daughter she'd never had.

One day when we went next door to see Miss Black there was a man there doing something with her television set. Mummy was talking to the man. They were laughing together. His name was Charlie. He was very funny. His job was mending televisions with something called valves.

***

We had a tiny front garden and a long thin back garden. All the animals we used to have had gone except our dogs Ruby and Penny.

There was a path and a flower bed that Mummy filled with flowers. And there was a pigeon loft for Jim to keep his pigeons. He made the loft out of wood. When I went in there, I could smell the wood. And there was sawdust everywhere.

Jim said I could have some sawdust as bedding for my pretend pets. He said he liked it when I went to see him in the pigeon loft. I didn't go to see him but to play with my imaginary pets – rabbits and hamsters. I gave them water which I spilt over the sawdust to pretend they'd had a wee. Then I had to clean out the wet sawdust for them and add fresh sawdust.

Then Jim held me close to him so I couldn't move and rubbed me inside my knickers. I ran out.

I stopped looking after my pretend animals.

***

I was a good reader and at school Miss Taylor asked me to sit in front of the blackboard and hold up cards with words on them. All the other children in the classroom had to say what the word was. Miss Taylor sat at her desk working on something else while I held up the cards for the children. I liked to do that. I decided that I wanted to be a teacher when I was a grown-up.

At Christmas time I got the biggest present. It was enormous and on top was a very small present. I opened the small present first. It was a box with ten sticks of white chalk inside. The big present was a blackboard on an easel. It was my favourite Christmas present.

I started to teach Annabelle and my other toys things I learned at school. They all sat on my bed while I stood at my blackboard teaching them. I loved playing schools in my bedroom and stopped playing pretend pets in the pigeon loft.

***

One day when Jim was out, Charlie came to our house. He had a Morris Traveller car and we all got in it and drove a long way away to a place called Boston that had a big fairground. Charlie paid for us all to go on lots of fairground rides like the Helter Skelter, bumper cars and the carousel with beautiful horses. We ate candy floss and hot dogs. Charlie was so funny. He and Mummy held hands and laughed a lot.

It was dark when we got home and we went straight upstairs to bed.

Jim moved out of our house and Charlie came to visit us more and more. He had his own rented house in a town nearby and had lots of children. They were a lot older than us. Some of them came to see us. There were two boys called teenagers and an older girl.

Miss Black came round too.

The older girl was called Jean. I told her that I didn't like it when Jim rubbed inside my knickers. I told her all the things he used to do.

"That wasn't his wrist," she said, when I told her about the pigsty, "That was his penis! Jeez!"

She said I had to tell Mummy but I didn't want to. I was frightened and felt bad. Jean held my hand and took me into the sitting room where Mummy was with Charlie and Miss Black.

"Tell them what you told me, Bess," Jeannette said.

I told the grown-ups what Jim had done. They made me repeat all the details like the time I was in the pigsty at our old house. I felt my face going very red. I was very embarrassed talking to the grown-ups.

It turned out he'd done the same kind of things to Melanie and Carol too. None of us had told tales though.

***

We were all watching television in the sitting room. The doorbell rang. "I'll go," I said and ran to the front door. I thought it might be Kim, come home to us. I felt very excited and shy. But Jim was there.

"Hello, Bess," he smiled. I felt sick with shame that I had told the grown-ups about him and backed away from the door.

"It's Jim," I told Mummy.

He left Christmas presents for us all. Mine was a tub of Stickle Bricks which he knew I loved to play with.

***

Mummy called us all into the kitchen. Charlie was there. He had his arm around Mummy's shoulder. She looked very happy. Mummy said she had something to tell us. She and Charlie were going to get married and Charlie would come to live with us now that Jim had gone.

Mummy looked at each of us to see how we felt about it. I was excited. I was shy of Charlie but he was kind and funny and loved Mummy.

"I'd give the world to your mother if I could," Charlie

said.

I plucked up my courage and went over to Charlie and put my arms around his tummy. It was a big tummy and there was a ledge on top where I leaned my arms and then put my head on my arm. "You've got a ledge," I said and Charlie laughed.

The wedding day was booked for 10th June. It would be at a Baptist Church where you were allowed to be married even if you'd been married before. Charlie had been married twice. His first wife was the mother to all his children. She died of illness. His second wife was horrible to Charlie's younger children and used to hit them with a wooden spoon.

Charlie wanted us all to meet his mother. She lived by herself in London. So we all squashed into the back of his Morris Traveller with the back seat down. We were like sardines, Mummy said. It was a long journey.

Charlie's mother lived in a flat on the ground floor of a two-storey building. She came out to meet us. She was very old and very small with white wispy hair and a wrinkly face. She wore an apron and fluffy slippers. She hugged Charlie and then hugged Mummy. She looked like she loved Mummy already.

Then she tried to guess our names. Charlie must have told her our names because she knew them all but she didn't guess right. I was taller than Melanie who was older than me so she thought I was Melanie. We all laughed and she laughed too. She stood in the doorway looking at us with delight, smoking a cigarette. As she breathed out her smoke, she said, “Hey! Innit good!” and gave Charlie another hug.

I wished Kim was there so we could smile together.

Some of Charlie’s sisters and their husbands came to meet us too. Charlie had nine sisters and brothers altogether. His father was dead though.

Charlie’s mum made us a huge tea of ham sandwiches, cakes and pies. Then we went to play outside where there was some grass. And then we went home again in Charlie’s Morris Traveller. It felt like a wonderful adventure.

Every night when we were in bed, Mummy would come and see each of us to kiss us goodnight and make sure we were tucked in properly. That night when we came back from our trip to London Charlie came with her to say goodnight to us. I felt very happy.

***

Now that we were all at school, Mummy was able to go out to work. She said she wanted to train as a nurse. Instead, she got a job at a factory where they packed vegetables like carrots, onions and potatoes.

One of the ladies who worked with Mummy lent her a dress that belonged to her daughter for me to wear at Mummy’s wedding. We were the same size. It was a beautiful dress with white puffy sleeves that fit tight at my wrists. The skirt part of the dress was red tartan and it had a wide red belt. I felt lovely in the dress even though it wasn’t mine.

Mummy had a cream suit and a big greeny/blue hat. Miss Black helped her choose her outfit.

All of Charlie's huge family came to the wedding. There were so many of them and they spread out in our sitting room, dining room and our kitchen. My job was to go around everyone with plates of things for them to eat while they talked to each other.

There was no-one from Mummy's family at the wedding except us, my three sisters and me (Kim didn't turn up like I thought she might). Grandfather sent her a letter.

Mummy and Charlie went away for a weekend as their honeymoon. Miss Black came round to make sure we were good. We stayed up extra late. Melanie and I wondered whether we would call Charlie 'Dad' now.

They came back late after we had all gone to bed. Charlie came into the bedroom I shared with Melanie.

"Night, night, Bess," he said to me. I was still wondering what to call him. I was shy and embarrassed. Then I said, "Night, night, Dad". I could tell he was pleased and he kissed my forehead and patted my arm.

Our house had no heating except coal fires and the Aga in the kitchen. There was also a paraffin stove on the landing of the attics to warm it up a bit. From where I slept in my bedroom, I could see the blue glow of the paraffin stove at the top of the wooden stairs going up to the attics. I loved to lie there watching the blue flame.

***

On Sundays Mummy always cooked us breakfast. Usually, we ate Rice Krispies or cornflakes and toast. On Sundays we had a cooked breakfast. We could have whatever we wanted. I always chose fried eggs and tomatoes. That was my favourite.

After breakfast we all walked to Sunday School. Mummy wasn't religious but she wanted us to go so she could have the house to herself and do all the jobs, she said. She changed all the beds, cleaned the house, did all the washing and made a huge Sunday lunch with loads of lovely puddings to choose from.

She would line up five 2p coins on the kitchen dresser for us to take 2p each for the Sunday School collection. Sunday School was at a Methodist Chapel. One of our school teachers who went there had suggested it to Mummy.

We would sit in the Chapel for a while with all the grown-ups. We sang hymns and said a prayer. And then the collection plate came around. We felt embarrassed we only had 2p to put in among the one and five pound notes the older people in the congregation had given. We covered our 2ps with the pound notes and quickly passed the plate on.

Before the vicar began his sermon all the children would leave to go to the room next door where we learned about Jesus, sang more songs and said more prayers. We had to close our eyes when we were praying or we'd be told off.

Then we walked home to play for a while until lunch

was ready.

One Sunday when we got home to our front gate, I found a small cream coloured teddy bear on the pavement. He had a lovely wet looking nose and a red felt mouth. Around his neck was a label that said 'I am Teddy Hayes' but there was no address to say where he lived. A baby must have thrown him out of its pram as they went past our gate. I decided to look after Teddy Hayes and keep him for myself.

On the first Sunday lunch after Mummy and Dad came back from their honeymoon, everything changed.

Dad was sitting at his new place at the head of our table.

When we'd finished eating all our puddings, I said, "Can I get down please?" as we'd been taught to do.

Dad said, "No. I've got something to say."

We all looked at him. Mummy sat quietly beside him, looking happy.

"There are going to be some changes now that I'm here to look out for your mother," Dad said. "First of all, there'll be no talking at meal times. I'm fed up with your constant bickering. Children," he said, looking at each of us in turn, "should be seen but not heard."

I looked down at Teddy Hayes who was sitting on my lap, not saying a word.

"Next," Dad continued, "you will all start pulling your weight. Your mother works so hard for you and none of you help her. You are killing her."

I looked at Mummy quickly, sucking in air. She looked

lovely. How were we killing her? I felt tears coming immediately to my eyes and looked down again, blinking them away.

"From now on," Dad continued, "you'll all do jobs around the house. No shirking! And some things have got to stop. There'll be no more cooked Sunday breakfasts. Your mother spoils you."

"Oh, Charlie," Mummy said, rubbing his arm.

"No, Evelyn," he said to her. "This has got to change. You spoil them. When I was their age, I was helping my father carry sacks of coal. I helped my mum constantly. There'll be a job rota and I expect you all to do it. Emptying the fireplace, cleaning the toilet, the stairs, you'll each have a room you're responsible for.

"And another thing! There'll be no talking about what goes on in this house. I've already had things come back to me from what people have heard."

We all looked at each other. What was there to tell? Who had told tales? Maybe it was about Kim. I could feel her near me but I never told anyone. Perhaps someone else had.

He went on and on, about how much he loved Mummy and how our laziness was killing her and how he would be making big changes. We all stared at our empty plates. I stroked Teddy Hayes' rough fur.

That night while I was trying to go to sleep, I cried quietly into my pillow so Melanie couldn't hear me. Mummy was dying and it was our fault. We were killing her! I decided that I would help her more to do housework.

Mummy came to say goodnight. "What's wrong, Bessie?" she asked feeling the tears on my face.

"What happens when you die?" I asked her. I couldn't imagine not being alive. The idea of being dead was suddenly terrifying. What would happen to Mummy if we killed her? What if I died too? What would it be like?

"I don't know," she said. "You are a funny thing." She kissed my head.

That night, I woke up with a sob from a nightmare. I instinctively looked for the comfort of the blue glow from the paraffin stove. And then with a sharp intake of breath, I saw Kim standing on Melanie's bed.

No, it was Melanie. She was asleep but standing on her pillow. I stared into the darkness at her shape which didn't move. Finally, I closed my eyes, buried my head in my pillow and went back to sleep.

***

At school my teacher smiled and said, "I heard you had celebrations at your house." I wasn't sure what she meant.

"The wedding?" she asked.

"Oh, yes, Mummy got married to Charlie," I said.

Now that Mummy was married, we had to pay for our school dinners. Every Monday morning, Mummy laid out four 50ps and four 10ps and we took the money to school to pay for our school dinners.

***

After every Sunday lunch, Dad would make a speech about new changes he wanted to see. We needed to make some 'economies' he said. Times were tough. We wouldn't be eating Anchor butter anymore. In his family they made do with Stork margarine. That was good enough.

Serving custard from a jug was wasteful he said. Serve it straight from the pan. Then you don't waste any.

One day at the end of his Sunday speech, Dad showed us a stick. It was around 2 inches wide and 2 feet long. If we were bad, he said, he would use this stick on us. If we were good, we'd get some pocket money. This week Melanie had helped him and so she could have some pocket money. He took a 10p piece from his trouser pocket and pushed it towards Melanie with the stick. As she went to reach for it, he lifted the stick and slapped her hand with it. He laughed.

He had seen me emptying the sitting room fire grate and I was given 10p too but he didn't slap my hand with the stick.

The following week, at the end of our Sunday meal, Dad looked very serious. Somebody had been talking about the family to other people, he told us. He had found out it was Louise. Louise had to be taught a lesson. When he was a boy, he said, his father used to take his belt to them if they misbehaved.

He stood up and took his belt out of his trousers.

"Come next door," he said to my sister. Louise didn't move. She looked terrified. Mummy didn't say anything.

She looked at her hands on the dining table.

"C'mon, Louise. Next door!" Dad got up really angry and grabbed Louise from her chair. He pushed her out of the door and we heard him shoving her into the dining room next door. Louise screamed. Then we heard "Whack! Whack! Whack!" She screamed some more and we heard her go running up the stairs. We sat in frozen fear listening, thanking Jesus it wasn't us.

Dad came back into the room, adjusting his belt in his trousers.

"Let that be an example to the lot of you," he said smoothing back his hair.

"Pass your plates," Mummy said, sighing. She didn't look at us.

***

In my head, my eldest sister, Kim, said to me, "Are you coming to Beauties tonight?"

"What's 'Beauties'?" I asked her.

I was a bit in awe of my eldest sister. She would be five years older than me and in my head she had friends who wore bras and talked about boyfriends and pop stars. Sometimes they came to tea.

We made our own tea when we got in from school. Mummy and Dad would not be home but we kept our back door key under a flower pot and could let ourselves into the house and make tea together.

We spread Stock margarine on a pile of bread and put it in the middle of the kitchen table. Then we found all sorts of things to make sandwiches with the bread: we cut Dairylea cheese triangles in half, we had Marmite, jam, sandwich spread, fish paste in a jar, peanut butter, golden syrup, slices of cheese with Branston pickle, sliced tomatoes with Heinz salad cream. Sometimes we ate mashed up banana with sugar in our sandwiches.

We made tea in a teapot with a tea cosy to keep it warm. And we finished our tea with 'cakieway'. "What's for cakieway?" we asked when we were stuffed with sandwiches. We rummaged around. It could be half a dozen iced gem biscuits or a slice of chocolate or raspberry Swiss roll.

"Well, are you coming to Beauties?" I distinctly heard her ask again. "It's a club. Donny Osmond's there and David Essex."

"I'll come to Beauties," I said. "How do you get there?"

"You just go to sleep and dream," she said.

That night I dreamed of Beauties.

The next day, as I caught sight of her out of the corner of my eye, I told her shyly, "I saw you at Beauties last night. You looked so lovely!"

***

Melanie had a friend called Lizzie whose dad was a bank manager. They had a lovely house at the top of our road. Lizzie's mum was a nurse and Lizzie had a brother and a sister who were grown up and had left home. They had tennis courts in their garden. We weren't supposed to go to their house – Lizzie said her parents didn't approve of us – but Lizzie let us in a side gate so we could play in the big garden.

"I had tea with Donny Osmond at Beauties last night," I told her.

"You're a liar," she said.

I wasn't.

***

Penny-Ann and James Cousins lived across the road from us. Penny-Ann was the same age as my youngest sister Carol and James was the same age as Melanie. They were very rich and went to boarding school. Their dad was a builder but their mum didn't go out to work. They had a swimming pool in their garden.

We went to play with Penny-Ann. She had beautiful toys and I showed her how to play schools with her dolls and teddy bears. Her mum made us a drink of Ovaltine with hot milk.

We weren't allowed to swim in their pool but they didn't tell us why. I was a really good swimmer. Penny-Ann told us she wasn't allowed to play with us anymore, her parents didn't approve of us.

We made light signals like Morse Code to each other at night from our bedroom windows. We could see James Cousins' bedroom window from ours. Melanie used the light from her toy slide projector that she got for Christmas and James and Penny-Ann used a torch.

When we had power cuts, Penny-Ann and James told

us they had a generator in their house so they still had lights. We had to go to bed with a small candle stuck in an aerosol lid.

***

I needed a brace to correct my teeth. My incisors were too high and needed to be pulled down so I had a brace fitted. I didn't want people at school to know that I had to wear a brace and so I always covered my mouth with my hand when I spoke.

One day I laughed out loud and forgot to cover my mouth. Someone saw the wire in my mouth and started jeering, "She's wearing a brace!" he sneered and others joined in and started to laugh.

My teacher, Mrs Marks, knew I had a brace but she said, "No she's not. Don't be silly."

Mrs Marks lent me some of her books to read.

We were learning all about graphs and one of the class graphs was to show all of our weights. We all had to line up to be weighed on the scales so our weights could be plotted on the graph.

I knew I was fat and would stand out on the graph. I didn't know how I could lose weight quickly enough not to stand out. But, before it got to me being weighed, Mrs Marks moved on to a new project.

I was relieved.

***

I went swimming at our local swimming pool every

Saturday morning with my friend, Timmy.

Timmy lived around the corner from us. I would knock on his back door to collect him on my way to the swimming pool and he would come out with his swimming stuff and we walked together to the pool.

Timmy had been born in Uganda in Africa. His parents were very beautiful and tall and were both maths teachers at the high school. I liked them very much. Dad called Timmy a jungle bunny when he came round to our house. Timmy was scared of Dad.

Timmy had lots of toy cars we used to play with in his bedroom or outside on his lawn sometimes if it was hot. His mum used to sunbathe with no top on.

Timmy was very clever. But I was cleverer than he was. I came top of our class in our end of year exams.

Mrs Marks gave me my school report addressed to Mr and Mrs Woods, Dad and Mummy. I gave it to them when I got home and waited to see what was inside. They didn't tell me. At last I asked Mummy what my school report said. She looked at Dad. He said, "We don't think you should see it. You'll get big headed."

"Please," I asked and started to cry.

He passed it to me. I had come first in class again and Mrs Marks gave me 'A' for everything. At the bottom she wrote, 'Elizabeth is a very intelligent girl and, knowing this, will often settle for less than her best."

I felt really pleased that she thought I was intelligent; I decided I wasn't sure what the rest meant.

***

That summer they tarmacked our road and put stone chips on the top. I went everywhere with bare feet. So did Timmy. But that was because he was a jungle bunny, Dad said. Sometimes I didn't know whether Dad was funny or cross. He had a little tremble around his mouth when he was joking but you had to look carefully to see it.

I walked round to Timmy's house in bare feet. The stone chips really hurt my feet. I had a new dress on. It was a hand-me-down from one of Mummy's friends whose own daughter had outgrown it. It had a very low-cut neckline and my chest was cold and goose-pimpled. Timmy's mum looked at me and said "Aren't you cold in that?" She placed her hand on my chest to see how cold I was.

Timmy and I went out in the road to play. He had bare feet too.

"Do your feet hurt on this new road?" I asked.

"No," he said.

"Neither do mine," I agreed, refusing to let him know my feet hurt.

"Don't you have any shoes?" the man asked at the corner shop when I went in to buy Miss Black's peanut crunch sweets. I gave him the coins Miss Black had entrusted to me and picked up the bag.

Before we went back to school in September, Mummy took us all to Hilton's Shoe Shop to get new shoes. We had our feet measured and then could choose a pair of shoes for school. My feet had been size 3 the year before. This year they were size 7, I had grown so much. The shoes Mummy chose looked enormous on my feet.

***

My best friend was Abigail Noble. She had a brother and sister who were grown up and left home. Her parents were teachers. They were old.

Abigail had a birthday party and I was invited.

We had a huge party tea and Abigail blew all her 9 candles out on her cake in one go. She made a wish with her eyes shut. Then we all sang "Happy Birthday to you!" We played lots of games like pass the parcel, musical chairs and statues. I won three prizes. Abigail's mum said I should let someone else win but I didn't want to. I liked to win.

We each had a goody bag of sweets to take home too. I remembered what Mummy had told me and said "Thank you for having me, Mrs Noble," to Abigail's mum.

We were never allowed to have a birthday party like that at home. Dad said he didn't want people noseying around our house. We were allowed to invite a friend around if we got permission from Mummy and Dad first. But we had to promise to be good. I imagined they didn't want anyone in to see Kim.

After Mummy and Dad got married we got a brand new car. It was a silver Toyota Corona estate car. People who lived along our road saw it in our driveway and made comments about having a Japanese car.

It was nice to have room for us all rather than in Dad's old Morris Traveller where we were like sardines.

We went on holiday in our new car all the way to Scotland. It was our very first holiday and we went away for two whole weeks camping. We had two tents: an old white tent that Auntie Megan had given to Mummy and a huge orange and blue tent. Mummy and Dad slept in the white tent. And the rest of us slept in the big tent.

Everything was packed in a trailer towed behind our new car. It was a very long drive and we stopped overnight in a lay-by, trying to sleep where we sat in the car. It was a horrible night. I was very uncomfortable and cramped.

But then as we drove on there were lots of mountains all around. It was very grand scenery that made me a bit dizzy at first. Where we lived it was very flat so it was very different but beautiful.

We put our tents up at last beside a river in the middle of nowhere on land that was owned by the Forestry Commission. We were allowed to camp there as long as we kept Ruby and Penny on the lead. There was bracken everywhere and mountains all around covered in pine trees. It was a very beautiful place and smelled of earth and pine.

We swam in the river and made up games to play. Every day we would leave the tents and go out in our new car visiting places. We had to walk up mountains for miles and miles. We would get to the top and find that it wasn't the top – the top was further off.

We spread our rugs and laid out our picnic and rested for a while before walking back down the mountain. There were flies everywhere which pestered us constantly and bit us all over the backs of our bare legs.

Mummy and Dad loved Scotland. They loved the scenery with the mountains, rivers and waterfalls. My sisters and I liked it a bit and loved to play in the river but we did get fed up walking up mountains.

One day when it was really hot, I was walking with Kim. No-one else could see her, I knew. But I took her hand and we walked on like that, hand in hand, for a long time. It felt really nice to hold her hand. But our hands got sweaty and slippery. We got to a gate we had to open. Kim took her hand out of mine to open the gate and laughed. "Finally, I found a reason to let go of you," she said. We carried on walking, our hands to ourselves. And then she disappeared again.

The best thing about being on holiday was that Dad was happy and relaxed and didn't tell us off or hit us with his belt. He liked to lie on a blanket with Mummy in the sunshine.

When we got home, we each got a present as a reminder of our holiday. It was a souvenir, Mummy said. Mine was Jock the Rock which was a little felt fairy man in a kilt on a spring. He rocked when I touched him. I said, "Thank you for taking us on holiday, Dad". He liked it when I said that.

At Sunday School they were pleased to have us back.

The four of us made up most of the Sunday School. We all had gnat bites all over the backs of our legs. "Whatever happened to you?" they asked.

***

We went to Grandfather's house every Boxing Day. Father Christmas would appear from Grandfather's study and present us each with a gift. It was usually a colouring book and new felt pens which I loved.

I would sit in the corner with my sisters telling them stories I made up while the grown-ups all talked about serious things.

We had to wash our hands before sitting down to dinner and be on our best behaviour while we sat round the table in the hallway and the grown-ups were in the dining room.

***

The next year we got a touring caravan and went back to the same place for our two weeks' holiday. Mummy and Dad slept in the caravan while we all slept in the orange and blue tent.

When we got back from our holiday, Dad inspected our bedrooms. Melanie and I were told to tidy up our room. We didn't want to do it and were grumpy. We started bickering and I shook my dusty duster over her eiderdown. Then she came over to my bed and shook her duster over mine. We started flicking each other with our dusters. We were called downstairs.

"What's going on?" Dad demanded.

"She started it!" Melanie yelled at me.

Dad got his stick and whipped us both over the hands with it. "Go back to your room and make sure it's clean and tidy," he shouted at us.

We ran back up the stairs laughing. We two were really as thick as thieves.

My youngest sister, Carol, had her own bedroom. It was the smallest bedroom. She wanted to play with Melanie and me in our room. We made a camp out of the clothes horse and blankets and tried to sleep in it. It was very uncomfortable so we got back into our own beds. Carol wanted to play in our camp too.

We told her she smelled funny and couldn't come in. We locked her out of our bedroom by taking off the door handle which was loose. She went to tell Mummy and Mummy told Dad and Dad yelled at us and told Melanie and me that we were too close and would have to be split up into different bedrooms if we weren't nicer to Carol.

***

Every Summer, Grandfather and Auntie Megan held a garden fête in their huge garden. People from the village would turn up and we would go too. It was fun: there was a Maypole, people played croquet and bowls and would smash old crockery hanging from a piece of string by throwing stones at it. Mummy said that was a terrible waste.

Auntie Megan organised races for children: sack races,

egg and spoon races and three-legged races.

I told a girl from the village that this was my Grandfather's house but she didn't believe me.

Auntie Megan died suddenly of a heart attack. She had suffered with something called angina and just suddenly died. It was very sad. I really liked Auntie Megan. Now Grandfather lived all by himself in his huge house and there were no more garden fêtes.

***

One day Melanie and I let Carol play with us in the garden. We were playing 'it'. One of us was It and we had to touch another person before they reached 'Home' so that they would be It. Home was the French door into the dining room.

Carol ran for Home, hit the French door and broke the glass, cutting her hand, her wrist and all the way up to her elbow.

There was blood everywhere and Carol was screaming. Carol had to go to the doctors to have stitches.

Melanie and I felt really bad even though it wasn't our fault.

I stamped on a beetle, then I felt really guilty that I'd killed it. I put it in a matchbox and buried it in the garden and said The Lord's Prayer as a funeral for it.

***

Dad had got a job as a fruit and vegetable quality control inspector with an American company that had shops in

England and Scotland. Dad had to go to the packing factories like the one Mummy worked at and check on the quality of the vegetables they were packing for the shops.

Dad's work had a big office in a place called Cambuslang in Scotland and Dad had to go there a lot. He would be away for days. We loved it when he was away. We gave our soft toys to Mummy so she wouldn't be lonely at night time, alone in her bedroom.

Mummy played records she loved which she couldn't play when Dad was at home because he didn't like it. She played songs by Gene Pitney and Simon and Garfunkel while she did the ironing. She played them over and over again and I learned all the words and would sing along.

***

The only thing I had as a reminder of my real Daddy was a wooden cot he'd made me for my dolls. Mummy must have got it for me, I didn't know how. I didn't remember him giving it to me. I only remembered his violence but maybe that was because Mummy used to talk about it.

Apparently, all of us (except me; I was the odd one out) took after Daddy – they had his ginger colour in their hair – and when they were angry and shouting, Mummy would snap in exasperation, "You're just like your father!"

The cot was perfect for Annabelle and she lay in it beside my bed as I lay looking at the blue glow from the paraffin stove before heading off to dream at Beauties.

I sometimes had nightmares too and had the same

nightmare every night where a thing appeared. It was so quick I couldn't describe it. It was a horrible thing. I woke up feeling relieved that I was awake and just lay watching the blue glow with Annabelle in the cot beside me.

I told Kim about the thing I'd seen at Beauties. She said that wasn't Beauties. That was a nightmare.

For my 10th birthday, Kim gave me a present of a mattress, pillow and sheets that she'd made herself for my cot. I loved them. "Thank you!" I said. "Did you make them at Beauties?"

"I was too busy being chatted up by Alvin Stardust," she said.

She had a poster of him in his black leather jacket on the back of her bedroom door that she'd got with Jackie magazine.

It was really Mummy who gave the present to me but I liked to think Kim would have made them for me.

***

Louise had a paper round. She used some of her paper round money to buy Jackie magazine. Dad found a copy and saw it had letters from teenagers talking about boys and parents that didn't understand. He said she wasn't allowed to buy it anymore.

She got a massive whop with his belt for that.

I could tell that Dad didn't like Louise. I didn't know why. Perhaps it was because she never stood up to him. She was 'a puny child' Mummy used to say. She was quiet. She had difficulty reading and had to wear glasses when she was just really small.

I played mostly with Melanie. I don't know what Louise did. I guessed she missed Kim. At one point before Melanie, Carol and I were born, there would have been just Kim and Louise. They probably used to play together just like Melanie and I did.

But Dad didn't like her. And every Sunday lunchtime when he took off his belt, it would usually be Louise who he hauled into the dining room next door to beat.

Apparently the head teacher of Louise's school had been in touch with Mummy and Dad to ask if everything was OK. 'Louise seemed withdrawn and slow', he wrote. Dad read out the letter after lunch in a sneering voice.

"C'mon Louise! I'll show them what withdrawn means." He stood up and yanked her by her shoulder. She yelped in pain as we all sat there with pitying glances, glad it wasn't us, hoping it would soon be over.

I stared fixedly at Teddy Hayes in my lap, praying for Kim to help. 'Let it be over, let it be over, let it be over,' I chanted in my head.

Mummy just sat there staring at her finger nails as we listened to the snap of Dad's belt in the next room. We heard Louise scream.

And then there was silence for a while.

Then we heard Dad called, "Evelyn! Evelyn! Evelyn!"

We all looked towards the doorway.

Dad stood there, his belt in his hand with the buckle pointing downwards. He must have been beating her with the buckle end.

He was breathing hard, his trousers falling down without his belt, his hair all ruffled.

"I need your help," he said.

Louise was dead.

***

Lou wasn't really dead. She was unconscious. We weren't allowed to see her.

"Go and get Blackie," Mummy said and I ran next door to tell Miss Black that Mummy needed her. I could hear Mummy crying in the dining room as I opened the door to let Miss Black in.

"Oh, Evelyn!" I heard her say.

Dad shouted at us all to go upstairs.

Melanie, Carol and I all sat on the landing trying to hear what was going on downstairs. I could hear Mummy shouting. The dining room door opened.

"Don't you EVER lay a finger on my girls again, Charlie!" she said and started coming up the stairs.

We scuttled into our bedroom. Mummy looked at us as if she didn't see us and walked on to Louise's bedroom. We followed her.

"Is Louise going to die?" I said.

"No, no, darling," she said. "Blackie's going to look after her for a while. I just need to get some clothes for her. I need to keep her safe."

We stood in the doorway while she opened drawers and put together a bundle of Louise's clothes in a pile on her bed.

I was still clutching Teddy Hayes. "Louise could borrow Teddy Hayes," I said.

"Oh darling," Mummy said. "That's so kind."

I put Teddy Hayes on top of Louise's clothes.

***

Louise went to live next door with Miss Black.

Mummy went to see her every day after work. But we weren't allowed to see her.

"We wouldn't recognise her, that's why," I told Melanie and Carol, certain that was the reason.

"How do you know?" Carol said.

Dad said we weren't allowed to tell anyone about what had happened. So we didn't.

***

Melanie started sleep walking at night times. I hadn't imagined it after all. I woke one night to find her trying to get into my bed.

"What are you doing?" I said. "Get out!"

She was asleep but woke up as I pushed her and, all groggily, got into her own bed.

"Melanie walks in her sleep," I told Mummy.

"What do you mean?" she said, looking at me shocked.

I told her.

"Your father used to do that," she said.

Mummy never talked about Daddy.

"What did he used to do when he was sleep walking?" I asked.

"Never you mind," Mummy said and closed her lips into a straight thin line.

***

Dad was away in Scotland again. I told my friend Timmy so he came round to play at our house after tea.

We played Kerplunk up in the attic.

Marbles were balanced above layers of plastic sticks and we took it in turns to pull the sticks out, trying to avoid marbles being dislodged in the process. Whoever ended up with the most marbles was the loser.

Timmy and I were very competitive. Neither of us wanted to be a loser.

"My dad says your dad beats you up," Timmy said as he carefully chose a stick to pull out.

I looked at him. "Why did he say that?" I asked.

"Your sister Louise. She's dead, isn't she?" he asked.

I laughed nervously.

"The teachers are talking about it in the staff room at Dad's school. It was in the papers," he added. "Ahh!" Marbles cascaded down the tube.

"Haha, I won!" I crowed. "She's not dead. She's just gone to live somewhere else," I said, gathering up all the marbles to play again.

"We were in the papers," I told Mummy that evening after Timmy had gone home.

"What are you talking about?" she said.

"Timmy said. His dad told him."

"It's just gossip," Mummy said. "Come here. Let me

brush your hair; it's all tatty."

My hair was long and thick now and got full of knots.

I let Mummy brush my hair wincing as she tugged at the knots to get rid of them.

"I'll plait it," she said.

"I haven't seen Kim for ages," I said. "Is she OK?"

Mummy was silent as she weaved my hair into plaits. "You're a funny thing. Why do you say that?"

"I don't know. I'd like to see her. I miss her."

"She's fine, darling. It's been seven years now since you saw her. I'm not sure I can get her yet."

It wasn't seven years. I'd seen her at Beauties just after Louise disappeared next door. She was crying and her face was all red. But I didn't tell Mummy that.

***

Mummy told us we were going next door to Miss Black's house to see Louise.

We walked in the back door.

"Woo-hoo!" Mummy called and walked through into Miss Black's sitting room which was the same shape as ours but much tidier.

Miss Black and Louise were watching television.

Melanie, Carol and I stood together looking at Louise.

"Hello," I said shyly.

"Hello," she said back.

"Can we sit next to you?" I asked. She moved over. She was holding Teddy Hayes.

Melanie and Carol sat on the other side of her. Mummy

and Miss Black watched us.

"Do you like Teddy Hayes?" I asked Louise, looking down at the small bear in her hand.

"He's lovely. Thank you," she said.

She looked pale and thin and her hair was pulled tightly back into a ponytail.

"Are you going to come back and live with us?" Melanie asked.

"Of course she is," Mummy laughed.

***

A photographer from the local paper wanted to take a photograph of the four Clarke girls having fun in the local recreation park.

We all sat in a row on the slide in our best clothes with our hair brushed tidily. We were in the paper the next week. The headline read, "All the Clarke Girls Having Fun!"

But Kim wasn't there.

***

Mummy and Dad had to go to Scotland and asked Melanie, Carol and me if we would like to go with them. We said yes. Louise stayed with Miss Black.

We stayed in a house that had a long driveway. It was owned by Mr and Mrs Lewis. We couldn't understand them because they were Scottish but they were very friendly.

The three of us all slept in a high up double bed with

a little window overlooking the long driveway and mountains in the distance. It was a lovely big clean house with velvet curtains that you pulled to open and shut with a cord.

Mummy told me that we were going to live in this house so that Dad didn't need to be away from home so much. We needed to get away, she said.

She asked me to ask Carol and Melanie what they thought. I said to Melanie and Carol, "Do you like this house?"

"Oh yes," they said. "Why?"

"Because I think we're going to live here," I told them.

***

And so we were told that we would be moving up to Scotland. Dad said that we weren't allowed to tell anyone. We would be leaving all our friends behind but we weren't allowed to tell them.

There were rumours going around about Dad killing Louise. I was walking around the playground at school with my friend Abigail's arm linked with mine on the left and my friend Karen's linked with mine on the right. Three kids much younger than us came up to us and started chanting, "Your dad's a murderer, your dad's a murderer!" We ignored them.

I was quite excited about our move. It made me feel that we were different and important. But I was quite scared too to leave my friends behind and our house and the town we lived in and Miss Black next door who loved

Mummy and was so kind to us all and had looked after Louise after Dad had nearly killed her. She gave me a pink tea cosy that looked like a dog because I came first again in the end of year school exams and got a good school report. I called the tea cosy Lucy and she joined in when I played schools in my bedroom.

We couldn't sell our house even though Mummy and Dad dropped the price they were selling the house for. So when the school holidays came to an end we had to go back to our schools again.

On the first day back to school, the headmaster stopped me in the corridor.

"I'd like you to read in our first assembly," he said.

"Thank you," I told him. I felt honoured and proud and excited and a bit nervous. He gave me a bible with the passage that I'd be reading

For a whole hour I practised and became more and more scared. I didn't know why.

And then the time came. I stood up in front of the whole school but nothing came out of my mouth. In the end I stuttered, "Ah, ah, ah, ah, ah, ah, ah …" I froze. My face was burning. I could see the teachers rolling their eyes and hundreds of faces staring at me. Someone started to laugh. Finally the word came out and I read the passage with tears of shame in my eyes knowing that I had let everyone and the headmaster down.

And so, I had a stutter.

I told Mummy that I had a stutter and had made a fool of myself.

"I had a stutter when I was about your age," she said gently. "I'm sure you didn't make a fool of yourself."

"How did you get rid of it?" I asked.

She shrugged. "It just went," she said.

I was very unhappy that term. My friends Abigail and Karen seemed to turn against me. They stopped talking to me and ignored me. Our teacher noticed and told them off.

"You've been friends all these years," she said. "What's going on? She's leaving soon so be nice to each other."

Timmy was my nearest rival in the school exams. I had come top of the class in every year and he always came second. He said he was annoyed that I hadn't moved when I was supposed to because he wanted to come first in the exams. I told him I would be coming first. Our teacher said, "Pride goeth before a fall", though I didn't really know what she meant.

I tried really hard in the exams and beat Timmy by 3 points in the end of year exams.

1976 – 1978

In June 1976 when I was 11 years old, we moved house again. We went to live in Scotland. We left all our friends behind, our neighbour, Miss Black, our schools, our church, our town, everything that we were used to, to move to a new country and a new way of life so that Dad wouldn't have to travel so much and be apart from Mummy. We knew there were other reasons.

Before we went, Dad and Mummy took us all to see our Aunt Lizzie, Mummy's twin sister.

Lizzie and Mummy didn't speak to each other. We didn't know why. But Lizzie had invited us for lunch. She wanted to see us before we went off to Scotland.

Mummy left us at the gate and said she and Dad would be back at 5 o'clock.

And so we were back at the house we'd stayed in when we'd escaped from my real father all those years before. Lizzie was lovely. She was nothing like Mummy even though they were twins. She was much taller than Mummy. She wore her long hair down with a kerchief tied around her head. She wore scruffy jeans and wellington boots. She loved working with animals. She and Tommy were self-sufficient.

Lizzie called us brats and showed us all her fabulous animals. She and Tommy had borzois and whippets, Siamese cats, an enormous goat, sheep, ducks, chickens and rabbits.

We had a lovely day. We didn't ask Lizzie why she

and Mummy didn't speak. We knew it was one of those things not to be discussed.

When we got home, Mummy told us to go round to see Miss Black. We were going to collect Louise to bring her home.

When we went into Mrs Black's sitting room, Louise was there with another girl. I knew her straight away. She was just as I'd seen her.

It was our eldest sister, Kim.

She burst into tears when she saw us all appear in the doorway.

"We've been to see Lizzie's goats," I said. "I thought you'd be there. But you're here instead."

"Who's Lizzie?" Kim said, sniffing.

I stared at her. I couldn't take my eyes off her.

"Stop looking at me," she snapped and blew her nose.

Her voice was different from ours, I noticed. She wore a beautiful blue dress and satiny pumps on her feet. "I haven't seen you at Beauties for ages," I said.

She looked at me. She smiled a beautiful smile and winked.

***

It turned out Kim had been living in a foster home with one of Mummy's old friends, Mr Rosolek, in Hertfordshire.

She laughed and talked a lot. She told us about her friends from her school. One had a beautiful black stallion called Black Beauty. She loved her horse so much she kept it in her bedroom.

"Really?" I said.

"I don't believe you," Melanie piped up. "A horse in your bedroom!" she sneered.

"She did. I swear," Kim said. "She put its mane in curlers at night time and put an eiderdown over its back!"

Mummy sat next to her holding her hand and smiling happily.

Kim carried on. "My friend Enid has been writing books since she was just seven. She writes at night while everyone else is asleep … "

"When does she sleep then?" I asked.

"She doesn't need any sleep," Kim babbled on. "Seriously, she's unbelievable!"

"Yes," said Melanie, "she is."

***

Our new house in Scotland was actually two houses.

On an enormous plot of land about half a mile outside a village called Newarthill, we'd bought the lovely two bedroomed house that Melanie, Carol and I had stayed in the previous year with the 2 bedroomed bungalow next door. The two were separated only by a narrow windy alleyway which Dad had plans to cover over and make the two buildings into one.

There was a long, long driveway off the main road leading up to the properties. We were on a hill and down below was our nearest big town, Motherwell, with its steelworks called Ravenscraig. At night we would see the flames and sparks flying out of the blast furnaces.

Melanie, Carol and I shared the large bedroom that we'd slept in during our visit the year before. Mummy and Dad had the other bedroom in the main house. Our rooms were separated by a small room where the boiler was. It became our walk-in airing cupboard.

Downstairs were three big reception rooms and a large hallway.

The sitting room had the beautiful ceiling-to-floor red velvet curtains over the windows that overlooked the front lawns. Another same-sized room was our dining room that we used only for the two Christmases that we lived there. It had the same velvet curtains, only in navy blue.

The third reception room was where we put our piano. There was also a sofa and some armchairs. Otherwise, it ended up filled with boxes that were never unpacked from the day we moved in. I was the only person who used this room – to practise scales on the piano and to poke through the unpacked boxes.

There was a bathroom downstairs and a kitchen. The hall was big and had a shiny wooden floor. There were French doors opening out onto the lawns.

Next door, in the bungalow, Kim and Louise had a bedroom each. They both needed personal space, Mummy said.

There was also a bathroom and a large kitchen/living room. This was where we ate our meals. There was a huge Aga stove with a fire that heated the house, the water and the cooker.

At the front of the house were huge lawns surrounded by beds for flowers. At the side of the bungalow were more land and outbuildings. At the back of the house the driveway led to a hard standing area where the two enormous removal lorries parked, with us all helping to empty the contents into our new home.

We were surrounded by farmers' fields. The nearest houses in Newarthill were half a mile away. We could see them in the distance from our back door.

A girl came bounding across the field with a beautiful Irish setter. She had a gorgeous broad beaming smile and said she'd just come to say hello. Her name was Morag and she lived just over there. She pointed to a row of houses across the field. I liked her instantly although I couldn't understand much of what she said in her broad Scottish accent.

***

School terms were different in Scotland. They finished early for the Summer holidays. They were also behind us in England. So while I had been due to move up to our secondary school when we lived in the Fens, now I had to do one more year in the junior school or, as they called it in Scotland, 'primary school'.

In Scotland you either went to a Protestant school or a Catholic school. I didn't really know the difference. Apparently we were Protestant and so would go to a Protestant school.

Mummy took me to meet the headmistress, Miss Smith. She was very kind and said she'd heard all about me and was looking forward to welcoming me when the Newarthill Primary School reopened in August. I would be in Miss Allen's class.

In the meantime, throughout our school holidays, Dad told us we had to help with the garden. It was enormous and there was a lot to do. He and Mummy were very excited about plans for the garden. We would grow all our vegetables. So we were to help prepare the ground for that.

It turned out that the whole area of the garden that they had planned for vegetables had been previously used as some kind of rubbish dump. The ground was stony. We had to dig a deep hole.

Dad made a huge sieve out of wire mesh stretched over a wooden frame. Our job was to sieve all the soil. The rubbish would be buried in the big pit and the sieved soil used to spread over the ground for planting the vegetables. It was the hottest summer we'd ever known and a heatwave melted us as we slogged away in the garden day after day of that summer, digging and sieving day after day.

The driveway had a ditch on either side. They were full of rubble: bricks and stones. Dad decided that he wanted the ditches cleared of rubble so he could plant bushes and flowers. So, we had to empty them. We dug out bricks and stones and heaped them into the wheelbarrow over and over.

Mummy loved the garden. She spent her days planting shrubs and flowers in the beds surrounding the lawns. She was happiest doing that.

In the evening we would all sit in the sitting room gathered around the television watching whatever Dad wanted to watch. He loved Westerns and war films. He sat in his armchair by the fire smoking cigarettes while Mummy sat on the floor between his knees, head on his leg.

And so we spent the Summer of 1976, the year of The Heatwave, working every day in the garden until late.

Mummy was in her element, completely oblivious to time or hunger, creating her beautiful garden out of the huge land they had bought: weeding, digging, planting shrubs that she knew would decorate the garden with colour all year round. She was a born gardener and knew the name of every plant, where they should be planted for best effect and how to look after them.

Mummy preferred being outside so Dad gave us all cleaning jobs to do inside as well as working in the garden. And we took it in turns to prepare late weekend lunches.

I cooked my first Sunday lunch for the seven of us when I was just twelve years old: it was a huge casserole layering sliced potatoes, fried diced beef, mushrooms, carrots (and other vegetables I found), tinned tomatoes, stock, salt and pepper, all topped with more sliced potatoes and cooked in the oven for a couple of hours. Then I sliced the runner beans and shredded cabbage.

Someone else made puddings. Everyone said it was nice.

Dad couldn't beat us anymore but he kept us under his command all the same. We dug soil that was packed hard from years of being undug. We sieved every inch of what we dug, throwing spade after spadeful of what we dug up against the wire mesh sieve he'd created. Day after day. We wheeled wheelbarrow-loads of bricks up and down the driveway.

I just wanted to sit in the sun to read my book or upstairs in our bedroom.

One day I put on my new red swimming costume, spread a rug on the grass and stretched out in the sun to get a tan while reading. I fell asleep and got terribly sunburnt. I woke up to hear Mummy's voice. She was standing with Dad leaning against the door into the bungalow.

"Wouldn't it be lovely to have nothing to do," she sneered.

I remembered I was supposed to be helping, grabbed the rug and went into the house to get changed back into my gardening clothes.

***

At school my classmates were delighted to receive an English person into their class. I was jeered at from my first day for being English. I found it hard to understand their local accent and said "yes" as a response to most things.

I liked my teacher, Miss Allen, who took no nonsense from anyone. We learned how to parse and how to do fractions.

The school was round with classrooms all around the edge and a round hall in the centre where we had assembly and did PE. There was also a library where I spent the break times. Miss Smith our glamorous headteacher knew I liked to read and asked if I could suggest books that she should buy for the library.

Normally the boys went out to play football in the playground and the girls played netball. One day it was decided that girls should join in with football. We had to change into boys' football kit. I was so tall and so wide that I found I couldn't fit into the boys' shorts and split them down the seams. Everyone laughed. I was so ashamed at being so big.

In the evenings at home while everyone sat in the sitting room gathered around the wood fire and the television, I would get bored and restless. I would sit behind the sofa, which had been pulled away from the wall to be nearer the fire, and read. After a while I would slip out of the room and go outside.

I loved to stand alone in the dark garden looking down the hillside to the orange lights shooting into the night sky from Ravenscraig Steel Works blast furnaces.

Then I would sneak into the kitchen in the bungalow and rummage through the cupboards. They were filled with tins of fruit of all sorts: peaches, plums, pineapple. I would open some tins and go and sit in the garden eating from them with my fingers and drinking the thick syrup. I was careful to put the empty tins straight into the dustbin so no one would know.

Having stuffed myself with sweetness, I would slip unnoticed back into the sitting room where the television continued and everyone was either glued to it or snoozing where they sat. Mummy always fell asleep in front of the television sitting between Dad's knees.

***

When Scotland beat England at rugby my day at school was misery. And I would search for sweet comfort in a tin of syrupy fruit.

With the new school term, Mummy went and got a job doing the cleaning and ironing for a family who lived in a town called Wishaw which was twelve miles away. She also looked after two young children. She couldn't drive so she cycled there and back.

Money was tight we were told. It had taken ages to sell our house in Chatteris and Dad and Mummy had had to take a 'bridging loan' to buy the house and bungalow and all the land.

The first Christmas we were there Kim was told to ask all of us if we would mind not having a Christmas stocking anymore.

"You don't believe in Father Christmas do you?" she asked. "Stockings are expensive you know and Mummy and Dad have a bridging loan to pay for."

We all agreed to do without our Christmas stocking.

I had stopped believing in Father Christmas when I found the ash-tray I'd made for him (out of a salad cream jar lid covered in silver foil stuck onto a length of material that was intended to be draped over the arm of Father Christmas' armchair) stuffed in a box of recycled Christmas wrapping paper.

I didn't mind much not having a Christmas stocking. But I didn't like it that we were poor. I wanted us to be rich like our Grandfather was and like Kim's friends at her old school.

"Did you mind coming back to live with us?" I asked Kim.

She had slid so well back into our family, it was as if she'd never been gone.

"You just have to adapt, don't you?" she said, plucking at the middle of her top lip (which I thought was an attractive habit to have). I felt secretly envious of her ability to adapt. I felt like a square peg in a round hole, lonely and outside of things.

***

Dad taught Mummy how to drive. He had a company car now and Mummy was able to drive the Toyota Corona.

Every weekend we would go out in the car to collect wood to saw up and burn in our fire. We would drive to some local wooded area and collect branches we found on the ground. We dragged them back to the car and stowed them in the back (seat down) and squeeze ourselves around them on the journey back home.

And then we took it in turns, in pairs, to saw the branches with a bowsaw over the sawhorse. Then we used a small axe on a wooden block to chop up logs to make kindling and stacked it all in the woodshed. We always had jobs to do.

I hated going wooding. It was cold and wet. My wellington boots leaked so I wrapped my feet in empty waxed bread bags with elastic bands around my ankles to keep my feet dry as we often had to wade into the burn to collect fallen branches.

There was an old woman who lived near the burn. Her name was Mrs Burn and Kim got a weekend job looking after her dogs. Mrs Burn had been friends with Beatrix Potter when she was a young girl, Kim told us. We'd stopped believing her stories. "It's true!" she said.

She lived in a big old fallen down house and had masses of dogs and cats which she fed on meat and bones she got from the local abattoir, Kim said.

When the wind was in a certain direction, we could smell the abattoir from our garden. It was a truly disgusting stench. Perhaps Kim was telling the truth, I couldn't help wondering.

Kim met a boy when she worked for Mrs Burn and he came on a walk with us one day when we were allowed out across the fields.

As we were walking back, Kim and the boy stopped to sit down and waved us on. "Go on without us," they said. When we got home Dad asked where Kim was.

"We left them behind," we told him.

"What do you mean? Where are they? Don't you know what happens when a boy and girl get together?" he demanded.

We were sent off to go and find Kim. She was walking home with the boy's arm around her shoulders. We told her what Dad had said and that she'd be in trouble. When we got back home, Kim went straight to her bedroom in the bungalow and refused to speak to Dad.

Kim went to the Protestant high school in Motherwell where Louise and Melanie went too and where I would be going soon.

There was a school disco evening and Kim was going. She was going with a friend. But when she went to leave and say goodbye, Dad said he could see her bra strap through her blouse and made her go and put a t-shirt on under her blouse so you couldn't see her bra strap.

Kim was really cross. She did as she was told though – now you could see her t-shirt under her lovely blouse. It looked strange! If I was her, I would wait till she got to the end of our driveway and take off the t-shirt. I think that's what she did, though I forgot to ask her.

***

Kim was very good at sewing and cooking.

She did "home economics" at school. She used to bring the food she cooked home in a tin or a Tupperware. She learned to cook sweet and sour sauce and one day when it was her turn to cook our late Sunday lunch, she made us sweet and sour beefburgers. They weren't very nice but I ate it all up as we were supposed to do.

The others argued and sulked and pushed the food around their plates. They had to sit there until they'd eaten it. But as soon as Mummy and Dad had left the room, they fed it to Penny, our corgi, who sat waiting under the table.

***

I loved making up stories in my head and writing them in exercise books I stole from the store cupboard at the primary school.

I didn't join in with my classmates at break-times. I was constantly teased for being English and for being tall and for the "boys' shoes" Mummy had chosen for me. I spent the lunch break in the school library or sitting in the store cupboard in our classroom.

I loved the smell of that cupboard with its stationery supplies, text books and mustiness. I helped myself to supplies that I could use at home when I ever had time to play schools which wasn't often now because of all the household jobs we had and working in the garden.

I was secretive. I had a heavy feeling of separateness from my family. I was bored and restless sitting in front of the television in the evening and would go upstairs to read in my bedroom or poke about in boxes that were still unpacked from our house move. I helped myself to things I liked and hid them in the small chest of drawers next to my bed.

We had an old piano that Grandfather's sister who'd

died had given to Mummy.

A friend at school was good at musical instruments and had piano lessons with a woman who lived quite close to the primary school. Mummy said I could have piano lessons. She was really pleased that someone would be using the piano at last.

I went to Mrs MacDuff's house once a week to learn scales and how to read music. I practised on our old piano which was in our spare room.

When I got bored with practising, I would rummage through the unpacked boxes. I found some coloured pencils that obviously no one wanted so I took them.

Kim had crocheted me a pencil case with lovely colourful stripes, the colours of a rainbow. I stashed my new pencils in there and carried them around in my school bag.

One evening when I was in bed dropping off to sleep, Kim came into our bedroom and started rummaging through my school bag.

"What are you doing?" I asked half asleep.

"You go to Beauties," she said. "I just need to borrow your pencil case."

A couple of days later while we were all gathered in front of the fire in the sitting room, Dad said, "Someone's been thieving from us. Some pencils have been taken." He looked at each of us in turn.

"Who has stolen the pencils?"

No-one spoke.

"Go and get your pencil cases," he ordered.

We all went off to get our pencil cases. He pulled my pencils out of my case. "Where did you get these?" he said.

"A friend at school gave them to me," I lied.

"Why?" he asked.

"I don't know."

"I don't believe you," he said. "These are English pencils. They can't be bought in Scotland."

Mummy was staring at me with her grey/blue eyes. She didn't believe me either, I knew.

"Get out!" Dad said and threw my pencil case at me.

I burst into tears and went upstairs to my room. I was sick with shame at being found out.

***

At school, one of the girls in my class started her periods. We heard her using the Bunnie machine in the girls' toilets that ate up sanitary towels. She was teased a lot.

She was 'developing' they said though I didn't know what that meant.

At home, Kim started her periods too. She would lie curled up on her bed in agony with what she called period pains. Dad told her to pull herself together. "Your mother never complains," he said.

Melanie and I wanted to know about periods. We plucked up courage to ask Mummy. She was outside on the lawn scrubbing the kitchen mat with a bucket of soapy water and a brush.

"Can you tell us about periods and the birds and the

bees?" we finally plucked up courage to ask her.

Mummy sighed and looked embarrassed and then told us about periods and eggs and sperm all the while scrubbing at the mat, not looking at us.

Soon after that, I started to develop too. My boobs began to grow. They were tender and sore. I asked Mummy if I could have a bra. Pubic hair appeared at my crotch. I was twelve years old and 5' 9" tall.

The Summer of 1977 was another hot summer – not quite as hot as 1976 but still a scorcher. I walked around in just my bra that I wore with pride (size 32AA) and my knickers.

And then I had my first period.

"I think you need to put more clothes on," Mummy said and sent me to speak to Kim about sanitary towels. Kim had a huge cash and carry sized box of Doctor White's sanitary towels stored behind her bedroom door.

She gave me a packet.

I began to notice that I gave off a smell from my armpits. I knew it was 'BO' that other people talked about. I asked Mummy if I could have some anti-perspirant deodorant so that I wouldn't smell. She bought me a Sure roll-on which smelled lovely.

***

When we had been living in Scotland for a year, Dad started having to travel down to England more and more for his work.

He would be away for a few days, sometimes a whole

week. We loved it when he went away. Mummy would put on her favourite music again that she wasn't allowed to play with Dad around.

And we didn't have to work in the garden. It was like a whole weight had been lifted from our house.

Kim had a boyfriend at school and he was allowed to come to our house when Dad was away. I saw him kissing Kim in her bedroom when I looked through the window. She and I didn't talk about Beauties anymore.

***

When the school holidays finished, I would be going up to the same school that Kim, Louise and Melanie went to. It was called Bradley High School. It was a huge Protestant school in Motherwell, three miles away so we had to get a bus to and from school.

Mummy had decided to go to secretarial college in Motherwell to learn to be a secretary.

We would all get in the car and she would give us a lift to the bus stop which was a mile from our house.

I hated my new school.

There were so many pupils. We had about 40 in each class.

I was terrified to speak because of my English accent and my stutter got worse. I learned to stop doing it by distracting myself. I would say a different sound over and over in my head from the sound of the first word I would have to read out. That's how I cured my stutter. But there was no cure for my English accent.

One day after school I had to go to our dentist in Motherwell so I didn't catch our usual school bus back home. I had to wait at the bus stop for a bus to take me back to Newarthill.

When a bus finally came along, I got on it and, as the doors closed behind me, I realised from the purple school uniforms that I was on a bus full of kids from the Catholic school.

I sat down at the front of the bus in terror, making sure I didn't say a word in my English accent to anyone throughout the journey.

***

We had a different teacher at school now for each different subject we were learning and had to move to different classrooms for each lesson. The school was huge and it would take some time.

A bell would ring to end a lesson, then we had about 5 minutes to get to the next classroom.

We learned maths, English, French, history, geography, PE, RE, science, art and home economics.

Our teachers were mostly bored and angry. Lots of pupils misbehaved and ignored the teachers and every teacher had what they called a strap. This was a thick strap of leather and when someone misbehaved they were called to the front of the classroom to the teacher's desk, required to stretch out their arms in front with the back of one hand in the palm of the other.

The teacher would then place a book over the pupil's

wrists (apparently to avoid serious injury to the tender veins there, the story went) and then bring the strap down on the open palm with all their might. Some teachers even gave a jump as they whipped the strap down.

It was mostly boys who got the strap. Some of them cried, some of them laughed their way back to their desk. I would watch in terror. It was horrible. It was a warning to all of us.

You got the strap if you were late to a classroom so we all had to hurry. But we weren't allowed to run.

It seemed there were so many traps you had to avoid to escape punishment for anything.

I kept my head down and did the work and the homework.

I had a couple of friends in my class and our neighbour, Morag Browning, remained a good friend with her Irish Setter dog called Tango.

But mostly I felt awkward due to my height, out of place due to my English accent and very troubled by my monthly periods that I didn't feel able to talk about with anyone.

I dreaded the arrival of each monthly period. It seemed that no sooner had one finished than the next began. They were so heavy that I had to change my sanitary towel between each class, usually discovering that my menstrual blood had completely saturated the sanitary towel and seeped through my knickers onto my school skirt. I would have to swivel my skirt round so people walking behind didn't see the walking bloodstains.

At night time I would wake to find my bed sheets soaked in blood.

Ashamed, I would rinse them under the tap with my blood red knickers and drape them secretly over the hot pipes in the walk-in airing cupboard to dry. It was nothing I felt I could tell Mummy.

One morning when I found I'd soaked my bed in blood, I stood at the top of the stairs waiting for Mummy to finish in the bathroom so I could clean myself up (she was always the first up each morning). She came out of the bathroom and climbed the stairs back to her bedroom. As she approached the top of the stairs, blood suddenly splashed out of me and landed on my bare foot. She pointedly stared at it and then stared up at me. "You'd better go and clean that up," she said.

I felt dirty and ashamed as if I'd done something wrong.

I had to ask Kim for more packets of Dr White's. I hated having to ask her.

"What are you doing with them?" she asked angrily as she threw another packet at me. "Lining your doll's cot?"

I scuttled off.

At school in PE, I had to ask Mummy to write a letter to excuse me from swimming. I loved swimming but I couldn't go swimming when I was having my period. After the third letter, my teacher said "You girls! I don't know why you don't use tampons!"

I plucked up courage to ask Mummy about tampons. She gave me a huge box of Tampax that she used herself.

I read the instructions and tried to follow them but I couldn't actually work out how to do it. I kept trying. It wouldn't go in!

Then, as I was working away with my private parts and the tampon in its cardboard casing, I suddenly experienced a terrible sharp pain and it went in. And it felt the most blissful sensation I'd ever had as the tampon entered me.

It suddenly came to me that I'd broken my own hymen with my tampon!

I'd read about hymens and losing your virginity in the historical novels I read. But how would any young girl know you had to do that first from the instructions that were given?

***

During my secret searches around our house, I rifled through the chest of drawers in Mummy and Dad's bedroom while everyone was working in the garden.

I came across pornographic magazines tucked under clothes in a drawer. I was shocked as I flicked through the photographs and put them straight back in the drawer. But I went back to them and borrowed them and read the stories in them and my sexuality was ignited. The magazines were sexually arousing and I instinctively learned masturbation.

***

During the winter of 1977, we had heavy snow. The fields

around our house were thick with snow which lay there frozen for weeks. Melanie and I dug out huge blocks and built an igloo in our garden.

The road to our house was cut off and impassable to traffic.

On Christmas Day our log pile had run out and Kim and I were ordered to go and saw up some of the stockpiled branches we'd brought home from wooding expeditions.

Kim had been given a blue transistor radio for Christmas and we listened to Radio Luxembourg as we sawed wood together, complaining about having to work on Christmas Day.

She started talking about her boyfriend. I asked her if she masturbated. She laughed and looked at me weirdly. "I think you know more about sex than me," she said.

"I just found it," I said.

***

Kim was in charge of us when Mummy went away to stay with Dad.

Dad had to be away for a few weeks and Mummy said she was going to visit him where he was staying in England. She caught a train from the village on the other side of the burn.

While Mummy was away, Kim was in charge. She was OK most of the time except when it came to mealtimes. We didn't like what she cooked and refused to eat it. She tried to be like Mummy and Dad and make us stay at the table until we'd eaten it, but we weren't afraid of her and refused.

We bickered and bickered and finally she shouted, her face red and looking like she was going to cry, "Why can't we all act like sisters?"

We laughed and mimicked her, "Why can't we all act like sisters!"

***

At school we had end of year exams which I revised for every night.

I came first in my class in eight subjects.

Mummy came home by herself on the train, leaving Dad still staying in a hotel in England.

She telephoned to tell us what time her train was due to arrive and we all went to meet her, crossing the fields and the burn to the train station.

It was wonderful to see her getting off the train. We'd missed her so much. We all ran to hug her. She was laughing and looked happy and hugged us all back. And then we all held hands and walked home together while we all shared our news with her.

I told her I'd won lots of prizes in the exams I'd come first in.

She told us that we would be moving back down to England.

Now that Dad had to be in England for his job, it made sense to move back down.

Dad had found a house for us in a town just eight miles

away from where we used to live in the Fens. Mummy had gone down to see it and they'd bought it at auction. I felt so happy to be moving back to England that I felt

I would burst.

***

Everyone who came top in an exam at school was given a book voucher.

We were taken to a huge wholesale warehouse full of books where we could choose books to the value of the book vouchers we had. It was like Paradise for me and I had eight vouchers to spend.

The books were discounted and very cheap so I came away with fourteen books.

Each prize had a copperplated handwritten book plate I could stick on the inside cover so that I could always remember that I'd won the book by being first in an exam at Bradley High School.

The Prize Giving event was on the last day of term.

All my family came to the Prize Giving: Mummy and Dad and all my sisters. I was called up on stage to collect my book prizes. Again and again and again my name was called.

I was called up eight times and ended up feeling very embarrassed. The people in the auditorium cheered and stood up and clapped. It was amazing! I loathed the school but it gave me a standing ovation.

***

We said goodbye to our friends, to the house and the bungalow (that we'd never been allowed to join together), to the amazing garden we'd created, to the blasts from Ravenscraig that would cease altogether in a few years' time, to the religious divides of Protestant and Catholic that I'd never understood, to the accent that I'd never truly got to understand.

I was brainy, that was confirmed. I was a teenager and emotionally confused. My hormones raged and I felt very alone.

I was excited at the prospect of leaving our Scottish nightmare behind me to be able to reconnect with our life in the South of England.

It felt like a new beginning.

1978-1983

In June 1978 we moved back down to England and arrived at our new home in the Fens late in the afternoon. The house was an old detached double-fronted building on the High Street but it was set back off the road with a low brick wall and lime trees marking its boundary. The front garden was an overgrown lawn. Iron gates opened up to a long driveway that ran beside the house with a Methodist chapel on one side next door.

The garden was huge with a long back lawn leading into two orchards and a big shed that had probably once served as a garage for cars. Everything was overgrown.

The house had stood empty for a while, previously owned by an antique dealer who had apparently embezzled money and been made bankrupt when he had to repay it.

We excitedly explored the house which was big but gloomy with wooden panelling in the hallway and dark wallpaper.

When you went in the front door, there was an L-shaped hallway. To the right was the dining room, the stairs going up, along the hallway on the left was the sitting room and next to that was a smaller sitting room we called 'the snug'. It had French doors leading out to the back lawn.

There was a walk-in pantry, a cupboard under the stairs, a long narrow room which became "the China cupboard" with Mummy's huge collection of dinner services, and the kitchen/living room with old servants' bells.

A door from the kitchen led to the scullery with a long low stone sink, a stone tiled floor and the backdoor leading out into the garden.

Upstairs there was a long narrow room like the one immediately below it downstairs. This became the place to store linen.

Next, on the right was a bedroom that we called the 'gas chamber' because it still had original gas light fittings. It was left as a place for unpacked items from our house move for years.

There was a separate toilet, then a bathroom. Mummy and Dad's bedroom was next to the bathroom. Then, at the front of the house were two huge bedrooms. Melanie, Carol and I shared one and Kim and Louise the other.

There was a nice landing where the ottoman was placed in the window as a window seat.

On our first night, the removal men hadn't yet arrived with our furniture so we slept in the car and the caravan.

I woke up early and lay there listening to the most beautiful bird song.

Melanie and I went exploring the garden. It was huge and overgrown and our hearts sank thinking about all the work we would be expected to do to get it under control.

***

Dad decided the grass was too long for mowing and ordered us to set to with garden shears.

We moved up and down the huge lawn on our knees

snipping at the grass. We moaned and complained bitterly. We wanted to get back in touch with our friends and explore our new hometown.

When it was done, Melanie and I plucked up courage to go to speak with Mummy.

"Do we have to work in the garden all the time anymore?" we asked her.

She looked surprised as if she didn't know we'd rather be playing.

"Of course not, my darlings," she said and we cheered and ran off, feeling free at last.

And so gradually some of Dad's vice like control over us began to loosen. Mummy became the go-between.

***

Schools in England were still open when we moved back down so Mummy said we had to go to school, even if it was just for a month.

Kim had finished school just before we left Scotland. She decided to do a catering course at the local Tech when it reopened in September. In the meantime, she got herself a job at the Nag's Head Hotel as a waitress. She always had a boyfriend and wore nice clothes.

Louise had also finished school and decided to do a course in childcare at the local College. She was quiet and pale and hardly said a word.

In September, Melanie and I would be going to the Grammar School. This was an academic school where the top pupils from surrounding schools went from age 13.

There was an open day event at the school and Mummy took Melanie and me to it.

As we walked into the Assembly room/gym, I immediately spotted my old childhood sweetheart Timmy Nixon and his mum. They saw us too. Timmy's mum looked really pleased to see us.

"Wow! How you've grown!" she said to me.

Timmy had grown really tall too and had lots of pimples on his face. He looked away and ignored me. I had no idea why. Perhaps he still believed the stories of Dad being a murderer.

I also saw my old friend Abigail Noble who was there with her parents.

I felt quite shy to be back with my old friends. Although I'd only been gone two years, I felt so different from my time in Scotland and by how much I'd physically grown.

It was now only June, though, and schools in England didn't break up till July.

We went off to the local secondary school for one month before the Summer holidays, to get out of Mummy's way and also to make some new friends.

I was now at the height I would be as an adult but I was still developing: I had long greasy dark brown hair and greasy skin with blackheads. Mummy and Kim used to take delight in squeezing my zits all down the sides of my nose, between my eyebrows and on my chin with their two thumbnails pushing together.

I had whiteheads on my shoulders which were also dealt with by Mummy squeezing the white pus out between her nails.

On my first day at the new school, I was standing in the queue to get my school dinner. Girls from my class gathered around me. They were curious about me and not unfriendly.

I felt one of them lifting up my thick greasy hair. When I turned round to see what she was doing, I caught her look of horror on her face. My hair was matted with grease from my oily head. I felt really embarrassed and blushed a hot deep red.

When I got home, I asked Mummy if I could wash my hair. We usually only washed our hair once a month or so. There was always a thing about rationing hot water to keep energy bills down. Now that we were teenagers, we really needed to do it more often.

Although we owned a huge house and garden, we had no money, Dad told us often. By now we had had it drilled into us that we had to turn lights off when leaving a room, close doors to keep the heat in and be sparing with hot water. Our water was heated by a gas boiler that only Mummy and Dad were allowed to turn on.

Melanie and I still shared a bath every Sunday evening. I was too big for this now and I also felt awkward showing her my naked body. Melanie was still as thin and scrawny as she'd always been even though she was a year older than I was.

I asked Mummy if we could have our own baths now. She looked surprised. "I didn't know you were still sharing the bath," she laughed.

***

I was very excited to be going to my new school, to see my old friends who came by bus everyday to the Grammar School and to make new friends. I loved school. There were only about twenty pupils in each class. I sat next to a girl called Pat Blake on my first day. She lived in a town about twelve miles away and came by school bus every day while I just had a twenty minute walk from our house. We became best friends immediately.

While we were in Scotland, Mummy had completed her secretarial course.

During the Summer holidays, she got a job as a secretary at a local grain laboratory. She would drive there every day in our Toyota.

Dad went out to work in his company car, driving around the local fruit and vegetable packing stations checking the quality of the produce for the company he worked for.

Every evening he would spend ages complaining to Mummy about the people he'd met during the day. And Mummy would talk excitedly about the man she was working for and the experiments on the grain she helped with.

Dad didn't like her working at the grain laboratory and told her they were over working her. She was doing much more than she was being paid for, he told her. He made her give up her job and go to work in a local packing station where she got a job as a supervisor. Now Dad got to pop in and see her a few times every week.

Mummy worked very hard at her job. She would leave home early, come home around 5.30, have something to eat and then go back to work for the evening shift and finally get home around 9pm.

Every Friday evening, Melanie and I would go to the mini market across the road from our house to do our weekly shopping. Mummy would give us some money and we would add up what we were buying as we went round the shop to make sure we had enough money to pay for it. Then we would lug the shopping home and put it away in the pantry and the fridge.

We had our main cooked meal at school. Our school dinners were lovely. When we got home, we would make ourselves a sandwich. Then I would go up to our bedroom to do my homework.

Melanie had made a friend in her class at school called Ava. Ava had long red hair and was very funny. She came round to our house after school so that she and Melanie did their homework together. They just laughed and messed around and drew in their school text books while I was serious and just cracked on with my work.

Occasionally I would chip in with them though and we'd be practically rolling around the floor laughing.

While Mummy was working her night shift, Dad would spend some time in his shed at the bottom of the garden where he made things, pottered or fixed things. Then he would come in for the evening and sit watching television. He would look at the clock a lot. "Your

Mother's late", he would mutter. When she was late, he wouldn't speak to her for a while as punishment.

***

Because Kim was at college every day and working at the Nag's Head in the evenings and weekends, we didn't see her much. She had a boyfriend. She said she was depressed and went to the doctor to get some pills.

"What's she got to be depressed about?" Dad said. "She's only 19."

It was strange. She'd been so happy when she'd come back to live with us.

"You don't know what it's like," she told me.

When Louise got home, she would curl up and go to sleep either on her bed or on the sofa. She had a boyfriend too: he worked on the railway like a lot of young men in the town. His name was Derek.

We pretty much did as we pleased now and no longer felt so controlled by Dad. His weekly sermons had stopped after he thought he'd killed Louise and if he told us to do something we didn't want to do we went to Mummy to ask if we really had to. And she said, "Not if you don't want to." And that was that.

***

One morning we got up to find that our corgi, Penny, had been run over. The milk man had found her body on the road outside our house and brought her inside our gate. Everyone cried except for me.

I heard Dad telling Mummy that I was the only one who hadn't cried.

I realised that I didn't cry anymore. It was like I'd forgotten how to.

***

Melanie and I decided not to call Mummy 'Mummy' anymore. I'd been teased at school for referring to her as Mummy. So I asked her if it would be OK to call her 'Ma' or 'Mother'. Melanie and I were both doing German at school and loved the German word for Dad, 'Vati'. We called Dad Vati and he actually smiled. Behind his back, Vati became 'The Fart' which is how we talked about him.

My friend Pat had been to stay at our house overnight. She came home with me on Friday afternoon and her mum came to collect her in her car on the Saturday. Now she invited me to say with her overnight. I was to go home with her on the school bus on Friday night and then catch the train back from her home town to mine on Saturday. Ma said that was OK.

On the bus journey to her house, Pat said, "We don't live in a big house like yours. I said we should tidy the house for you but my Dad said that you should take us as you find us."

Pat's mum and dad were lovely and so kind to me. Pat had a younger brother too. His name was Harry but we ignored him. Instead, we went up to Pat's bedroom. She had a double bed and we were going to share it that night.

While we sat talking about school and boys and music and teachers and Ian Benson (the boy in the Lower VI we both fancied), Pat's mum came up with a tray with two plates of fish fingers, chips and baked beans, orangeade and two KitKats. It was amazing!

Pat's mum was lovely: she wore green eyeshadow and pink lipstick and had a lovely short haircut. My mum never wore makeup now. She told me that Dad didn't like her wearing it even though I remembered she used to wear it before they were married.

"There you are, darlings!" she said as she put the tray on the bed for us. "Enjoy!" she said.

It was such a gorgeous meal. My mum never did anything like that. I felt a pang of jealousy. Pat's mum didn't work. Pat said she didn't know what she'd do if her mum wasn't there when she got in from school. My mum hadn't been at home when I got home from school ever since I could remember – since I first started school.

We stayed up late talking and laughing and plotting how we would attract the attention of Ian Benson.

I had such a lovely evening feeling cared for and free. In the morning Pat's mum cooked us eggs for breakfast. And then Pat walked me to the train station to catch my train back to my home town

It was a 45 minute walk from the station to our house. There was no-one in the house when I got home. Ma was in the garden and Dad was in his shed. I made them both a cup of tea and went up to my bedroom to do my homework.

***

During the Summer holidays, Melanie and I worked as strawberry pickers. We took our bikes and cycled up the road a couple of miles to the strawberry fields.

Then, on hands and knees, we worked our way up and down the lines of strawberry plants, picking the glorious red fruit. When we'd had enough, we took our baskets to be weighed and were paid for every pound we'd picked. It felt so wonderful to have earned some money. We were able to buy Christmas presents that year for the first time, rather than having to make things for everyone.

***

When I was fourteen, I went across the road to the mini market and asked the owner if he had any part time jobs going. He said he didn't and then asked me where I lived.

"Across the road at number nine," I said.

"What? That big double fronted house set back?" he asked.

"Yes," I said.

"OK," he said, "you can have a job."

And so, after school on a Friday and all day on Saturdays, I worked in the mini market, filling shelves, sticking price labels on biscuits and packing customers' bags. It was a really busy shop and there was always a lot to do.

At break times I sat in the staffroom with the full-time workers and had a cup of tea and a biscuit. Cynthia was the boss. She had a squint so you didn't really know whether she was looking at you or not.

I just drank my tea in silence, listening to the young women talking about their violent relationships, pregnancies and holiday plans.

I loved earning money so I could spend it. On Mondays after school, I would go to Woolworths to buy makeup and to Lucy Shop sometimes to buy new clothes.

At school some of the girls in my class talked about their boyfriends. I decided I wanted a boyfriend. I was lonely and dreamt of having a boyfriend. Every afternoon when I walked home from school, a boy would pass me cycling in the opposite direction, going home from the secondary school. He was good looking and always looked at me as he cycled past, his school blazer tails lifting behind him in the wind.

"There's a boy I pass when I walk home from school," I told Pat. "He stopped and asked me out. His name's Andy."

"What are you going to do?" she asked, believing every word I made up.

"I'm not sure," I replied.

In our class at school, some of the boys talked about the disco at the Conservative Club that happened every Friday night. I decided I would go. I really wanted a boyfriend. I was ready. My body was ready. I asked Ma if I could go out on Friday night to meet some friends from school at the Conservative Club.

She said, "Yes, but don't be too late".

I bought myself a new outfit from Lucy Shop: black silky looking trousers and a tight-fitting pink, white and turquoise striped cap-sleeve t-shirt. I felt a million dollars! I didn't have a nice coat to wear so even though it was nearly Christmas I decided not to wear a coat.

I was a few months away from my 15th birthday, 5'9" tall, a voluptuous size 14 with a 36B bra size.

When I kissed goodbye to Ma as she sat on the floor between Dad's knees, she whispered 'blusher' in my ear. She could smell that I was wearing makeup.

"Will you be warm enough, Darling?" she asked, seeing I had no coat on.

"I'm not going far," I said. Dad just stared at the television screen.

I went out by myself, heading to the Conservative Club.

I had never been out in the evening alone before. I found myself walking with determination towards the Conservative Club where school friends said they went on a Friday evening. I wanted to be more like them, to belong, to show them I wasn't just a school swot. Above all else, at the back of my mind, I had decided it was time for me to find a boyfriend.

In the Conservative Club, the disco blared. I found some friends from school and sat talking with them for a while. I danced a bit too. Amanda and her friend Nicky said there was a disco on at the Nag's Head Hotel that they were going on to. It wasn't far from our house so I said I'd go with them.

The slow songs had come on at The Nag's Head disco. As I stood with Amanda and Nicky a boy came up to me and said, "Can I have a dance?"

We danced a couple of slow songs and then he took me by the hand and found us some seats. He said his name was Dan. He looked about 19, had sandy coloured hair and beautiful teeth. He smiled a lot. He was taller than me and quite thin. He wore the trendy clothes of that year, maroon waffle sweater, jeans, white socks and maroon tasselled shoes. We got up for another slow dance.

He pulled me really close to him and started telling me jokes in my ear. He was very funny and I found myself laughing out loud.

"You have a gorgeous smile," he said, looking straight at me. And then he just kissed me, a proper snog that went on for ages. It felt amazing. My first kiss with a boy in full view of everyone on the dance floor!

When I opened my eyes, I could see that the dance floor was full of couples hugged together snogging like we were. Lots of people stood or sat around idly watching us.

Finally, Dan said in my ear, "Do you want to come back to mine for coffee?"

"OK," I said. He took my hand again and we walked to the exit. It was bitterly cold outside now. Dan took off his jacket and wrapped it around my shoulders.

"Aren't you cold now?" I asked.

"Doesn't matter," he said.

He told me where he lived. It was a small semi-detached house. When we got there he let himself in and we went straight upstairs to his bedroom.

"It's just my old lady in downstairs," he said.

He pulled me down on to the bed and we started kissing again. I broke free.

"How about that coffee?" I said.

"Do you really want coffee?" he asked.

"Of course. That's why you asked me here isn't it?"

He looked disappointed but got up and said, "OK". He disappeared out of the door. He was back very quickly with one mug.

"Where's yours?" I asked.

"I don't drink coffee," he said.

We both laughed. He took the mug back from me.

"Is that you Andrew?" a woman's voice shouted outside the door. Dan quickly moved a small chest of drawers in front of the door so she couldn't get in.

"Yes Mum. I'm trying to get some sleep," he said.

He pulled me to him and we started to kiss again. Before I knew it he had his hands inside my clothes, inside my bra groping at my breasts and then trying to undo my trousers.

"Stop!" I said.

"What?" He sat up and looked at me. "Don't you want it?"

"That's not what I came for," I said.

He sat on the edge of the bed staring at the floor. I felt a bit sorry for him. He looked like a sad little boy.

"OK, alright," I said.

He brightened immediately and came back to me.

And so I let him take all my clothes off.

"This isn't your first time is it?" he asked as he stripped himself. He sort of sneered as if it was a bad thing to be a virgin.

"No," I lied.

"Are you on the Pill?" he asked.

"Of course not," I said. "What do you think I am?"

"I'll have to get a jonny."

He sighed and got up and rummaged in the drawer that was now a barricade over his bedroom door.

He parted my legs with his knees as he ripped the condom wrapper with his teeth.

"Ah no! I've lost it!" he said as he tried to put the condom over his limp penis. "It's your fault."

I lay watching him as he crouched between my legs and fumbled with himself, feeling a bit guilty and sorry for him. Finally he succeeded in pushing himself into me. With a few thrusts in and out he was done. It was over. He lay there on top of me for a bit, breathing hard and then withdrew himself.

There was no condom. He groped around the messed-up bedclothes.

"It must still be in you," he said. "C'mon. I'll walk you home." He started to get dressed.

It was still very cold outside. "Next time you should wear more clothes," he said as we walked along the pavement towards my house. He cracked jokes as we walked. He was very funny.

"This is me," I said as we got to my house. The light was on in the sitting room and I could see the flicker of the television screen.

"You live here?" he asked, peering at our house. "It's big. Do you want to meet next Friday?"

"OK," I said.

"I'll wait for you here at 7.30 next week then," he said and kissed me on my lips.

"By the way, what's your name again?"

"I'm Bess," I said opening our gate. I was no longer a virgin and had a boyfriend.

I was a bit worried about the missing condom and prayed that I wasn't pregnant. But the very next day my period started.

When Friday came, I spent ages getting ready for my date. My period was still very heavy. I wouldn't be able to have sex, I'd have to make sure that Dan knew.

I told Mother I had met a boy. She didn't say anything. It was a cold night again and this time I put on a big thick coat over my outfit. Looking out of my bedroom window I saw Dan standing behind the trees at the front of our house.

I said goodbye to Ma. She was sitting in her usual Friday evening position on the floor between Dad's knees watching television. "Don't be late," she said.

Dan looked me up and down. He didn't seem that pleased to see me.

"Did you have a good week?" I asked. He'd told me he worked at Perkins Engines.

"Not bad," he said.

He decided we'd go to the Nag's Head disco again where we'd met the week before. He was quiet. He bought me a Babycham and we stood sipping our drinks. People he knew came passed.

"Hi Dan!"

"Dan the Man!"

"You alright Dan?"

They looked me up and down.

"Why do people call you Dan while your mum calls you Andrew?" I asked.

He shrugged. "They always have."

Finally Dan said, "Do you want to come back to mine again?"

"Not tonight," I said.

He stared into his drink. Then he said, "I think I want to go and join my mates. I don't want to go out with you." It felt like my heart had dropped to my stomach. I didn't say anything. It suddenly dawned on me that he'd just wanted sex with me and that was it. I got up and walked home.

When I walked into the sitting room, Ma looked at me and said, "You're home early."

"Yeah, I didn't really like him," I said.

***

Ma came home with a new dog. She was a small black cross called Penny just like our old corgi. She looked like a small, sleek Labrador.

Someone at Ma's work was having problems coping with Penny. She had so much energy. Ma said that we would have her. We'd always had dogs. Ruby had had to be put down when we lived in our old house. She was very old and had gone blind and deaf and then had developed arthritis. With Penny our corgi gone, it was strange not to have a dog.

It didn't take long before Penny loved Ma. When she saw her, she would just leap into Ma's arms and lick her face happily.

The problem was that Penny hated being left alone. When we were all out of the house, she would rip away at the chair she slept in in the kitchen and leave diarrhoea all over the kitchen mat.

She would be looking out of the window for whoever got home first. That lucky person would have to clear up behind her while Penny cowered in the corner.

***

Louise's boyfriend Derek used to come round sometimes. He asked me if I'd like to go on a double date with him and Louise and one of his workmates whose name was Kenny. Louise giggled.

I said yes. I was still only 14 years old but had a yearning inside me for something I couldn't really explain. It was to be more like other girls I knew and not just a school swot, I thought. I wanted to be noticed, to be wanted, to have fun. Unconsciously I also wanted something else more harmful.

I dolled myself up for my blind date. Louise said Derek would pick us up in his car and we'd go to play pool at the Station Hotel.

When we got in Derek's car, Kenny was in the passenger seat. Louise and I got in the back. "Hi," Kenny said trying to look me and up and down but the car was dark.

When we got out of Derek's car at the Station Hotel, Kenny hung back to walk with me. He was good looking but very short – about three inches shorter than I was.

I was shy with him as we walked into the pub.

Derek bought us all drinks and then he and Kenny played pool while Louise and I just sat and watched. It was very boring.

Louise and I didn't really have much in common, apart from being sisters.

We'd never really talked much. She'd definitely never talked much after recovering from Dad's final beating. It felt strange to be out with her. And the guy I was supposed to be on a blind date with was playing pool with another guy. I was really bored.

Derek and Kenny took it in turns to go to the bar and buy us drinks. I drank Babycham which was the only alcoholic drink I knew based on Christmas time television adverts.

Finally, they put down their pool cues and suggested we should be off. I agreed.

We all got back in the car except this time Louise got in the passenger seat and Kenny got in the back seat with me. We drove off. It was like there was some secret agreement I wasn't a part of. I was a bit scared but excited.

When Derek stopped the car, I saw we were in a deserted lay-by goodness knew where. He turned off the headlights and we sat in silence.

And then Kenny slid his arm around my shoulders and pulled my face to his and started kissing me, a really lovely sexy kiss. It felt delicious.

I was conscious of Louise and Derek kissing in the front of the car.

Kenny's hand crept into my blouse and into my bra and he started fondling my breasts and nipples. It felt amazing. But I couldn't do anything with my sister sitting in the front of the car.

Finally, Kenny unzipped his jeans, wriggled around a bit and placed his very hard penis in my hand. I didn't know what he was expecting me to do. It was laughable and embarrassing.

He pushed my head down to his lap. I realised at last that he wanted me to suck his dick. But I wasn't going to do much with Louise in the front. It was very embarrassing.

I just stroked his (very big) dick like you would a cat while he bent down to my nipples and began to suck on them one at a time while he squeezed the other between his finger and thumb. I felt exquisite sexual pleasure but just couldn't bring myself to give him anything in return with my sister sitting there.

Finally he sighed, put his penis back in his trousers, Derek started the car and drove us home. It was all very weird to me.

Louise and I walked into our house without a word.

I kept playing the scene with Kenny in the back of the car over and over in my mind, the smell of him and the creak of his maroon, soft leather jacket.

I wanted to see him again and explain that I couldn't do what he'd wanted me to do with my sister just a foot away.

I got Derek to give me Kenny's work number and I tried to track him down at work.

Finally, I managed to get someone to call him to the telephone.

"I wondered if you wanted to see me again?" I asked him.

"You're too young," he said. He spoke kindly and he was right. I was only fourteen and he was twenty-two even though he was shorter than I was. Still, I felt bereft again, discarded.

***

Melanie went on a blind date with one of Derek's friends too. She met him at the Nag's Head Hotel and told me they'd gone on to the Cock Inn which was the pub opposite our house.

A few days after her date, our phone rang. It was a man's voice asking for me.

He said his name was Adam and that Derek, Louise's

boyfriend, had told him about me. Adam knew Derek because they both belonged to a karate club. Derek had invited my sister Melanie to meet Adam by mistake. It was supposed to be me.

Adam said he really wanted to meet me. I was immediately flattered and we agreed to meet in the lounge bar at the Nag's Head on Sunday evening. Adam said he'd have a red rose in his lapel so I knew it was him.

I wondered what Melanie would say. I told her about the phone call. She said it was fine. She hadn't really liked him.

I told Ma I was going to meet someone. It was a friend of Louise's boyfriend, Derek. She didn't say anything. I kissed her goodbye. "You look nice," she said. "Don't be late."

Adam was good looking and I liked him straight away. He had brown wavy hair, green eyes and wore an earring in one ear. He wore grey trousers and a black leather jacket and smelled of Brut aftershave. He had a moustache.

He was sitting at the bar when I arrived. He looked me up and down and smiled.

"What are you drinking?" he said.

"A Babycham please."

Adam was nineteen and worked as a butcher at a local supermarket. He went to college one day a week. He lived with his mum and his sister. His dad had died. He was very funny and told endless jokes.

We talked and laughed for hours it seemed. It was

lovely to be with him. I told him I was 15 and he asked when would I be sixteen.

"Next month," I told him. He smiled, moved closer and kissed me really gently. There was no-one else in the lounge. He put his hand in my hair behind my head and we kissed for about five minutes. When we came up for air he grinned.

"Do you want to go on somewhere else?" he asked.

"OK."

"Let's go to the Cock, opposite your house."

We walked up to the Cock and had another drink there. When it was time to go, he said, "Come with me" and led me to the ladies' toilet outside.

We went in and he locked the door and pulled me to him, kissing me with his tongue while his hands went inside my clothes.

He pulled down my jeans and pants and sat me down on the toilet seat. Crouching in front of me he spread my knees open and began kissing and sucking between my legs. It felt really sordid to be sitting like that in a public toilet but I didn't stop him.

Finally, he stopped and I tidied up my clothes.

He walked me to our front gate. "I'll give you a ring," he said and went off up the road.

When I went to bed that night, Melanie asked me if I liked Adam. "Oh yeah!" I said.

"Did he take you into the ladies' loo?" she asked.

I laughed.

I ran through the whole evening again and again,

reliving it in my mind as I went to sleep.

***

I used to go round to Adam's house while his mum was out. We'd sit in his bedroom while he played ACDC on his record player. Sometimes he'd show me his karate moves!

On my sixteenth birthday Adam invited me to see the latest Jackie Chan film that was showing in Peterborough. We went with a couple we'd been out with together a few times already. We had a few drinks before and after and finally Adam walked me home.

It was late and everyone was in bed. Ma had left a lamp on for me in the sitting room.

Adam had been teasing me all day about the fact I was now 16 and so he could now 'have' me as he said. "I'm not on the Pill", I said.

"That's alright, I can withdraw." He grinned.

I made us both a cup of coffee. I felt quite drunk from all the alcohol consumed throughout the day.

Adam put the coffee to one side and pulled me onto the floor.

Before I knew it, he'd pulled off my jeans and pants and was lying between my legs.

"Not like this," I said.

He was heavy and I couldn't move. He pushed himself inside me. I just lay there and let him fuck me. True to his word, though, he did pull himself out before he ejaculated.

He stood up smiling and doing his trousers up. He gave me a peck and left.

He came round to our house after lunch the next day. We went up to my bedroom. He said, "I had a dream last night," grinning from ear to ear.

"What?" I smiled.

"I dreamt I had you at last," he said and kissed my ear. "But we'll call it quits now. I don't want a relationship. I was just waiting. It was just fun. I'll give you a ring sometime."

And that was it. He left!

***

Our friend Ava was going out with a boy from the Lower VI called Graham. They were going steady.

Ava told us that she'd gone to the Family Planning Clinic at the doctor's surgery to get the Pill. Anyone could get it, she said. The problem was that her mum, who was a Catholic, had found her packets of pills and thrown them away, calling Ava a slut.

The week after Adam dumped me, I decided to go on the Pill. I went to the Family Planning Clinic after school.

The doctor was a kind looking lady with silver hair and glasses on a chain around her neck.

"Are you in a relationship?" she asked, smiling at me.

"No," I said. "Do I have to be, to be on the Pill?"

"It's usual," she said. "Otherwise, why would you wish to be using contraceptives? Of course, some girls choose the Pill because it can help regulate messy periods." She peered at me.

"I get them," I said.

There was silence.

She looked steadily at me with a kind, concerned face. Then she said, "Were you abused as a child? Sexually abused I mean?"

I was taken aback by the question and didn't see the relevance.

"Does that matter?" I said, looking down at my hands on my lap.

"What do you think?" she asked.

I didn't reply. I couldn't see her point.

"Does your mother know you're here today?" she asked gently.

I felt tears spring to my eyes.

"I guess not," she sighed, "otherwise she'd be with you, wouldn't she, helping you make this choice."

She continued to look at me in silence, waiting for me to speak. I was afraid to speak in case my voice cracked with tears.

"There are patterns in these things," she said finally. "When you allow yourself to be abused as a child – not that it's your fault of course – sometimes that can continue into adolescence and adult life. I've seen it so many times. But, technically you're of an age of consent for sexual intercourse. And, of course, if you did want to regulate your menstrual cycles, the Pill can help."

She gave me six packets of the Pill in a paper bag.

***

Melanie and I were revising for our 'O' Levels.

Kim had left college and got a job in catering at North London Polytechnic. Now that she'd left home, Carol moved out of our bedroom and went to share with Louise. Melanie and I had more space now.

I would sit at the desk in front of our bedroom window that looked out over our front garden to the High Street beyond.

I was sitting there revising one Sunday evening when I looked up and saw Adam limping along holding hands with a girl I recognised from school who was in the year above me. Adam looked up at me and smirked. I knew he'd come walking past deliberately so I'd see him.

The girl he was with I knew only as a quiet reserved girl, quite plain I thought and a strange shaped body in that she had a very long torso. I felt a stab of jealousy as I watched them both walk into the Cock Inn. I knew what they'd be up to.

I went back to my revision.

***

The fair came to town and Melanie and I went to see it.

Melanie didn't like the rides – they made her sick – but we walked around enjoying the music and the atmosphere. As we stood watching the waltzers, a gorgeous looking man with blond hair and a lovely tan and tight jeans came over.

"Wanna ride?" he said. We shook our heads. "Why not?" he asked. "A gorgeous girl like you," he said looking at me. "You need a ride."

I blushed. "My sister doesn't like the rides," I said. "That's not your sister," he said looking from Melanie to me. "Anyway, who cares about your sister. Do you want to go for a drink later?" he asked.

"Alright," I said.

"How old are you?" he asked.

"Guess," I said.

"Nineteen?"

"I'm sixteen," I said.

"No!" he smiled. "Tell you what. Meet me here at half seven and I'll take you for a drink. I'm Billy."

"I'm Bess," I said.

"You're not going to are you?" Melanie asked as we walked off.

"Why not?" I asked. "He's gorgeous."

So I went back at 7.30. The fair was closed. Billy was there waiting for me. He had changed his clothes and looked even more gorgeous.

"My car's over here," he said and led me to his car.

"Where shall we go?" he asked. "I don't know this town."

"How about the White Hart? I'll show you where," and I gave him directions as he drove.

We had a great evening. It was fascinating hearing Billy's stories of the fair and how he'd grown up in it. He'd never been to school and couldn't read. He was 25 and had ambitions to buy a brand new ride for the fair. He wasn't supposed to mix with people outside the fair. When it was time to go home, we got back in his car.

The car park was empty. He leaned over to me and kissed me. He smelt gorgeous. His hand went inside my blouse and inside my bra cupping my breasts and teasing my nipples.

"You've got a gorgeous figure," he said. "Do you want to do it?"

"What? Here?" I asked.

"Yeah. There's no-one around," he said, looking around.

"I would love to," I said, "but I'm having my period."

"Would you really, even though you don't know me?"

"Yeah."

"Why don't you take out your tampon and chuck it out the window?" he said taking my hand and pushing it down his trousers. He wore boxers. He unzipped his trousers and pulled his boxers back to show me his huge erection. I stroked it softly.

"Do you do head?" he asked. Apparently I did now.

Billy drove me home and said he'd call me in a few weeks. He had some business to do in the area and would call when he was passing.

Sure enough he did. He drove me to the car park in the town centre which was empty. We moved to the back of his car and I allowed him to abuse me as the family planning doctor had predicted.

***

During May and June, Melanie and I sat our 'O' Level exams.

I did English language, English literature, maths, geography, history, German, French, chemistry and physics. Then school was out.

I left my job at Maurice's mini market. Maurice wanted me to work every day during the school holidays which I had no intention of doing. So we agreed I should leave. Now, on Saturday mornings Melanie and I did casual labour at the factory where Ma worked. She put us on the potato graders where we'd stand for four hours picking dodgy spuds off the conveyor belt as they moved to the next stage of the process to be weighed and packed into plastic bags for the supermarkets. We chatted with the older women on the line. Everyone loved Ma who was the supervisor. One woman swigged gin out of a flask from time to time.

***

Kim came home with a new boyfriend. According to Kim he was 'Persian'. His name was Jaffa and he was an Iranian. He was smaller than Kim but seemed nice. He was studying at the Poly that Kim worked at along Holloway Road in London.

Kim said how happy she was with Jaffa. He would buy her gifts all the time and take her out to expensive restaurants.

"I'll never go out with an English guy again," she said. "They don't know how to look after a woman."

She looked at me. "Why have you got that stuff on your eyes?" She went to pull at my mascara laden eye lashes. "You'll get yourself a reputation," she said seriously as I stepped back.

"Maybe I want a reputation," I said.

"Mummy wouldn't like that," she said.

"Mother doesn't care," I said. "She's never here!"

***

Melanie went down on the train to stay with Kim and Jaffa one weekend. She said she'd had a wonderful time. Kim and Jaffa had introduced her to one of Jaffa's Persian friends and they had slept together. They'd had sex all night long, Melanie said. She was worried that she might be pregnant even though her periods hadn't yet started. She was seventeen.

And then, the same week, her periods started.

"That was obviously what you needed to get going", I told her.

***

Mother used to collect burnable rubbish from all the waste paper bins in the house and burn it in an incinerator at the bottom of the garden. One day, after gathering the rubbish and lighting the fire, she came into the kitchen where I was and shoved my unburned Pill foil at me.

"Is this yours?" she asked angrily.

"No," I lied instinctively.

"Well, whose is it?" Ma demanded.

"I don't know. Ask the others."

I told Melanie that Ma had found my Pill packet.

"Yes, she asked me if it was mine," she said.

"What is it?" I said." I realised I shouldn't have known what it was.

I felt the usual shame of being found out but also felt she should be pleased that I was taking precautions not to get pregnant like she had. And she had never had a conversation with us about sex, birth control or anything. She was too embarrassed or just not aware that we were growing up and sex was what happened these days as part of growing up.

She never mentioned the Pill again. She just left us to our own devices.

Some of my friends and people I knew in school and on the pub scene were in long term relationships.

And then there were girls I knew who slept around – the boys called them 'nymphos'.

My first teenage experience of men and sex were heartbreaking to me. I gave myself and was then cast aside and spent sleepless nights wondering what I'd done wrong. Where were they now? Had they found someone better than me? What was wrong with me?

I understood young men seemed to want to boast with their mates about their sexual conquests and weren't interested in having an actual relationship and I was falling straight for it like something tattooed on my forehead.

***

Our 'O' Level results were out. We would receive our results through the post but they were available to see on the noticeboard at our school the day before.

We all scrambled back to school to see. I had passed all nine 'O' Levels with six 'As' and three 'Bs'. I was overjoyed.

While I cried with joy at my great results, Melanie hadn't done so well and did her own crying. I didn't feel I could really celebrate.

A few days later, my old friend Pat rang to ask how I'd done. She was surprised, she said, that I hadn't rung her. The truth was that I'd moved on from Pat. I envied Pat her lovely cosy family life where her mum and dad and brother were so tight knit and looked out for each other. Boys were my distraction from my fractured family and Pat had yet to have a boyfriend. She said she'd talked about me with her mum and that her mum had told her I'd developed faster than her. Secretly I wasn't so sure about that.

I hung out more with my friend Ava at school than with Pat because Ava's family was more like mine.

***

We went on what turned out to be one final family holiday in our Monza caravan.

We towed the caravan to Ogwen Caravan Park in

Wales in the Summer of 1981 following our 'O' Levels. It was just Melanie, Carol and me and Penny the dog, Kim and Louise having now left home.

Dad was moody and complained of feeling "leggy" meaning he didn't want to walk. We left him in the caravan smoking while the four of us went out for days without him. We had a great time.

We climbed Snowdon, we sunbathed on blankets under the hot sun and we visited castles. It was like a weight was lifted without having Dad around.

But then we returned to the caravan to face his sullen silent stubbornness.

We abandoned our holiday and went home early.

***

I had never been close to my sister Louise but she invited me down to stay with her in Stanmore. The family she lived with were on holiday in their house in the South of France so Louise had the house all to herself. It was enormous.

It turned out that Louise had two boyfriends on the go. They were friends and were both at Hatfield University. They both rode a motorbike and had long greasy hair and wore black leather.

One night while I was staying with her, she went out with them both leaving me alone in the house. I watched a couple of Barbara Streisand films in the huge games room and helped myself to different spirits from the drinks cabinet.

Louise was an enigma. None of us ever got close to her. I asked her what happened when Dad beat her senseless all those years before. She looked at me blankly.

"I can't remember," she said.

"Really? Nothing about it?" I persisted.

"I've forgotten it," she snapped. "You should too."

"Why have you got two boyfriends?" I asked.

"Well, it's better than you," she said, "You haven't got one!"

She had a point.

"Both at once?" I asked, trying to imagine how that would work but preferring not to know.

***

Back at home, Dad had been asked to take early retirement. Ma said it was because he was so critical of everyone and didn't help the company's reputation.

Now he spent all his days in his shed at the bottom of the garden while Ma worked all day and every evening, apparently because she loved what she did and wanted to earn extra money for us, or because she didn't want to be at home with us all.

Dad told us when we were gathered with him in the sitting room watching television, that she was having an affair. He said he, 'knew it in his water'.

It was true Mother worked long hours all week. We hardly saw her. Melanie and I went to work with her on Saturday mornings. When we got home we took it in turns to cook some lunch and then Ma would start the weekly wash and get into her beloved garden. We didn't see her much or get to talk to her much.

Dad told us she was having an affair.

"My penis is my god," he told us as we tried to watch that week's episode of 'Dallas'. "All the times I spent in hotels," he carried on, "I had loads of opportunities. But I love your Mother and my penis is for her alone."

We looked at each other and smirked silently. But we felt uneasy. What was she up to? We started avoiding her when she came home between shifts.

Finally, one evening when she was just about to go back to work and we were in the sitting room (Dad was in his shed) she came in and said ,"What's going on?" We didn't say anything. "Look," she said, "no-one's speaking to me. What's going on?"

"Dad says you're having an affair," Melanie piped up.

"Look! Don't you dare side with him," she snarled. "Who brought you into this world? Who saved you from your miserable psychopath father? Who bought this house? Who puts food on your table? Don't you ever side with him!"

She walked out and went back to work. We all felt miserably guilty that we'd fallen into the trap of believing Dad's stories.

***

Melanie's sleepwalking began again. She hadn't done it for a few years that I'd been aware of.

It was a very hot night. I woke to find her standing at

our open bedroom window carrying the quilt from her bed.

I leapt up. I'd learned that you weren't supposed to wake someone who was sleepwalking but just guide them back into bed. This was different. It looked like she was about to jump out of the window!

"Melanie, come back to bed, come back to bed, come back to bed," I repeated gently as I moved towards her, got between her and the open window and shut it.

She woke up and looked at me startled. "I was dreaming I was jumping so I threw my quilt out so I could land on it," she said.

I helped her get back into bed and pulled the quilt over her. She was asleep instantly. In the morning she didn't remember anything about it.

I told Mother about it. She looked worried. She was quiet. She looked like she was making her mind up about telling me something.

Finally, she said, "Your father tried to kill himself while he was sleepwalking – a few times – before they put him on medication."

***

Melanie and I went to stay with Grandfather. Ma arranged it all and took us over to his house one Sunday. We went out for lunch and then had a long walk at a nearby reservoir and then Ma went home, leaving us with him.

Grandfather lived in an enormous old house. He owned an enamelling business that had two factories and had won the Queen's Award for Industry. He still worked even though he was now 81 years old.

I was very shy of Grandfather. He was the most intelligent man I had ever met and I was always afraid of saying the wrong thing. When we got up the next day, he offered us a glass of orange juice while we were preparing the breakfast table.

It was delicious. I said, "That really wakes you up!"

"Don't be silly, child." He said, "You're already awake."

He had a way of looking at you, his eyes the same as Mother's and his thin lips pressed into a straight line. You had to look away feeling sure you'd done something stupid.

But we were here to get away from home and Grandfather kindly put up with us.

He had a board meeting at his factory. He drove us there and we stopped off for lunch at an Inn called The Pheasant. Grandfather recommended that we choose the vindaloo curry that was on the specials board. We'd never eaten curry before. It was so hot that our faces went beetroot red and our noses ran. Grandfather laughed as he slowly ate his quiche salad.

When we got back to his house, Melanie and I decided to do some cleaning for him. His house was beautiful and full of wonderful furniture and antiques. He had a cleaner who came in every day but she was very lazy so we decided to help.

Grandfather seemed surprised that we should take

it upon ourselves to clean his house but he didn't say anything. He went to his study to make some telephone calls while we willingly became his char ladies.

Once we'd finished cleaning, we made some fruit scones and ate them straight from the oven with a pot of tea.

"These are very good. Thank you," Grandfather said, spreading butter over his scone.

After a while, as we ate happily, he asked us about our plans going forward, now that we'd finished our 'O' Levels.

Melanie said she was going to follow Kim's example and go to catering college.

"Ah! Just like your mother," he said, "that's all she was good for too." He laughed.

I looked at Melanie sitting beside me. She had her head down as if she'd been slapped. I rummaged for something to say.

"Do you wish you had boys and not girls?" I asked politely.

"Who's been telling you that?" he asked.

He paused and said, "Well, girls have their uses, I'm sure. But we need more science. Girls just seem to want to get married. A boy would have been nice – as an heir. They can do so much more than a girl."

In the evening we played Scrabble. (Grandfather didn't own a television.) He absolutely thrashed us at Scrabble. Ma came back the next day to collect us. She did a tour of the garden and neglected greenhouses, watering the over-dry geraniums and dead-heading.

Grandfather apologised for the neglect. "I haven't had time to look after things," he admitted. "I need to speak to the gardener!"

"I hope they haven't been too much trouble, Daddy," Mother said laughing as we went to leave.

"It's been lovely to have them come and visit their old Grandfather," he said, with one hand on Melanie's shoulder and the other on mine. "So nice to see them turn into such attractive young ladies," he said. "You must be doing a good job, Evelyn. Or is it in spite of what you're doing?"

He had a way of adding a smile to a barbed comment that left you wondering what he really meant.

"Bye Daddy!" Mother kissed his forehead. He solemnly shook Melanie and me by the hand and pressed a five pound note for each of us into our palms.

***

When we got home, our dog Penny was gone.

Carol came in with her boyfriend.

"Where's Penny?" we asked her. "We thought you must have taken her for a walk."

"I took her out," Dad said.

He was watching television, flicking cigarette ash into the empty fire grate. He said he was fed up with the mess Penny made. He'd taken her for a ride in his car to the other side of some wetlands, let her out of his car and driven off.

We just stood and looked at each other, too shocked to speak. We knew he'd done this cruel thing to punish Ma because Penny loved her so much. It was such a terrible and cruel thing to do.

"How could you?" Ma finally said, looking at Dad in disgust. She went upstairs. Melanie and I went to unpack our bags.

We were quiet for a bit, lost in our thoughts as we emptied our weekend bags.

"I hate him," Melanie said at last.

"He's getting worse," I said. There were occasional times when Dad could be a bit mellow. But not these days.

"He's evil," I said. "There's something wrong with him." A thought came to me. "Or is there something wrong with us? Do you think we've been programmed to be victims?" I asked her. "Do we just allow ourselves to be victims and put up with all this shit? Some people are bullies and the rest are victims? Is that it? or are bullies victims too and victims bullies?"

"You're doing my head in," she said. "You think too much."

"You sleepwalk too much," I laughed, but only half joking.

Despite our change of scene, staying with Grandfather, Melanie was up sleepwalking again that night.

The next term Melanie went off to do her catering course at Peterborough Tech just as Kim had done. I went back to school to study for 'A' Levels.

***

A boy at school I fancied, Nigel, invited me to the pub to meet up with some of the guys from school.

We had a few laughs and then they began to tease me. They knew me only as a swot at school who did all her homework, revised for exams and was liked by the teachers.

When one of them who smoked lit up a cigarette, I asked if I could have one. I could see they were quite shocked by that, or perhaps I chose to believe they were. Then they started making little jokes about whether I was a virgin. And then Nigel joined in their laughter. They really began to annoy me. They knew nothing about me.

"You're really beginning to annoy me," I said loudly. Even though I had fancied Nigel for years (I thought he was handsome and polite and respectful and funny) I stood up and said, "You know nothing about me" and walked out.

I went over the road to the Red Bull pub. Some girls from school were in there and there was a disco going on.

I sat down next to a guy called Bernie. He was a quiet guy who often appeared in the pubs I went to but didn't say a lot. He was tall and slim and blond, quite good looking with a quirky way of walking. I started chatting with him.

Bernie worked on the railways. He was 24 and loved to read. His dad, Archibold, had got him the job on the railways and he was training to be a train driver but he hated it. He only did it to please his dad.

A hit record called 'Pig Bag' was playing and a friend and I got up and danced to it with sheer joyous abandon. It turned into a fun evening.

Bernie asked if he could walk me home and I said yes. "So this is your house," he said. "Can I see you again?" he asked. "Next Saturday?" "That would be lovely," I said.

I started going out with Bernie which was my first proper boyfriend relationship.

Bernie and I saw a lot of each other. I really liked him. His parents were away one weekend to see his sister who lived in Devon. He suggested we might go back to his house after a couple of drinks at the pub. I said yes.

We sat on the sofa listening to music and he kissed me for the first time. And then he did the most amazing thing. After kissing and caressing me all over, he gave me oral sex and I experienced my very first orgasm from a guy. I cried silently, so moved that he had given that to me. Then he took me by the hand upstairs to his bedroom where his bed was a mattress on the floor and made true love to me. It was exquisite. "I bet none of the others have done that for you," he said. He was right.

***

One night Kim rang. She spoke with Ma. She was in a terrible state. Apparently, her boyfriend Jaffa had decided she was having an affair with the local handyman who was a bit of a simpleton that Kim just chose to be friendly with. They'd had an argument which led to Jaffa holding two cigarettes to her face unless she confessed. She'd managed to escape out of her bathroom window.

Ma was distraught. "I knew this would happen! I just knew this would happen!" she said. She rang the local police to report it. When a policewoman rang back to let Ma know that Kim was OK, Ma decided she had to drive down to see Kim for herself.

She brought her home with her. They got in around 4am absolutely exhausted.

Mother had a couple of hours' sleep and then went off to work. She came to say goodbye to us before she left.

"Look after her," she told me. "Please look after her."

I took a day off school. Kim was sound asleep in her old bed. I sat reading a text book sitting on a chair next to her.

Around midday she opened her eyes. I looked up and saw her watching me.

"What are you doing?" she asked in a small voice.

"Just reading." I held the book up. It was a play I was reading for my French 'A' Level, Molière's 'L'Avare'. "The Miser," I said. "How are you feeling?"

She closed her eyes.

"Can I get you anything? Squash? Soup?" She nodded. "What?" I said.

"Squash," she said. "Please."

I went and got her a jug of squash and a glass. "What happened?" I asked.

She told me how they'd gone to bed and were having

sex when Jaffa suddenly stopped moving in her to say 'Is this how it is with Benny?'

"I asked him what he was talking about and he just went mad. Jumped up and lit a cigarette and told me he knew, people had seen me talking with Benny and told him I was having sex with him. He made me light another cigarette for him even though he already had one lit. Then he held the two cigarettes near my boobs, then up to my face, telling me I had to confess.

"I screamed for help. He jumped back and I got away and locked myself in the bathroom. I managed to get out of the window."

"Aren't you on the fourth floor?" I asked.

"Someone must have called the police," she carried on, ignoring me. "The next thing I know the door was kicked down and Jaffa's in handcuffs…" She started to cry.

I pretended to believe her and put my hand on her shoulder, stroking her.

"Guess what? I said, suddenly remembering. "I finally got an orgasm off a man!" That made her laugh.

After a while she went back to sleep.

I watched her for a bit and went back to my book.

She stayed with us for a couple of weeks and then got a job at Tooting Bec Hospital in South London and disappeared again.

***

One day our French teacher asked us who was going to apply to university.

I didn't put my hand up. I'd never thought about it because I assumed it cost a lot of money. No-one had ever asked me about University or my education or career plans. At home Mother always seemed pleased with my school report and it had seemed logical that I should carry on at school to do 'A' Levels. But, beyond that, I didn't know.

After the class, Miss Pearl our French teacher asked me to stay behind.

"Why didn't you put your hand up?" she asked. "I've never thought about University. We couldn't afford it. And, we have problems at home …" I tailed off.

"You have to go," she said. "You're too clever not to. You'll get a grant to go. And the fact that there are problems at home make it even more important that you should get out. You need to start thinking of your future."

It made sense. I didn't know what Mother would say though.

That evening I told Ma what Miss Pearl had said.

"Can I go to University?" I asked. "Apparently there are grants to pay for everything."

Mother seemed surprised.

"Nobody's been to University since Daddy and Mummy," she said. "Daddy didn't seem to think any of us were up for that. And of course it was very obvious that I was too thick. But I don't see why you shouldn't apply if you want to."

I was excited at the thought of being the only one in our family to get to University since Grandfather and

Granny and of leaving home.

I told Miss Pearl that I would apply for a place at University.

I found a French degree course at York that sounded perfect. I applied.

***

It turned out that Ma was having an affair. It didn't bother me. I was wrapped up in my boyfriend, Bernie, and studying for my 'A' levels. Ma was home later and later and Dad carried on telling us tales.

Sometimes in the summer evenings while it was still warm and at weekends Ma suggested a trip to the seaside. I was busy with Bernie and homework but Melanie and Carol would go with her and our friend Ava would sometimes go too.

It turned out that Ma's 'boyfriend', Brian, had a caravan at Hunstanton on the Norfolk coast.

One time, Ava had waded into the sea with her granddad shirt on. It got mixed up with all the wet swimwear that went into the washing machine when they got home. A week or so later she asked if she could have her shirt back but we couldn't find it anywhere.

"Your Mother's having an affair," Dad told me while I was (unusually) sitting watching television with him. "I don't know why. When I think of all the opportunities I had when I was staying away from home, all the women throwing themselves at me. I was never unfaithful to her. I'd give the world to your Mother. And now she's out all the time. I rang her at work but she wasn't there. The worst thing I ever did was teach that woman to drive!"

"I've been to see a solicitor," he said. "I know she's having an affair. He told me to keep a notebook of what's going on. So I keep one in my car."

Dad had stopped eating meals with us. He'd stopped washing. He took to taking his worn clothes out of the dirty clothes basket. He'd lost a lot of weight and his wrinkled stinky clothes hung off him. He didn't shave and looked wild.

I told Ma I thought Dad was having a nervous breakdown.

"He probably is," she said. "He's his own worst enemy. But he won't talk to me. When I ask him what's wrong, he just says, 'You know!'"

He started going to bed really early around 9 o'clock.

Mother complained to me that he smelled terrible.

"Why don't you move out of that room?" I asked her.

"Why should I? It's my room. He'd probably put a lock on it if I did," she said.

***

My birthday was the same day as Mother's Day that year, just as it was the year I was born. We decided we'd go out to Sandringham for the day. We put together a huge picnic and packed blankets and cushions into the Toyota. Dad was in his shed at the bottom of the garden. We hadn't even bothered asking him if he wanted to come. He never went anywhere with us.

The car wouldn't start.

Mother got out and went down to the shed to tell Dad. When she came back she sighed and said, "Well, we're not going anywhere today, girls. He's taken the rotor arm out and won't give it back".

"You ruined my birthday," I told Dad when I saw him later. He looked surprised. I don't think he realised it was my birthday.

"I'm sorry," he said, "But she needs to be taught a lesson."

***

"He's told me he wants a divorce," Ma said. "I think he wanted me to beg him not to but I told him to get on with it."

When Dad left his job, he'd been able to keep his company car. One day when I walked past it on the driveway, I tried the handle for some reason. The car wasn't locked so I got in. I opened the glove box and found the notebook Dad had said his solicitor advised him to keep. I read it.

"No dinner again," he wrote. "Evelyn not home till 9.30. I was in bed and heard her come in.

"No clean pants so I had to take a pair out of the dirty clothes basket.

"Evelyn out again all evening.

"Found his shirt on the washing line so I burned it in the incinerator..."

Oh my God! He'd burnt Ava's granddad shirt thinking

it belonged to Ma's lover! The notes were mental. I put the book back in the glove box and went to tell Melanie what I'd found out about the missing granddad shirt.

That night she was up again sleepwalking. I woke to find her walking fast out of our bedroom door. I got up quickly and followed her.

She went into Carol's room. I followed her. She spun round and headed down the landing.

Dad was just coming out of the loo. He stood there in his vest and pants, looking confused at what was going on.

He stood at the top of the stairs as Melanie headed towards him – or maybe it was the stairs she was heading for. I don't think she saw him. She went careening into him as I grabbed her, otherwise she would have gone down with him.

Without a word, Dad went flying down the stairs.

I had my arms tightly around my sister and Mother appeared in her nightie.

"What's going on?" she asked and flicked the light switch on.

Dad was in a heap at the bottom of the stairs, his arms and legs at strange angles.

"Oh my God, Charlie!" Mother shouted. "We need an ambulance!"

We ran downstairs. Mother began calling Dad's name and slapping his face gently. "Charlie, Charlie, Charlie, can you hear me?"

He'd crapped himself on the way down. The smell

was awful.

I picked up the phone and dialled 999.

It turned out that Dad had broken his legs, some ribs and his back and had damaged nerves in his spinal chord.

"You're very lucky to be alive!" the ambulance man told him. Dad was unconscious but breathing.

He was paralysed from the waist down. ("So much for his penis", I said to Melanie.)

"They're not sure whether he'll walk again. But it will be a very slow recovery," Mother reported the next day when she got back from the hospital.

She looked tired and shocked and complained about her own back.

"Maybe you should go to bed and get some rest," I suggested to her. "There's nothing you can do."

"I need to get to work," she said. It was Monday.

***

As I got near to our house on my return home from school that day, I saw a black dog sitting by our gate. She saw me and began to wag her tail faster and faster. It was Penny! I couldn't believe it.

"Oh you beautiful dog!" I said delighted as she jumped up at me and began to lick my face and hands.

"How did you find your way back?" I couldn't comprehend how she'd got back to us having been dumped miles away and the other side of flooded fields by Dad weeks earlier.

When Mother got home later she squealed with delight

to see Penny.

"We mustn't tell Dad," Ma said.

"How will he know? He's not here!" I said.

We were sitting drinking tea at the kitchen table. Penny slept soundly, exhausted in her old chewed up chair.

"Do you think this is Karma?" I asked Mother.

"Calmer?" she asked.

"No, 'Karma', K, A , R, M, A. Dad did a really awful thing - now he gets his just deserts. And lovely Penny comes home."

"Darling! That's awful. It's not 'just deserts' – no-one deserves that."

"Penny might have died," I tried to point out. "Just because of his jealousy…"

"But she didn't. I don't want to talk about it," she said. "I need to get back to work." She winced as she stood up.

"How's your back?" I asked, concerned.

"Not good," she said. "However, I'll survive."

***

That summer, Bernie and I went down to stay with his sister for a weekend near Totnes. She and her husband had a gorgeous cottage built into a hillside. They ate organic food and smoked pot up the chimney.

It felt really good to be on holiday with my boyfriend and meeting his family.

Bernie's sister and I were in the kitchen preparing a meal. She said, "I'm so grateful to you, Bess. You've changed Bernie's life. You know, he had a hard time getting over his last girlfriend's treatment of him. And he talks about you all the time. I can see the change in him. It's like you've brought him back to life."

***

It turned out that Ma's boyfriend, Brian, had ended their relationship.

"He was a chicken," she said.

She'd told him about Dad's crippling accident and Brian had gone strange after that. She decided that he was scared she might be suggesting he leave his wife.

***

Dad was still in hospital. He was slowly recovering from his fall down the stairs but he couldn't walk and was suffering from mental health problems, the doctors said. They advised against visits and decided it was better right now that he stayed where he was. We all agreed.

Except for Dad, everyone came home for Christmas for what turned out to be the last Christmas we would all be together. And we promptly bickered and argued as we had as young children.

Kim was in tears and Mother shouted, "Why can't you all be nice to each other?"

Over the Christmas holidays I revised hard for 'A' Level mocks and I got three As. I was getting excited about the prospect of being accepted at a university. Being the 'brainy' one was my way of getting recognition and being noticed and approved of which I craved.

I had completed my UCCA form. We got to apply to five universities. York was my first choice to study French. Then Sheffield, Leeds, Exeter, Manchester, in that order.

I told Mother.

"Oh darling," she said, "You make me feel so inferior." I was invited to York for interview, and to Sheffield and Manchester for an open day. We'd had a school trip to Manchester to listen to some lectures on Shakespeare. Based on that experience, I decided not to bother to go to the open day. I didn't like it there; I wouldn't be going.

But they offered me a place anyway.

I caught the train to York. I went by myself. Then I caught a bus from the station to the university. It was wonderful. I had a letter afterwards offering me a place on the course provided I got two As and one B in my 'A' Levels.

I also went to the Sheffield open day. The course was big on drama which I wasn't that interested in. They offered me a place if I got three Bs at 'A' Level.

It felt wonderful to receive multiple offers of a place at university.

***

I decided to have a party for my 18th birthday. I'd never had a birthday party in my whole life.

I hired the function room upstairs in the White Lion pub and asked a friend of Bernie's who was a part time DJ if he'd provide the music at mates' rates. I would do my own catering.

I made my birthday cake. Ma gave me £10 to buy some party food. My birthday was a Friday and the party would be that evening. I made invitations and posted them out.

On the day of my birthday and party, I skived off from school to make all the food.

Bernie turned up with a gorgeously wrapped box. Inside was a beautiful emerald green dress with matching flimsy underwear he'd chosen for me.

"I love you," I said and meant it in that moment. No-one had ever given me such a beautiful gift.

He helped me cart all the food to the pub, "Who needs to go to catering college?" I said out loud, admiring the spread I'd prepared.

The pub landlady donated a huge bowl of punch which people added to throughout the evening.

Ma showed up at the party just as I was giving my welcome speech inviting everyone to get completely drunk and have a fabulous evening. ("Darling!" she said, appearing shocked.) She presented me with a birthday cake she'd had professionally made for me which was a really lovely surprise.

***

Our exams started.

Each morning Ma would say, "Make sure you read the question, Darling," and give me a peck on the cheek.

I had revised endlessly, practising essay writing, learning great quotes from all the books by heart. I just had to stay calm.

My last exam was Economics. I had revised all I could and decided to go to bed early. I was there ten minutes when Carol came in to tell me Bernie had arrived. I went downstairs.

"Come out for a quick one," he said. "I really need to see you."

"OK, just one," I said and went and got dressed again. We went to the pub. He was quiet.

"I thought you needed to see me," I said. "I should really be in bed getting some sleep for tomorrow. You know I have an important exam."

"I love you, Bess," he said and took my hand. He didn't look at me, just stared down at my hand.

"What, Bernie?" I said. "You're scaring me."

"Will you marry me?" he said. He looked up and saw my face. My mouth had fallen open in surprise. I had assumed he'd brought me out to dump me.

"Well?" he prompted and looked back down.

"Why?" I asked. "You know I'm off to university.

We might not last that long!" It came out involuntarily. "Sorry," I said. "But we can't think of marriage yet. I'm only eighteen."

"You said your mum married at eighteen…"

"Nineteen," I corrected him. "I don't want to be like my mum. I don't want to repeat her mistakes." I was really putting my foot in it, I could hear myself.

"I think you'll break my heart. And I don't want my heart broken again. So…" he paused. "I think that's it then."

I sat silently, staring at him. Then I got angry.

"So you drag me out of bed the night before the most important exam of my life and tell me that if I don't repeat what my mum did – the thing that ruined her life – we're finished? Is that what you're saying?" I was livid.

I picked up my bag and ran all the way home. I could hear him chasing behind me, calling out my name. But I slammed and locked our front door before he could reach me.

I got back into bed.

***

Once the exams were over, we had a couple of months to wait before the results came out.

Mother was in increasing pain with her back. She had no idea what was causing it and her doctor was not being helpful. I suggested she should ask Grandfather if he would pay for her to have her back checked out by a private consultant to get to the bottom of it.

"Well, he knows all about it so I guess he would have offered by now if that was an option. I can't ask him for help again," she said.

She carried on working long hours every day. I hardly saw her.

I asked if there was any casual labour needed at her factory. There was and I got a job. So at least I could get to see her there.

***

One evening I went out by myself to the local night club where I used to go regularly with Bernie.

I went to the bar. Jon, who was Bernie's best friend, was sitting by himself smoking cigarettes. He seemed pleased to see me and paid for my drink. We sat there chatting away.

I told him I was waiting for my 'A' Level results before going to University in October.

He said he'd lost his job in the pub he'd been managing in West Sussex. He'd lived above the pub so had also lost his home. He'd come back for a bit to live with his parents. His girlfriend who I'd seen him with before was a nurse in West Sussex and was still there.

Jon was good looking and very popular. He was 25, very charming and funny, everyone liked him.

He had a reputation as a heavy drinker. His fiancée had died of leukemia a couple of years earlier. They had both run a pub together in town. He wore her engagement ring on a chain around his neck.

"I drink to forget," he said, "What is there to forget you ask? I don't know. I've forgotten." He laughed.

At the end of the evening, he asked if I'd like to go back to his place. His parents were away. He drove me there in his car which was an old Beetle. He let us in and we talked some more and he carried on drinking. Then he took me by the hand and led me into his bedroom. He lay on the bed and promptly fell deeply asleep. I let myself out of the house and walked home.

The next evening I went to the White Lion which I knew was Jon's local. I was at the bar when he came in. He apologised for crashing out the night before.

"Give this beautiful young lady a drink" he said to the landlord. And we resumed our conversation from the night before.

And so the rest of the summer played out. Jon and I became an item even though he was officially still going out with his girlfriend in West Sussex. Everyone knew Jon and now everyone knew me.

Jon became a regular at our house too. He was such a sociable guy. He was a great hit with Ma too and called her 'Marmie' as you would if you were trying to get around your mum. (The name stuck and I called her that too, from time to time for the rest of her life.)

When it was Ma's birthday, Jon and I made her a birthday tea for her to gobble down before she went back to work for her evening shift. Occasionally I would go back to the factory with her for a second shift to earn some extra money.

'A' Level results were due out at any moment. "When are they due?" Ma asked.

I told her when we would be getting them in the post. "But the school gets them the day before," I foolishly told her.

I had taken a day off and was lying on a rug on the grass sunbathing on the afternoon before the results were due to arrive in the post. Ma came home and walked across to me.

"Right," she said, "I rang your headmaster at the school. I'm sorry, I couldn't wait for tomorrow. There's so much riding on your exam results. He told me you got two As and an E. E for economics. So you didn't get the grades you need for York. He's been pleading with them to let you in," she said, "on the basis that you got an A for French and you'll be reading French. But they won't budge because the competition's so tight. So he's calling round the other universities who offered you a place."

I cried for the first time for ages.

I cried because Mother had ruined my anticipation; I cried because she was finally showing an interest in me; I cried because I had allowed myself to go out with Bernie the night before my economics exam and had flunked it and lost my place at York; I cried because I'd got an 'A' grade in French which I'd been told was unheard of. I was so proud I'd got top marks. Finally, I cried also because my headmaster had busted a gut to argue my case with York University.

In the end he got me a place at Manchester, the place I'd not bothered to visit because I decided I didn't want to go there. My French teacher consoled me when I went to meet with her.

"It's their loss," she said of York. She gave me a massive carrier bag of key texts that she fished out of her store cupboard. "These will get you ready," she said. "Get ahead with your reading over the summer."

Jon had been ditched by his nurse girlfriend who'd

heard stories about him and me. He went down to West Sussex in his Beetle to collect his belongings from her place and we met that evening.

I went to the bar to get some drinks. Bernie was there.

"I'm off to Manchester Uni," I told him.

"I thought you were going to York?" he said.

"I didn't get in," I said. "Their loss!" and smiled.

***

Now it was my turn to get ready to leave home.

Manchester University had sent me a list of things I should bring with me when I moved into my Halls of Residence in October.

Ma drove us down to Brent Cross Shopping Centre. We went to the huge M & S there and bought me towels, tea towels, a mug tree and six mugs, duvet covers and matching pillow cases, wooden spoons, a saucepan, cutlery, plates, bowls, an egg cup.

And then it was time to go. I said a sad farewell to John but promised to write.

We finally arrived at the halls of residence. It seemed I had chosen a university a long way from home, deliberately or by chance, who knew?

We humped all my stuff up to my room. The building was full of people milling around with parents and luggage, finding their rooms.

We dumped my stuff on the floor of my new home and looked at each other.

"You don't have to hang around, Ma. It's a long way

home," I said.

"Take care, darling," Ma said. We had a long wordless hug and Ma sighed.

I walked with her back to the car. Then she was gone. I was on my own.

Dad came home shortly after I left. Finally, he had Mother all to himself, just as he'd always wanted. But it didn't work out. He found out she was having another affair and they were divorced within a year.

Part Two

27th July 1987

Darling Marmie!

Hope you got home OK last night, and that your bones aren't aching too much today? Thank you so much for your absolutely invaluable help, ma: I cannot thank you enough, ever!

Did you get to see Gramps on the way? I hope he was in but, there again, I hope you didn't linger too long ... You really must try 'n' look after yourself for me: early nights, lots of food and Horlicks, curling up with books, visits out, swills out with Corsodyl after that gum disease treatment – and a little self-indulgence (a shopping spree? Evaporated milk in your coffee? ...) every now and again! And a visit to that hip specialist!!!

Sorry about the awful writing, ma; my writing is just too rotten for words these days – my mind tends to work faster than my hand! But it means that this letter should last longer as it'll take you longer to de-cipher it!

Anyway, here I am in my new home and it feels really good. It's just a Tube ride away from work so I'll have lots of time either side of work to do my writing.

I didn't think about it at the time (consciously) but isn't it weird that I followed in your footsteps to do that secretarial course? Mind you, at least I'm doing something with my new skills in my job. I never imagined working for the BBC or in personnel come to think of it. All I ever wanted to do was to be a teacher. Anyway, I guess that's what happens when you have a mental collapse at Uni – get derailed from your dreams and have to rethink everything. And the main point of this job is so that I can earn money in the day to write by night. I'm thinking maybe I could work like Kim's old school friend and not need much sleep! I never believed those stories of Kim's anyway... well, maybe some of them, ha,ha! (Where was she all that time? Truthfully, I mean! Maybe you'll tell me one day.)

As I write, it's 7.15 on Monday morning, and I'm sitting at my desk with the window wide open – I haven't closed it at all; this house is boiling!! I have an excellent view into all the houses across the way, but nothing exciting seems to be happening yet. It poured with rain all last night, but it's quite pleasant out there at the moment.

Will carry on with this this evening!

My room here, as you know, is just perfect. The fitted cupboards with wardrobe go the whole length of the room so everything is stored away neatly. And I love this workbench with all this space to spread out books and papers. I have my little television and my bookcase with all my books which have multiplied by about 500% since I went off to University.

My bed's very comfortable and I have my sofa too. It's all very nice (though very hot which I'm not used to!) I have my own bathroom and Maureen the landlady says I can share the rest of the house with them.

The garden's very small but pretty and my window looks directly down into it so I can just sit and gaze ...

Anyway! My boss started today and I officially started as her PA. She's very nice and I feel quite guilty that I've filled her diary up so tightly for her v first week. The 'Big Boss' is "Dragon" (that's what we all call her but not to her face!); nobody likes her and everyone sighs with relief whenever she has to go out to a meeting. She definitely puts a blight on what would otherwise be a really great working environment! However, I s'pose there has to be one of them in every organisation; I'm lucky there aren't more, but work is really great and I thoroughly enjoy it! I've just got back upstairs after your very welcome 'phone call – so good to hear you, ma! – and 2 glasses of wine. My landlady, Maureen likes to drink a lot in the evenings and there's a friend of hers staying here at the moment so I was forced to share some wine! However, they're still at it, while I came back here to do some writing. Maureen's a producer for the BBC, by the way,

and the friend is a director.

Maureen is going down to Bristol tomorrow for a couple of days, to do some editing; it all sounds fascinating but television's not really my scene – radio, p'raps (?) one day, but books are my first love & I'm getting really int'rested in personnel since I'm working in personnel. My 'personnel secretary's course' is Nov 24-27 and I typed a memo today, requesting a place on an AXS Word Processor Course ['AXS' = the name of the system, like 'Amstrad' or 'Commodore' etc]. And I shall make enquiries tomorrow about these after-work shorthand lessons I told you about. And the library's just up the road, so I shall pay a visit and discover what amenities are at hand! I want a swimming pool and some sort of aerobics class to get this flob off me.

[Uh-oh! A man with a guitar has appeared in the window opposite mine, nearly naked!!!].

My phone number at work – in case you should ever need to ring me / feel like speaking to me there is 01-580-576 ext 2773 and you'd get me as that extension = the 'phone on my desk! I'm sure it'd be OK as another secretary's boyfriend and friends are always ringing her and the temp used to spend her working life ringing her friends.

I'm sad to've left you, ma, and hope you're OK. I hope you'll be given lots of attention by People That Matter(!) but that you'll also soon get used to being self-sufficient in your lovely little house – ie living for yourself more, rather than others always. You're such a wonderful, selfless person, mother, and I do love you lots and demand that you take care of those Bones of yours! I can't believe that what started as a backache is now in your hips!

Anyway, I shall be home with you at the w'end and have worked out the train and bus times and should be at yours at around 8.30 – sounds OK, doesn't it? So then I can find my way to your place and you can leave the key for me around. How about under that mat outside your back door?

On Saturday morning, I could go to work with you,

couldn't I? and sit somewhere and read/write letters/sleep while you work. Perhaps we could go to see Gramps on Sunday and then I could go straight to the station from there – ie early!!!!

Anyway, there's a whole week to go yet!

Hope you're well and happy, ma; all my love goes to you and looking forward to seeing you soon!

***

27th August 1987

Dear Marmie

Since you were so kind and generous to buy me the electronic Brother typewriter, I decided it's really time you had a sample of my handy work, too! So I've got out my Brother typewriter – who fancied a chat with you anyway! – and shall let him loose with you! However, he's pretty tired, I ought to warn you, so, if he makes the odd booboo, and his speech is slurred, you'll know why!! It was lovely to hear you today when you rang me at work, but I was sorry to hear that you weren't too happy! (Sorry I had to rush away, too, but it was pretty hectic today and I had a load of stuff to catch the last post.) (I never do know where the full-stop goes with a bracket: Confessions of a Graduate!!!) ... Anyway, I'm afraid I won't have time to finish this letter 's evenin' which means that you won't get it till next week – the Bank Holiday 'n' all that – and that's not very good, as I wanted to try and cheer you up with a liddle note from me... I s'pose

I could finish it, only I won't be able to tell you all the things I wanted to; ne'er mind, I'll write you a full-length saga next week to accompany your Radio Times I'll send you – we get a free copy as a perk of the job but I don't need it. I feel sorry that I can't be with you to provide an ear for your probs &c – I think we two understand each other pretty well, don't we? Must come from living together last year 'under difficult circumstances', and you've been through so much with me – since I was born in fact. I do think you're the bee's knees, Marmie!!

This week, as I think I've already mentioned, I've had this whole house to myself which has been quite nice as I can leave my doors open and let some air in my quarters! But Maureen's husband Bill comes here tomorrow. I've met him once already; he's very nice but, if he's here when I get home from work, I hope he doesn't give me the 'Maureen treatment' that I had last time as soon as I got in from work!! (ie half a bottle of sherry).

It was my first Friday evening living here. People at work invited me to the pub but I was so tired (burning the candle at both ends all week with my sec-by-day/writer-by-night double existence) that I said no. Got home ready to run a bath and lie in it for an hour, but Maureen was in the kitchen and said, "Oh! Let's have a sherry and you can tell me all about your week ..."

Before I knew it, it was 9.30, we'd finished the whole bottle and I hadn't even taken my shoes off! I went up to my room, lay down on my bed and woke up at 2am with a disgusting taste (half a bottle of sherry!) in my mouth.

I have great plans for this weekend, and am looking forward very much to it since this week has been very hectic at work and I'm pretty tired (I know you are too, but this is my Brother wingeing on here and there's no stopping him once he gets going!!) I'm going museum-visiting and am specialising in London history this time, the Victorian era in particular since I'm reading Trollope at the moment. So I thought: the Victoria and Albert Museums, the London Museum, the Trocadero and ... whatever else I find in my little book! Marmie, you really must come and stay with me sometime – it's much more fun going round these places with someone who also appreciates them! Anyway, all these places are free – makes you wonder how they keep them up! So I shall be getting maximum use out of my Season Ticket and paying nothing extra for some excellent fun and stimulating exercises. (Can't wait!)

And now I must go – as I see that I've passed one of my pencil marks in the margin I was taught about in my typing classes! Lots of love to you my Darlin' Ma and hope that you're feeling a bit better for my Brother's chatter!!! Get your leg seen to, please, NOW! and I'll write again soon.

***

8 September 1987

Dear Marmie

I enclose a snippet of paper, torn from one of those

magazines they throw at you as you emerge from the Underground ('Ms London', '9 to 5', 'Girl' and the like...), not because I had anything specific in mind, but because I thought you might like to see the type of thing 'on offer'; would you like to tell me what your particular likes/dislikes are, musically, as I really don't know and it might be handy for me to know in case something stupendously wonderful turns up. And then I can get your approval and buy good tickets – and then you'll have to come and see me!!!

Has Kim decided yet whether she's going to give up her job to go and live with her Greek guy in Greece? Can you influence her at all and tell her not to? I'd love her to come and see me in my London squat (if she'd like to examine my squat, ie) so p'raps you could both come down for the day and we could go out somewhere fabby-do... What d'you think, Marmie? Anyway! Something for you to discuss/reflect upon over the delicious meals I'm sure Kim is concocting for you while she's home!!!

I had a nice – and hectic – weekend (and am still tired from it!). Sister Melanie and her man Roy brought Sister Louise with them on Saturday, which was very nice of them. We all had coffee and bickies – freshly purchased from M & S that morning for the occasion – and then, as the weather suddenly brightened, I insisted they take me out somewhere, so we went to Richmond Park. A lovely and enormous park with spectacular views (as I know you know) and deer wandering round all over the place. However, the brightened up weather didn't stay bright for very long so we couldn't stay all that long, and Lou had to get home to cook her hubby Peter his dinner – I've heard the excuse about feeding the dogs, but... Anyway, a very brief visit but quite pleasant.

You'll be amazed to hear that we actually didn't fight at all or say one tiny cross word to each other! I asked Melanie whether she still sleep walks. She actually denied she'd ever done so which was hilarious because it made me wonder whose version was correct! Did I imagine her sleep walking? Did I make it all up? She says she doesn't remember anything from our childhood before the age of 16. Surely that can't be possible? I remember everything– or do I? Maybe I made it all up in my head – just cling on to made up memories! That's a bit weird isn't it? Can we make up our past or redesign it maybe? There's a thing called "false memory syndrome" I've read about where shrinks can put ideas into your head about things that never actually happened.

Anyway, I wanted to ask you what did you think about the sleep walking story I sent you? It was a bit wicked wasn't it! I laughed out loud while I was writing it, I have to admit. Gosh! I wish it had been true! (I can hear you saying – shocked! – "Bessie! What a wicked thing to say!")

On Sunday I got the train to Carol's. She had the day off from her work in the pub restaurant and we just sat and talked all day and ate Smarties. I asked her about the time she cut her wrist open on the French windows and she denied it ever happened. She said the scars she has are from when one of her boyfriends tried to knife her. Bloody hell! (scuse my language) – never heard that one till now. It seems I'm the only one who remembers what really went on in our family (though I have lots of questions I need to ask you some day – to help make sense of so much of it). I think I'll have to write it all down in a book some day just to set the record straight. But there again maybe my version is just my version ... Carol said she was amazed we all turned out OK in the end. I said, "It's not the end yet. Let's wait and see ... " Full of mirth, your beloved daughter, eh?

Anyway, I'm off now as I've reached the end of this side – and sides are rationed! But I shall write again very soon and hit you with some more, Man! Lots of love to you as always and hope to hear from you and see you very soon!!!!!

***

13th September 1987

Dear Ma

Today is a foul day outside: drizzle! And I bet it drizzles all day long – so it will do now I've made that bet! Ha, ha! So I've decided that I'm going to stay in the snugness of my London pad all day and study! Art.

(There is a rather nice smell of toast coming upstairs: it's 9.35 and I had my bowl of Sultana Bran at 7.30 but I could just go some toast ...)

I've been round several galleries &c since my visit to

the Tate all those weeks ago. I really feel that I want to organise what I've seen to make it more comprehensible. That, by the way, is why we humans like to organise, you know: the World, saith the Philosopher, is such a huge and incomprehensible phenomenon that we tiny Beings need to arrange and organise and catalogue and tick off lists and study the History of Art to make our own little worlds more secure. This is why some people catalogue their carrier bags or arrange their jam jars in order of size... She probably wouldn't like me for saying it, and definitely wouldn't agree with me, but I suspect – this is really HEAVY! – that Kim is helping you straighten out your house &c because, when she goes to Greece she needs to know, subconsciously, that she has a secure root to which she can return... What do you think?

...

Maybe instead, I shall write today. I have about 4 short story started efforts here which I've written in about 2 hours each. I can only write for about 2 hours at one time and, in the evenings, this is all the time I have really, once I've been fed, watered and bathed and then, when the next evening comes I do something else or ... whatever. But I seem to've been caught up in the World of Work and so have lost sight (for the time being only, I hope) of why I originally did that awful secretarial course. I write letters, of course, and keep an erratic diary but I'm not really dedicated enough to write stories. It really is frustrating: I have these ideas but can't sit down to commit them to paper and, before I know it, I'll be struck down by a thunderbolt and nobody'll know what these ideas of mine are!! And I s'pose I read too much which isn't really good for would-be writers as their ideas interfere with your own.

[I do believe the drizzle has stopped! But it still looks incredibly grey!]

I'm sorry my letters to you are always so egotistical (I – I – I !!!) but my letters to you are really means by which I sort out my thoughts. I have little time now to sit and think and decide what I'm doing, so writing down things helps to organise (agghh!) myself. When I'm on the Tube – a potentially ideal place to do some thinking – I usually sit (if I'm lucky) / stand, clinging onto whatever's handy, in a stupor. And then there are so many interesting people – with their different attitudes, dress, expressions, habits (!!!) – to gaze at. So I hope you don't mind, too much, if I use you as my confidante with whom I can sort out in which direction I'm going!

But enough! At home: Maureen and Bill have been in residence for Ages now. Maureen came back from 2 weeks in Plymouth to take another 2 weeks' holiday here! And Bill has also had 2 weeks' holiday here. They don't seem to've done anything thrilling but I expect it's nice for them merely to be at home together since they don't usually see much of each other. Maureen cooks sumptuously for them every evening and then they usually drink and drink ... and go to bed. Maureen is definitely the loner of the 2: she tends to come upstairs at about 9-ish to shut herself away for a while to enjoy her own space for a few hours. Their relationship seems ideal to me – more like companions than the usual portrait of a married couple. Bill is definitely The Boss but it's nice, somehow, to see Maureen cooking in the kitchen, preparing the evening meal. Hmmm! I do miss that, actually: having my mummy getting my dinner for me. I think (getting heavy again, here) I do hanker after a settled domesticity but I only realise this at odd occasions: eg I get peculiar sensations – of security and peace and things like that – when I see you ironing or reading, and seeing Maureen cooking seemed to reawaken that.

I've gone off men completely (I think). Fed up with being leered at with crude comments. There's no-one at work I fancy and I don't actually feel a need for a boyfriend which is strange after so many years chasing them. I have gone the complete opposite way now. I stopped taking the Pill since there isn't any need to take it. I haven't had a period since then. I actually went to see my GP just to check that that was OK. He told me my libido needed kick starting!! – not sure whether he was offering but I'm happy to have no libido for now!

It was a very long and stressful week last week and did not end well either. A friend from University, Fred, rang me at work on Friday morning to say he was off back to Italy; his coach from Liverpool came into Victoria at 6.35 and he didn't have to catch the coach to Italy (!) till 9.30 so would I like to meet him for a drink after work?

The silent answer was, "No; I wanna go home and flop", but I said "yes", and got to Victoria coach station at 6.00. It was cold and wet and I was tired and hungry and there were no seats and my back ached and it got to 7.30 and it was dark and I was getting angry because my whole Friday (usually a blissful event) was ruined! So, Stuff Fred! I thought ("how very rude", I hear you say!) and came back home; I got drenched as the Tube wasn't working properly and I had to walk! I was not too happy!! As I got in, Maureen poked her head round the door: "Fred rang. He's very sorry but his coach was late." I just looked at her, the water dripping on the floor! I told you: sod men! Unreliable and useless. Just break your heart – or get you wet! How are you getting on with Mr W by the way?

Anyway, Ma, I'm not going to start another page – I could go on for ever! So I shall say bye-bye and "See you soon!" I'm going on the Word-processing Course Sep 30 – Oct 2 and am on leave the next 2 weeks. We'll have to liaise to see when I can come and see you – asap preferably.

***

20 September

Dearest Ma

It was really lovely to have Kim stay over last night. Bill and Maureen were out. I met her at Kings X and we bought pizzas from Sainsbury's on our way back here. We had a lovely evening reminiscing – she is so funny the stories she tells. She was telling me these horrendous stories of her time at Tooting Bec with the antics of the patients there. I went to bed eventually and so did she. But then she heard Bill and Maureen come home and got back out of bed to go and speak with them. I could hear her voice for hours talking with them. Lordy knows what she was telling them! Then I took her to the Tube for her to get to Heathrow for her plane to Greece. She said it's very cold there at this time of year so I gave her my old camel-coloured winter coat to take with her. She got on the Tube all fake smiles and I was holding the coat as the doors closed!! I saw her clamp her hand to her mouth as she realised that I still had the coat I'd promised her. I stood there looking after the train for ages. Then another one came and went and I walked home. Then I realised that I should have followed her on the next train! So I went back and got on the next train to Heathrow. It's a long old journey when you're clutching a coat and worrying whether you're going to be able to find your sis! I found her in Tie Rack tears pouring down her cheeks as she flicked aimlessly through the ties. "Where have you been?" were her first words. "I got off at the next stop and waited for you but you didn't come." We had a big hug and she now has the coat. But there were lots of tears and wailing. I really don't think she wants to leave you again and go to Greece. Couldn't you stop her? She seems so sad and mixed up. I think you need to tell her. We'll all miss her craziness!

***

20 October 1987

Dear Marmie

Here it is, a little note. I'm munching huge grapes from Kim's new father-in-law's vineyard, thinking of you and hoping that you're OK.

First I must thank you tremendously for enabling me to go Greece with you for Kim's wedding; I'm so pleased we were able to go – I'm sure it must've finished off her perfect day that some reps (especially you) from her family were able to go. I don't think I'll be able, ever, to thank you enough for being so wonderful to me but I hope that the following expresses a little of how I feel:

THANK YOU THANK YOU THANK YOU THANK YOU THANK YOU THANK YOU THANK YOU THANK YOU THANK YOU THANK YOU THANK YOU THANK YOU THANK YOU THANK YOU

How was your day at work? Did you get to bed last night at a reasonable hour? (Don't bother to answer that!!!) Anyway, I hope you're not feeling too anti-climactic after our whirl wind trip to Greece! This morning at work I felt yuk! and wondered how I'd ever be able to be happy at work again after all that excitement and emotion, but this feeling soon wore off as the day progressed and I feel OK now: work is still hectic and we're moving offices next Monday so, what with builders building around me, packing up for the move and still trying to get the day's work done – typing letters, answering the 'phone (which never stops ringing), writing out ID cards, organising Appointment Boards, smiling sickly at the Dragon and all the other duties of a Personnel Secretary ... phew! there's no time to wish the phrase 9.30 – 5.30 had never been invented!

Sis Melanie 'phoned me about ½ hour ago and was very nice and chatty which was very encouraging! Invitations to go and visit her, enquiries about our Greek Adventure and News about herself. I've also just had a little chat with Maureen – told her a few anecdotes, gave her a bag of sugared almonds from the Greek wedding which she was very pleased with, and apologised for not making it here on Friday and for you not catching her yesterday. Apparently, they were worried about us because of the Hurricane but she seemed very pleased that we made it to the Wedding. I told her in all the glorious detail how you had to stay behind because the roof was blowing off the factory and then our arduous, heart-in-our-mouths trek down the A1 with all the trees down and how we JUST got to the airport in time but had to park in the short stay car park because we just had 15 minutes to leg it the terminal. It was very exciting in hindsight I guess: the Great Hurricane of 1987 and how we very nearly didn't get to Greece for Kim's wedding.

But then how beautiful, unimaginably blue the sky was above the clouds considering what was going on beneath the clouds! I hope not portentous! as in Greek mythology! I have to write to all the aunties and the Gramps now – well, I don't have to, but I'm going to tell them about Kim and Christos and their gorgeous wedding! Look after yourself for me and see the doc soon and Chin up! Oodles of love to you (and an oodle for your man, Mr W!) Hope to see you soon.

***

2 November 1987

Darling Marmie

How are you feeling now? I hope, I hope you're much better – please don't go back to work until you really are well again, and then see if you can get to the Doc's! (Sorry about the nagging but I love you so much, Marmie, and hate to think of you so ill, especially being so ill all by yourself ... So forgive me!) You never complain, you never talk about how you really feel. I don't think that can be good for you, keeping all that stuff all pent up.

I'm sending you a goodie to keep your energy up and I've put a special spell on it to make you get better extra fast, so eat it all up like a good girl!

I hope I didn't "disturb" you by having a moan about work yesterday. I am happy at work and still enjoy it – and especially the people I work with/for – but I do want (need!) to have my brain appreciated, and also I'd like to earn a bit more so that I can at least have something to show for my efforts! But I hope I haven't made you worry about me because I am alright! And I have a lovely warm house to live in too!

However, I have a feeling I'm pretty feeble, really, and I know I've caused you far too much worry in the past:

I'm so sorry, Ma, but thank you HUGE HEAPS for being so lovely to me always – you are very much appreciated!! I've written a story which is enclosed. Love to hear what you think.

Thanks for all my goodies – these grapes (munch, munch!) are delicious: bursting with juice and goodness! I go on my Personnel Secretaries' Course on 17 Nov (till 20 inclusive), to which I am looking forward very much. And I hope to come home to stay with you on

Friday evening of 20th – if that's OK!

Please think seriously again about becoming Companion to Gramps and p'raps re-suggest it to him... ??

The weather here is very cold (but lovely and warm in the house!!) and definitely feels like winter! The pavements along our road are thick with wet fallen leaves.

Get better soon Ma and much love to you.

***

8 November 87

Darling Marmie

Guess what? I've just finished another story!! And it's all typed up (1½" margins, double-line spacing and one side of the paper only) and looking pretty good; I think I may let you read it; it's taken me all day to do it (it's now 8.45 on Sunday evening) and I'm feeling pretty good about it.

It's not all that good really, but I think I've managed

to say what I wanted to say. That's always the difficult bit – I have ideas, but it's getting it into The Written Word that's such an ordeal.

Altho' a whole day's gone by without my venturing forth into the World – except for a 10 minute walk to post a letter to Lizzie (!) and to buy a can of coke – I feel as if I have actually done something today! It's a great feeling, finishing a story! Here it is: I'd love you to read it and see what you think.

TUG OF LOVE

By Elisabeth Henderson Clarke 1987

The door opened and Helena stood before her children. There was a tall man behind her. The four girls all looked up together from their tea and cried out excitedly:

"Hello Mum – " "Guess what, Mum – " "Mum!"

Only Rose, the youngest, said nothing. She left the table and ran to her mother, hugging her mother's legs with her short plump arms.

"Look, Darlings!" Helena's usually strained face was animated. "This is Francis." She stepped aside revealing the tall man to them. His hand rested on her shoulder, laying claim to her.

***

"Diana, Louise, Julie, and you must be Rose." Francis took each child's hand in turn and gravely shook it. "Four beautiful ladies," he chuckled, looking across, above their heads, at Helena. He didn't laugh but chuckled in his low deep voice. "You have four lovely daughters," he told Helena. Helena linked her arm around his and hugged it to herself delightedly.

"Francis," she said, relieved and smiling. "I'm so glad."

"Now then." She relaxed noticeably, letting out a deep sigh of breath. "Let's all have a cup of tea."

***

The four girls are also glad. It is a new experience to have a man in the house for, nine years ago, their mother had gathered them together, ordered a taxi and fled from her violent husband, their psychotic father. After that she had had to struggle for nine years to bring her four girls up single-handed: to feed, clothe and love them so that they would grow up into healthy women, marrying wisely, she hoped, when their time came, to have their own children.

While her daughters were at school, Helena went to work. It was there that she had met Francis. He watched her day after day, his admiration changing slowly to physical desire. She was a tall elegant woman with black hair piled up on her head, showing the soft white skin of her neck. Her face had been beautiful once, but now her brow was faintly lined and her mouth turned down a little.

One day Francis said to her, "Helena, come to dinner with me?"

"Whatever for?" Helena asked astonished, her

eyebrows raised. Helena's father was a famous chemist and she had been expensively educated. She spoke in a gentle, cultured voice,

"I want somebody to talk to," Francis told her simply.

Francis was fifty-three. His first childless wife died ten years ago and he remained stubbornly celibate. Now, at last, he was lonely and admitted his loneliness. He was tall and good looking and had thick iron-grey hair. His shoulders were broad and muscly from years of heaving coal sacks in the East End of London. Nowadays he was a salesman and dressed in dark suits which stretched tightly across his wide back.

To her surprise Helena fell in love with Francis from the East End of London.

"Call me Frank – everyone does," Francis told her as he held her fingers with one hand and nursed a mug of his favourite over-sweetened tea with the other.

Helena shook her head, smiling gently but slightly reprovingly. "No; Francis is a lovely name," she told him, and watched him gulping at his tea.

"Come and meet my girls," Helena suggested. Francis agreed, wanting to know all about her and her private life.

The girls were charmed with him. He worked as a fruit and vegetable salesman and brought them trays of soft golden peaches and bunches of fat yellow bananas. Wide-eyed, they took the gifts and ate them excitedly, the peach juice dribbling down their chins.

And one weekend in May, they all climbed into Francis' company car and he took them to the fair. They sang happily, 'My ol' man's a dustman, he wears a dustman's hat,' and Francis chuckled. Helena took Francis' large hand and squeezed his fingers happily.

Francis and Helena were married in June.

Helena had to organise her own wedding. Her mother had died shortly after the first one and her father, disapproving of Francis' East End origins, pleaded an arthritic knee. He would not be attending the wedding. So Helena had to conceal her hurt and asked Miss Peters to give her away. Miss Peters was the elderly spinster who lived next door. She was Helena's adopted mum.

Invitation cards were sent out with the letters RSVP in gold paint on the bottom left corner. They came back from Helena's family: 'We regret –", "- because of other commitments", "The baby has measles –". Francis did not seem to mind.

"I'm marrying you, not your stuck up sisters," he told her, kissing her worried forehead. And Helena smiled at him and kissed him back. But her family's snubs struck deep wounds in her heart and she cried to herself a little, locked in the bathroom. The message from her family was unspoken but painfully clear: "Him or Us." If I have to choose, she thought, splashing cold water onto her face and staring at herself in the mirror, I choose a husband for me and a father for my little ones. And the thought that her daughters were to have such a kind and generous father after so many years softened the pain a little.

"I'm so sorry, Francis," she said to him when they were alone. "When they do meet you, they'll all love you." She was more upset on his account than on her own.

***

Helena was awake before she opened her eyes. Emerging slowly from sleep her mind gradually adjusted itself to re-establish its waking consciousness. This gradual reshaping of her Self, however, was interrupted when the realisation of being married again formed into a thought sentence. She was lying next to her husband. She jerked suddenly wide awake; her eyes blinked open.

But the room was silent. Francis lay sound asleep on his side, one arm curling over her thigh. Helena turned her head to watch him for a while. Then she stretched her body beneath the sheets, flexing her toes, wiggling them. She smiled contentedly. The June sun shone through the curtains and specks of dust danced in its light. Helena could hear the distant rumble of traffic far away outside the hotel room. So peaceful, she thought, what peace! And the man at her side stirred and softly stroked her thigh. "Hello Darling," he said, his voice thick with sleep.

The telephone beside the bed began to ring, shattering the still moment. "Bloody hell," Francis grumbled pushing his face into the pillow. "Who the hell is that?"

Helena sighed and reached for the receiver. "Good morning," she said cheerfully. It was beyond her to be rude to anyone.

It was Reception. There was an urgent call for her. Would she take it? "Yes, of course." A pause, a click and Miss Peters' voice was on the line. She felt dreadful about disturbing them, and she hoped it wouldn't ruin their honeymoon but it was the little one.

"What's the matter?" Helena demanded sharply, instincts immediately alert. She sat up straight in the bed, letting the sheets slide so that her white shoulders and breasts were exposed. Francis watched her, this desirable woman, Helena, his wife. But Helena was speaking urgently into the telephone: she would be there as soon as possible. No, of course it didn't matter. They'd got nothing planned anyway. (Francis had planned a day in bed.) No, Francis wouldn't mind – Helena glanced down at Francis who lay, furious, listening to the conversation. "Tell her Mummy will be home this morning," Helena said. She put the receiver down.

And now Francis sat bolt upright, his grey hair ruffled so that he looked almost like a mad man.

"What the hell's going on?" he demanded. "Can't you leave those bloody kids for a minute?"

"I've left them for more than a minute," she replied quietly. "Rose is being sick and won't stop crying and won't tell Miss Peters what's wrong." She paused, her face pleading with Francis. "She's very sensitive, Francis darling. It's most important that she knows nothing's going to change now that we're married. We did agree," she added.

Before Francis could stop her she had slipped out of the bed and was quickly dressed.

"But things have changed," Francis insisted watching her. "You're my wife. You're mine now."

"I know Darling," Helena told him. "I am yours." She refused to raise her voice but spoke quietly and patiently, as if explaining to a child.

And all the time she was doing up buttons, putting on face cream, brushing her hair. "But I'm also their mother and they need me too."

Her quietness was infuriating. Francis' anger flared. "They're spoiled," he shouted. "This is what happens when you pamper them. Spare the rod, spoil the child. What they need is a good hiding!"

"Francis Darling," said Helena reproachfully. His words had struck home but she would not show her hurt to him. "Come on. Get dressed. We have to go."

***

Helena sat on the edge of the bed. Rose was crying silently, the tears streaming down her red and swollen cheeks. Helena stroked her shoulder gently and said, "Hush, Hush." Eventually the little body ceased to shake beneath her hand. Helena went to the kitchen and made up a drink of squash.

"There," she said to her daughter. "Sit up, there's a good girl."

Rose obediently sat up and sipped at the mug her mother held for her.

"Now don't cry," Helena murmured, infinitely patient.

"I... I thought he'd taken you a... away," the little girl stammered, looking up at her mother. Tears appeared again in her big brown eyes.

"Don't be silly," Helena said, smiling. "I couldn't leave you, could I?" The child smiled at last and gulped again at her drink.

Francis sat sullenly on his side of their bed, staring out of the window. Helena came cheerfully into the room. He didn't move.

"Francis darling," she said. "I've brought you a cup of tea." She sat beside him, holding the mug. Steam curled up from it. He was silent, unmoving.

"Francis darling," she said again and stroked his shoulder softly. She put her head against his shoulder and was quiet. The room was silent. She could hear a lawn mower going outside.

At last he took the mug and sipped his tea: strong and sweet as he liked it. His tense body relaxed as the anger ebbed away. He put the mug carefully on the carpet and turned to his wife.

"You're beautiful," he told her pressing his mouth to the soft white skin at the base of her neck. "Don't ever leave me."

"Silly," she said.

THE END

Anyway, that's what I really wanted to tell you but, while I'm here, let me tell you that I trotted along to Burlington Lane yesterday (off Piccadilly) to visit the Royal Academy. The "Age of Chivalry" exhibition is already underway but I didn't look at it. The woman at the ticket office was most put out when I announced that I didn't want a ticket. (They're £4 by the way – I'll treat you; that'd make a change, wouldn't it?) but did she have a leaflet or something on the exhibition? She gave me the "or something" which I enclose for your perusal. So now I await your decision: ie when are you coming to stay so that we can hit Piccadilly? Might I add that Christmas decorations are now going up in the vicinity, if you fancy a liddle looksee at those too.

How are you, my Darling Marmie? I'm really shocked to hear about the diagnosis of osteo-arthritis, but I s'pose I knew all along that it was something pretty ghastly. I haven't had a chance yet to consult any learned books about the disease but, don't worry, I will! We must scout around and keep eyes and ears open for any cure/ alleviation, and it's your responsibility, my poor damaged Marmie, not to overdo things! I love you so much, Mother Dear, and know that you've been through so much – much much more than you ever speak about – and I just want you to be happy and well now.

So! Take care of yourself and I'm looking forward very much to 20th!! (They've turned the central heating on here and it's unbearably hot – I had to take a cold shower!!!)

***

17 November 87

Dearest Mother

How are you? I hope you're feeling OK and managing to find time for a couple of minutes' relaxation every now and again!! Not long before I see you again – it seems Ages since I saw you last! – and I hope to find you bursting with Good Health!

I got nabbed by the Sherry-Pusher landlady last night – although I managed to get away fairly quickly after only one glass and a handful of Twiglets! She seemed in a friendly mood as she slaved over cauliflower cheese (that woman even manages to look dainty when she's making cheese sauce – not like me, with flour on my behind, where I've wiped my hands, and grated cheese over the floor...) and was asking about you. I mentioned that you'd like to see the Age of Ch. and she thought that a splendid idea – and p'raps we could all go out for supper ...

My landlord and his lady spent last weekend at their other house so I was all on my ownsome. It wasn't an especially thrilling weekend because I wasn't feeling too well and I think this was mostly in the mind because I had a story in my head and just couldn't write it! I'm not joking! I always feel ill! When I have an idea – it's all written in my head but it's not much good there is it? I finally sat down on Sunday afternoon and got it written and typed within 2 hours!!! It just flowed from my pen! I'm going to send it to a writing magazine I get and see what they say.

***

25th January 1988

Darling Ma

I'm glad you got Home safely after our lovely day together. It was so nice to see you again and so good (and brave and energetic) of you to do the journey! I hope you're not too tired and aching as a result! But it was a really wonderful exhibition, wasn't it? and I can only thank you, once again, for taking me there.

Anyway, you've revived my enthusiasm for London again – it had never really gone but I was wallowing in lethargy!...

*Today at work was fairly satisfying; if it wasn't for the **** money, I'd be quite content to stay where I am. Our Super Sec had the day off so I was doing her boss' work as well – which included the letters to staff about the decision to make them all redundant! There were 78 letters and envelopes to type but I did the letters on the word processor! And all the time I had to answer 2 'phones, send off application forms – requests for these were coming in thick and fast as we have some "popular" jobs currently advertised – and keep up with my own boss's work...*

I bought Melanie a lovely card today for her b'day and have just written her an accompanying note. I hope she's alright and is happy. I wish I weren't so sentimental sometimes; I can't help remembering past times and yearning for them – not very healthy, I s'pose! Eg I remember 'Elderberry House' which was a little nook she and I discovered in the graveyard just over the fence at our old house, among some elderberry bushes, and we made bows and arrows and had target practice, using some ancient gravestones as the targets! And we formed "The Adventurers" which was our club; we were s'posed to do adventurous feats and planned to climb that tree in the front garden! Carol was definitely not allowed to join! Trouble is Mel tells me she doesn't remember anything from our childhood so maybe I just made it all up – reinventing my childhood with things I wished we'd done perhaps. Who knows?

Aren't I so morbid? I think you must've dropped me on my head when I was a baby! It couldn't have been anything horrible because I love you so much. I hope you're having a good day and are in happy spirits. I hope to be able to visit Home soon!

***

3rd February 1988

Darling Ma,

Thank you for ringing me again today; it is always so nice to hear you, and I was pleased to hear that, at long last, people (ie your man, Mr W and your doctor!) are beginning to take note of your serious "condition". I'm glad you've got painkillers which actually work (at the moment anyway!) but please be careful what you take – and if you detect the slightest, intsyinsiest side effect, you must promise me that you'll shout!! (Sorry about all the underlining, but it is just to show how strongly I feel about the whole Bizz!)

Apart from your aching bones, I hope you're feeling fine and fairly contented. What have you been up to? I was pleased to hear that you'd been to that Garden Centre; I like to know that you're doing things you enjoy.

I have felt much better ever since you came to take me out that Sunday...

I've been cracking on (grinding on – it's a slow process!) with my short story writing. I write one, put it in a drawer for a while, rewrite it, then send it off to a magazine. Then a couple of weeks later, back it comes. There's a sort of rhythm going on! But it's just about keeping going until someone says yes!

I do love writing. I'm sure I'll move onto more sophisticated stuff. At the moment it's my therapy – making sense of crap from the past (I'm sorry but there was A LOT of crap), finding meaning in it if you like and as long as the names are changed I think that's fine! And sometimes I like to re-imagine/redesign the past – create a new story, turning out in a new way.

Recently I've been reading a fab book from the library on classic fairy tales. I have a thought – probably been done already I expect – to write metaphorical stories as modern takes on old fairy stories. 'Rumpelstiltskin' always appealed to me. I love the idea of the strange little man tearing himself in two – such violent fury in response to having had his name found out so the queen didn't have to give up her baby. I guess there's some significance in ripping yourself apart like that ...

'Rapunzel' too is a favourite of mine. I remember when you used to read it to us. She reminds me of you with your long long plait. She was given away by her parents too – a theme I'm finding of parents being forced to give up their babies for whatever reason. Anyway! Maybe I can put you into a modern fairy story! All with a happy ever after ending!

In the meantime, I need a job with more money!

Do you think it's wrong to work merely for money? I know that was the original idea, anyway, but it seems wrong in a way. I wish you'd tell me what you think as your ideas/suggestions/advice would mean a lot to me. One thing is for certain, I cannot continue in my present job and shall not rest now until I've found another one. It is absolutely ridiculous to be as constantly broke as when I was a student, and I work (pardon me: it's for emphasis!) bloody hard too and would like just a little reward – and a BIG reward would be wonderful!

Anyway, fingers crossed! And here's hoping!

What else? At work, The Dragon's temporary secretary leaves next Wednesday and Super Sec leaves to start another job in the Beeb on 11th! and Hugh leaves on 11th March! which means that my boss will have to look after Hugh's people until another personnel officer is found and I shall have to work for the Dragon as well as for my boss... I wouldn't mind because it'd mean piles of glorious work but I really do detest that "woman" and I can't abide the thought of having to be subservient to her!

At the moment, I manage to ignore her most of the time but it is becoming a bit difficult to keep polite – and my boss (I'm going off her too now) told The Dragon that I was looking for another job!!!!! So it is getting a bit dicey now and, really, the sooner I get a new job and can hand in my notice, the better. I do, tho', manage to forget all this while I'm working – I get so engrossed – and, believe it or not, I still love the work and the staff I "look after" are all so nice and come to me with their problems and queries and it's all very satisfying.

***

22nd February 1988

Dearest Mother-of-Mine

It's about time for me to leave your lovely house so I thought I'd just write you a quickie to say thank you for letting me stay. I don't want to go back to London and would love to stay here for a whole week more – or forever! It's such a lovely sunny day and the thought of the Office tomorrow does not appeal.

Please take care, my ma, and try to get a bit of sleep now 'n' again. And also, think of yourself a bit more, my Darling, and be "Looking After No 1".

I love you lots, marmie, and I don't want to go back to London...

***

5th March 1988

Darling Ma

I'm feeling quite satisfied as I've just finished a story! It took me 3 solid hours to do and I now realise that the day has gone! (It's 6.45pm on Saturday evening.)

It was a lovely day as well and I went out this morning – just exploring Chiswick. It was sunny and not too cold and I wore that lovely red, yellow and grey tracksuit top and went exploring. I found a great "Health" shop that sells sacks and bottles of interesting things; I spent about 20 mins poking around, looking, but to my shame didn't buy anything! The cheek of the girl! And it smelled healthy too!

Maureen has gone to Essex for the weekend so I have the house and the budgies to myself. (They were making a lot of noise – talking to each other I suppose – so I said, "Hello Birdies," and they haven't made a peep since! I hope I haven't stunned them!!)

As I said, Maureen and Bill were extremely nice and interested about my new job and were very kind to give me the freesias and wine to say congratulations. A 50% pay rise just for moving 2 inches further right in the A-Z! I bought myself a T-line shorthand text book as well today and hope to have the patience to look at it and "brush up" on my "short forms". I think I'll be using my shorthand lots in My New Job and I hope my new boss Nigel is going to be patient with me as I am a bit rusty – and the words'll be more technical, won't they?

I'm really looking forward to starting (I got my P45 from the BBC today; they are efficient in that respect anyway!) but I must confess to more apprehension than I remember feeling when I started with the BBC (8 months ago!)

My last day went well. The Dragon wasn't in which was Great – we had an extra long lunch hour! And my boss was only there in the morning which was also Great as she couldn't give me any last minute, urgent stuff to do. I think I left everything in good order for the new girl...

6th March 1988

Hello again, Dear Ma. It's now 12.30 on Sunday and I've just typed up the "story" I wrote yesterday. (It's called "Home" and is pretty deep stuff – I might let you read it...) Also, this morning I've done all my ironing, so I've been pretty busy.

While I was ironing, Melanie rang to wish me Good Luck for tomorrow, which was very nice of her. I had only just been thinking about her, too, as I ploughed my way thro' umpteen blouses, so I think she must have caught my vibes. [I'm eating a juicy apple while I write and trying not to let it drip on this paper; I was eating a jam doughnut yesterday while walking up the stairs and imagine my horror when, later, I saw that I'd left a trail of jam splodges all the way up!!!]

Anyway, Melanie and I had a nice little chat and it was good to hear her.

Today I discover that my freesias have opened overnight and are really lovely. And my amaryllis is now leaning alarmingly so I'll have to search out a piece of string. Yes? (The amaryllis is looking decidedly obscene at the moment!!)

Did you see 'Butch Cassidy and the Sundance Kid' last night? or were you still chez Gramps? It was excellent; I really enjoyed it. Effective end I thought.

You may have gathered that I am not gadding around anywhere this weekend and this is because I'm trying to make it last as long as poss. If I do anything (ie culture vulturing) the day goes too fast and I can't believe that I'm starting my new job tomorrow! In fact, this time tomorrow I may be spending my first Luncheon Voucher ...

I'm really looking forward to my new salary tho' and am determined to save as much as I can, spend the rest wisely and generally be more responsible about money for the 1st time in my life!

I hope you're feeling OK, Ma. How are those blessed bones of yours? I do so wish I could help you in some way!

However, I think you're so brave and wonderful, Ma. I just hope something can be done pdq (pretty damned quick!) so that we can go on our holiday together. I haven't forgotten the Cruise by the way!

I'll see you at the weekend, ma, and speak to you before then.

***

22 March 1988

Dear Marmie

I've finished all the work I found waiting for me on my typewriter this morning and Nigel's on the 'phone again! So I thought I'd write to you. I'm actually writing it in shorthand because he's liable to pop out of his office any second (he often does this!) and will probably try and peer at what I'm up to! But when you get this letter it should be nicely transcribed and I hope to have time to type it up tonight. (It may be slightly altered by the time it is typed up but you are not to know, are you?)

Anyway, first I must thank you very much for your lovely b'day card and the pressie. It was very good of you to give me a cheque rather than cash; I put it in the Halifax yesterday and felt very pleased with my self as I haven't put anything in there for ages! So thank you very much for that: that may be the first contribution towards my mortgage ... (I'd love to be able to buy a flat in London, and a house eventually so that I could rent it out and live in the country).

My birthday was very quiet but it was lovely to be remembered by so many people. I don't care what Dad used to say about not caring if nobody liked him. It is nice to be remembered and I think I would have felt quite miserable if nobody had. (With four sisters, though, I think I'm guaranteed a couple of cards at least!) Maureen realised it was my birthday because of the pile of cards waiting for me when I got in on Sunday night; the first thing she said was, "Is it your birthday?" so I had a card waiting for me when I went down for my breakfast the next morning and it was a really lovely card: a girl sitting at a desk surrounded by books. She must have had it all ready somewhere because she had no chance to go out and buy one.

I happened to mention it at work last week that my birthday was on Monday; we were discussing ages and Susan (who used to be Nigel's secretary) thought I was 23 because Nigel had told her I was. So I said, "I'm 23 in March". She asked, "When?" and I told her. But that was a week ago so it was extremely nice to have 2 cards (one from a very nice girl called Ros and the other from Susan) and Ros also gave me a chocolate orange! I had been all prepared to forget it was my b'day while at work but it didn't turn out like that! Because my cards were on display, people kept saying, "Is it your birthday today?" Mind you, Nigel still made me stay late!

I didn't go out last night but had all my washing to do: two massive loads which took me till 9 o'clock, so tonight I've got piles of ironing to do. I really didn't feel up to it on Sunday night you see and now I'll spend the week trying to catch up. (Where have those elves gone to? They never seem to visit my washing pile anymore!!)

I had two b'day telephone calls last night: from sis Louise (!) to tell me that she kept forgetting to post my card but I did have one (on the window sill!) and from my old friend Ava. I must have cost her a fortune because we were talking for about half an hour but it was nice of her to ring me, I thought. And of course, there was your 'phone call in the morning and a friend from the BBC rang me too to suggest we go out for a celebration on Thursday which I'm looking forward to

(Sorry this letter reads in a stilted way! It's quite difficult typing this shorthand back but I'm managing and haven't changed a word yet!!)

Gramps rang me on Sunday night to wish me a happy birthday for the next day and to say that my card was in the post.

My real birthday treat though was over the weekend and thank you as always, my darling ma, for having me to stay in your nice little home.

By the time you get this letter, you'll have been to the physiotherapist doobrey. How did you get on and was it worthwhile? Oh Mother, Mother, Mother, I hope it's not too long before we can get you better again.

I've just had my lunch and am waiting for Nigel to finish dictating a tape for me – he's quite a sweety really! and I can hear Lil with her trolley: we get tea and biscuits now! Lovely Lil comes to our desk and pours it for us from an enormous teapot.

I haven't really got any news for you at the moment because I haven't really done anything since I left you on Sunday. Thank you for taking me to the station and

I hope you had a good journey home again. While you were acting out your sign language outside the train, the man opposite me said, "She wants you to ring her" and another one said, "You'll have to learn sign language"; what helpful people there are about!! I hope you know all about thought language because I think about you most of the time and I hope you pick up the occasional wave! You are a really wonderful person, Dear Ma, so brave, so gentle and so giving. I do appreciate you and wish that I could be more like you: the atmosphere in your house is you through and through and that's why I love to visit you.

***

Easter Monday 1988

Dear Ma

The last day of the Easter weekend! I hope you've had a good one – it sounds (from your 'phone calls) as if you have, so I'm pleased. Congratulations for getting the gardening done: you must be very satisfied about that, but I hope your bones aren't suffering as a result!

Our weather here has been first class, although it looks

a bit dull today. Perhaps it will brighten up later.

It has been a weird weekend for me. 4 days is quite a long time, really, to sit writing and I think I'd go loopy if I attempted a longer stint! All the time my mind is rummaging around in the Past for suitable "material", editing it and adding souped-up bits and imagining characters, and now I'm feeling a bit pulled-to-bits!

I've been out a few times. On Friday, as I told you, I

went along to the Hayward Gallery (South Bank Centre: Waterloo) only to find that it was shut for Good Friday! I was very disappointed, as it's quite a long journey, but I walked back over Hungerford Bridge in the sunshine and got a really breathtaking view of the City skyline along the Thames. So that made it all worthwhile.

And on Saturday morning I discovered Chiswick House (postcard enclosed). I had the whole place to myself at 10.30 and it was wonderful. The grounds are enormous and very well-maintained and I wandered around feeling quite ecstatic. Squirrels scampered around quite unafraid and I took 2 photos of one – one with him (her?) sitting on a tree stump eating a nut and looking straight at me! A very obliging squirrel!

And the house is truly incredible. I have never seen one like it before: it's a true villa in the Ancient Roman style with pillars and long, low-ceilinged, cool corridors. Upstairs the rooms are lavishly decorated with everything possible painted gold and everything carveable, carved! The walls were hung with that furry paper and I was asked "Please do not touch the wallpaper" – I s'pose it would've disintegrated. (I was the only person there by the way, and I felt like a naughty child, looking in some secret rooms.)

The domed ceilings were, of course, painted and there were enormous paintings everywhere. Completely unfurnished but sumptuously decorated!

And that is 5 minutes from Sainsbury's! It was wonderful and so amazing to be the only one there. Was it a dream p'raps? Perhaps I am going potty and just making everything up!

Easter Day, I felt less exuberant and merely went for a long walk, first to Ravenscourt Park and then to the Riverside Studios in Hammersmith. It was a lovely sunny and warm day. I gave Maureen and Bill an egg and they gave me a bottle of Piat d'Or. I have a sneaky feeling that I am using up their cellar! It's very nice of them but I really don't like red wine and now I have 2 bottles. Perhaps, one day when I'm desp'rate?

I think I'm having a crisis! I am 23 and have done nothing and it doesn't seem as if I will! When you were 23 you'd had 3 children(?) and had something to show. I have a drawer full of stories and a headful of dreams. I want to do something real! That's my crisis.

And now I will stop being a selfish bag and will go away and come back when I feel better!

I started another story this morning but after 3 pages I couldn't think of what was actually going to happen, so I've given up for the weekend and shall let things mull over in my subconscious this week – things often get worked out for me that way.

I've told Carol that I'm going to visit her next Sunday (10th) as I want to give her a book to give to Kim when she goes to see her in Greece next month. I haven't bought it yet, but I'm sure she must miss books, so I'll buy one in the week. (I guess they do have books in Greece, come to think of it but maybe they're all in Greek!)

Our little garden looks lovely here: loads of daffodils

with long stems and lots of other things which look nice but whose names I have not an inkling – niceties I neglected to pick up from my darling ma! There's a nice yellow thing which may be a forsythia??

I look forward to seeing your nice little garden soon: it's going to be lovely! I hope it's still OK to come to visit you on weekend of 15-17th?

I miss you miserably, ma!

***

11th July 1988

Darling Ma

James Last's 'Firebird' is playing at the moment and I love to just lie there listening to it; it always reminds me of that lovely evening when you were asleep and I was nearly asleep while I taped some of your records. I always feel very contented – if a bit (lots!) homesick too – when I'm listening to those lovely high notes ...

Thank you very much for ringing me this morning – as ever, you sounded so bright and cheerful on the 'phone; it makes me feel extremely useless for being such a misery all the time but I s'pose you're you and I'm me

– or summat like that! (As I've said before, I think you must have dropped me on my head when I was a baby.) Anyway, you do cheer me up.

However, although you always sound so cheerful, I do remember the pain you're always in and I hope that it's not getting worse; please take your painkillers sometimes,

Ma, to give you a bit of relief. You are so brave; I would have gone to pieces long before now.

I hope this letter doesn't seem too full of 'oohs' and 'aahs' but I have so much to thank you for and I'm never sure if you know how grateful I am for you; in fact I think, I believe I worship you, Ma, which is probably not too healthy but it is so. So there!

Elf Bags full of love to you and I hope to be able to see you very soon.

I've written another story. I'll send it to you!

THE MISSING SHIRT
OR
PIGGY-IN-THE-MIDDLE

By Elisabeth Henderson Clarke
1988

I had never known my mother to be so happy or to look so lovely. She had begun wearing stylish clothes again and taking more care over her appearance. Her dark hair was elegantly bobbed and, dressed simply in cord trousers and a large 'granddad' shirt, I thought how young and happy she looked. Her face was flushed and her grey eyes, usually so dull and tired, crinkled as she smiled at me. I felt strangely proud of her.

We were on our way to meet my mother's friend, Bernie, who was taking us out for a ride in his new Rover Fastback.

***

The next morning, however, I moved stealthily about the house as I got ready for college where I was doing English 'A' Level. My mother always left very early for work but my father now lingered until late in the morning. He was waiting for the post to arrive and hovered near the letter box in the hallway.

I was trying to avoid having to face him. A party, as I was, to my mother's affair with Bernie, I felt acutely embarrassed in my father's presence, particularly as I was almost certain he knew what was going on. I darted now from room to room anxious not to have to speak with him. He stood in the hall, toying with the telephone. I slunk guiltily past him. He was wearing his dressing gown and his iron-grey hair stuck up around his head, uncombed. He whirled round suddenly and I jumped, my heart beginning to race. I looked at him, frightened.

"What's going on, Diana?" he demanded, his eyes blazing. "Who is he?"

His chin was unshaven and grey I saw.

"I... I...," I began. I stopped and looked away, not knowing what to say. "Nothing," I said and, turning, bolted upstairs.

The day before had been a scorching hot day and my mother's boyfriend had taken us to the local seaside resort in his new Rover.

His name was Bernie and he was a senior manager with the fruit packing firm where my mother was the Personnel

Officer. He was about the same age as my mother while my father was quite a bit older. Bernie was quite short really but very good-looking: short, light brown hair and huge brown eyes.

I loved adventure and sat, watching excitedly from the back seat as the needle on the speedometer swung to the right. It was a wonderful car and an exhilarating breeze blew in through the fully-opened windows.

Bernie owned a wooden hut along the beach. There was a tiny kitchen with a sandy floor. A camping stove and a kettle stood on the table and there was a cupboard stacked high with tins of soup. A door led through to another small room where I saw a camp bed made up.

After coffee I left my mother there with Bernie and went off to lie reading in the sun. Occasionally I got up and dipped into the sea. It was a beautiful day but the beach was almost deserted. What bliss, I thought, staring up at the vast cloudless sky. The sound of sea gulls along the beach and the gentle movement of the waves soon lulled me to sleep and I dreamed peacefully until late in the afternoon.

When I got home from college on Monday my father met me in the street outside our house. He was smoking furiously and his suit was crumpled and stained. He smelled unwashed. I tried to smile hello and said, "Hi dad," but felt tired and depressed suddenly. He grabbed my elbow eagerly.

"I've been to the solicitor's, Diana," he told me.

"What for?" I asked mechanically. I carried on walking

but waited for him at the front door. He ignored me and waved his hand importantly.

"I'm not coming in," he told me. "Two can play at her game." I didn't really understand what he meant and opened the door, wanting to get to my bedroom, to shut myself away. But he went on, "I have to keep a diary. As evidence." I shut the front door between us and leaned back on it, closing my eyes for a moment.

Dully, I made myself some coffee and wondered what to eat. As I went through the hallway on my way upstairs, I noticed a small black notebook on the telephone table. I opened it curiously. It was the 'diary' my father had just mentioned and he had already made some entries.

"Good God," I muttered and, putting my mug down beside me, I sat on the bottom stair.

'Friday, 8th July,' I read. 'Late again – 8.30 pm. Went without my evening meal. Could not sleep because of worry. She did not speak with me.'

'Sunday, 10th July. Diana went out with her but I think Maggie dropped her off somewhere. Gone all day. Did not eat again. They did not say where they went.'

'Monday, 11th July. Found his shirt on the washing line so I threw it on the bonfire.'

I stared at the page for a long while before closing it slowly and returning it to the telephone table. I felt detached and empty, and walked upstairs through the silent house. The clock tick-tocked loudly on the landing.

THE END

***

23rd August 1988

Darling Marmie

How are you? It already seems Ages since I saw or spoke with you but I hope you're not feeling too bad. How is your leg and have you used your stick yet? More importantly, have you managed to get to see the doc yet? This end, things are OK (I suppose). I met Kim – as you know – for "lunch" yesterday with Christos on their way from yours to the airport. It was lovely to see her again but we didn't get much time together because their coach was late. Christos was nice and they seemed on good form together but quite a lot of digs going on and I got the idea of a cultural divide though I could be imagining. I managed to quaff 2 cups of coffee in ¼ hour at Kings X Coffee Shop and I left them at 10 to 2 and got back to work on the dot at 2.

Yesterday, Nigel had wonderful plans for me which meant I didn't finish work till 6.30 because of this BORING 10-page letter. It was interesting when I first typed it but, several amendments later, God! Was it BORING!!! All about the law related to a recognition of union dispute. And, since Nigel once wrote a book on the subject, you can imagine that he was eager to exhibit his in-depth knowledge! Did you know that ... ? No, I won't go into the details.

Last weekend was pretty grim really. Maureen

disappeared again on the Thursday and, as usual, I was full of exploring plans but the weather was so yuk that I really didn't fancy it. However, I managed to get some of my ICS (International Correspondence School) creative writing exercises done so I can send them another story now. I have 3 more test papers to get done by October. The course has to be completed by then so – only 2 months so I've got to get cracking.

***

14th September 1988

Darling Ma

At last it looks as if I can begin a letter to you; I so miss not being able to write letters with this postal strike going on! I've just heard that another 30,000 PO people go back to work today so, altho' the post boxes around here were still sealed yesterday, I should be able to post this to you fairly soon.

The radio has just informed me also that a computer failure means that there'll be trouble on my Tube line this morning. So that's something to look forward to and, together with a beastly, snotty cold that I have developed (first one in more than a year!!), I could quite cheerfully stay in bed today, particularly as it is a real winter's day out there today – bitterly cold!

Thank you for 'phoning me yesterday pm. It was good to hear you and I'm sorry I couldn't stay to speak longer but Nigel had done his favourite thing – given me some work at 5.15 after an idle afternoon! – and was hovering! I've told him time and time again about hovering but he persists, especially now that we've moved offices and I am once again bang outside his door. But he goes on holiday next week, for 2 weeks, (to Devon; I wrote to book the cottage and to order 2 pints of milk per day!) so he'll be out of the way then at any rate. (He said he'll ring in to see what's happening! And I thought you were a workaholic!)

***

15th September 1988

I've just heard that the London POs have refused to break their strike – obviously enjoying their holiday! As Dad'd say, "Get the Army in ..." So it looks as if this could grow into a fairly long letter by the time I come to post it.

And I'll give you a running commentary on the progress of my cold if you like. (If you don't like, it's too bad!) This morning I woke up with crust stretching from my right nostril (it's always only one!) to my chin – like the crust on the lava of a volcano, so you can imagine what happened when I scraped it off ... (Did you really bring me up to be like you?)

Anyway, I haven't thanked you yet for a lovely weekend, have I? I hope I didn't pick this bug up from your house because that'd mean you have it too. I hope you're well.

It was good to see you and it was lovely to get home again – I'd forgotten how nice your house is, so it hit me again when I walked in the door on Friday evening. So much like home!

That was a lovely lunch on Sunday: yum yum! Thank you v much for that: Sausage & Yorkshire – I'll have to remember that combination! And thank you, too, for all my smellies and the food parcel.

I wonder how Kim's b'day went à la Greque? Poor sis, I do feel sorry about it all. Having to leave you like that, though I guess she didn't have to – just must have wanted to. I know she likes to be sensational. I really feel that she and I get on well now. Looking back it seems as if there's a big gap in my life when she simply wasn't there; I s'pose I was too engrossed in growing up to think about her much, but I'm glad we're proper sisters now. But I do remember when I was little (and she literally wasn't there) feeling her close to me. Maybe we'll get to talk about that someday. It was strange – I used to feel her there. I could see her. I wonder if you did too?

The bad news is, my Darling Ma, that all the post boxes are still sealed, but the good news is that the postmen should be back to work tomorrow morning! So I hope to be able to post this tomorrow and you might eventually receive it! All my news will be hopelessly out of date, but I hope you won't mind.

I hope you're managing to get home at a more civilised hour now but suspect not: I'm not sure I like your new job!! How is your leg? Do you have enough pills? Have you managed to get to see your useless doctor yet? (I'm not surprised you're not all that bothered about seeing him – worse than useless!)

What else do I need to tell you?

I'm cracking on with my writing course.

Did you read "Mind the Gap"? What did you think?

I thought it was my first really "saleable" story to date – probably because I made it all up! I was quite pleased with it anyway and hope you were too.

***

22nd September

It's Thursday already: the week has zipped by again. Peculiar how the week seems interminable on a Monday or Tuesday but, once Wednesday's over, wow! It's the weekend again – and then Monday again all too soon!

Here, it looks as if it rained in the night and this morning is grey and damp. An umbrella day. Have you used your brolley/walking stick yet? And how is your leg anyway? In fact: how are you feeling truthfully? I wish you would take a holiday. I haven't forgotten the cruise, by the way, and, in fact, I have a (very) little contribution to it which you shall have ... when I see you.

Do you think – would it be possible – Could you tolerate – Can I come a-visiting 1-4 October please? If not, it doesn't matter dreadfully; I can cope. But if yes, it'd be soopa-doopa for me, at least.

***

5th October 1988

Dearest Ma

Today was a good day at work and I was pleasantly busy all day. Nigel was pleased to see me – well, he seemed to be – and I went out for lunch with the other girls to the Red Lion (our local). We have one day there (or lunch time, rather) a week which is good fun. They are a great bunch and everyone is so friendly.

What else to tell you? I went to the library yesterday afternoon and got a book out on embroidery.

I'm determined to do this seriously so, with my next salary, I'm going to kit myself out with blunt needles and material and thread and perhaps a frame too. And then I can think up suitable ideas for stories while I sew. It might also be good for relaxation (soothing, like being at home with you) because I think that perhaps my inability to relax could be one my problems.

I love the Greek myths where the ladies stay creating tapestries while the gods fly off and create mayhem. There's a lot to learn from ladies with their needles and thread I think!

I had a huge pile of post awaiting me which was very nice including one of my test papers (sent out before the postal strike) back from my ICS tutor. I got another B+!! He (I assume it's a "he"; it sounds like one) wrote glowing comments about my answers to the critical/

analytical part of the question. (I think I've told you that each test paper has 2 parts: questions on a short story by a famous author, and your own creative story.) The story was EM Forster's 'The Machine Stops' and he wrote to me "You have been very much at home with your reading and have written on it with great confidence." I should hope so! Anyway, I was pleased with that. And now I have 2 papers to do by the end of this month: eek!

Our work Christmas do is on 9th December at a night club in the West End. I can't wait: it should be really fun. I'm feeling much better now; hope you didn't mind too much my unburdening myself.

***

22nd October 1988

Dearest Ma

I'm sorry I haven't written all week I haven't even thanked you properly for such a lovely weekend last week. As always, it was lovely to see you and to be at home and thank you for the swag and the lovely Sunday lunch.

However, it is terrible to see and hear how much faster your hip is deteriorating: how much longer d'you think it can last out? When you see Mr Picker again, you really must tell him the whole truth and nothing but the truth or what are we going to do about our holiday? What do you really think about my suggestion that I come back to live with you? At least I'll be able to keep an eye on you and help with the difficult chores. If you do get selected for the op, you won't have to worry about taking time off work, because I'll be able to pay the bills while you're convalescing.

And anyway, I have decided that I shall save up and pay for your operation. So there's no way you'll have to wait till you're 55, OK?

Nothing would please me more than to be able to get you a new hip joint, ma, and to give you a new lease on life. I would feel at last as if I were actually doing something useful and, because I can never say thank you thank you enough to you for everything you've done and had to endure for me, and for my 4 siss-pisses, your new hip would be my gratitude to you. I would simply love to be able to do it and only wish I could hand you the dosh tomorrow! (We may have to forego the cruise for yet a few more years, though!)

Anyway!

I was getting a bit apprehensive about having to tell Bill and Maureen that I'm leaving them to come back to you. They've been so nice to me lately. Eg Maureen gave me that lovely Nefertiti gold thingy I told you about from Egypt and then these clothes began to appear in piles outside my door and I was instructed to take what I liked and leave the rest. (All designer labels though mostly too big for me.) And then, today, Maureen got back from work in celebratory mood because she'd seen the "rushes" of her Egyptian film and was thrilled with them and I was asked to give my opinion on a bottle of wine they'd bought. I really couldn't let this go on!

Then they asked me to join their dinner party (tonight) in double celebration of their 21st wedding anniversary and Bill's b'day (which Maureen missed because she was away). So I had to tell them. And – relief! – it wasn't so bad, especially since, as I told you, they will be selling this place early next year anyway, to go to live in Essex.

So things are much better already.

[I think we have caviar as an "eat" with our aperitifs as I just noticed a jar of it in the fridge!]

Anyway, I'm now off to do my shopping and to stroll along Chiswick High Road. See you later! 7.30 pm, Saturday evening

Maureen has been chopping and stirring since dawn (practically!) and nice smells have been filling the house. It's lamb something. And I saw a note stuck on the fridge reading, "NB chill wine" which sounds promising and also means, since it has to be chilled, that it's white which is amazing since they usually knock back the red. I have bought them a bottle of red "Blue Nun"; I didn't know you could get red Blue Nun, but obviously you can!

Sunday morning

Well! I survived the party (just) but am feeling a bit peculiar today: "hungover", I think would be the most appropriate adjective to describe my condition. I didn't get to bed till 2.45.

The evening/night, though, was very successful and the meal was stupendous. There were 6 of us: Bill and Maureen, Mark and Deborah (2 friends: she's a teacher and he etches), Susie who's 40 but looks 30 and is really nice, and me.

We started promptly at 8 with champagne and delicious canapés: shells filled with taramasalata, caviar and a mint leaf, all exquisitely packed in. And then: Melon, parma ham and figs as a starter, this gorgeous lamb dish (which tasted really professional and was a bit like Lamb Pasanda) on brown rice and calabress, with sesame sticks to munch and red or white wine flowing very freely. Then apple pie and cream, coffee and finally a cheese board and port. It was reeeeeally great and I enjoyed it. Oh! I almost forgot, with the coffee we had dates and Turkish Delight too.

But to get back to yesterday pre-party. After I left you in the morning, I went out shopping. It was a lovely day – quite hot – and I decided to explore Hammersmith (the opposite direction to Chiswick High Road) as I've never been shopping there on a Saturday. Anyway, it's quite good for shopping really and the fruit stalls had good bargains, as it was about 4pm by this time, so I bought 2lbs of satsumas for 50p. And I also bought Carol's 21st b'day pressie at last! So I can finally hand it to her when she asks next time, "Have you got my birthday present?" I knew all along what I wanted to get her but never really got round to finding one, and never had any pennies either. It's a Nottingham lace tablecloth for a square table. I always like the way you get things out (eg a tablecloth or a vase etc) and say, X gave me this for my 21st b'day! Or whatever occasion. So I thought I liked the idea of her telling her brats in years to come, "Your mad Aunt gave me this…".

I've got something about lace at the moment anyway. When I went to Covent Garden the other Sunday and discovered the lace shop there, I was really impressed by the beautiful designs made out of something so fine.

But I think I'll stick to embroidery. I haven't started yet because I haven't found a hobby shop where I can buy all the gear and not get ripped off in the process. But I'm looking forward to starting.

Anyway, I had a really interesting conversation at the dinner party.

Turns out that Maureen goes to bed so early because she has ME – I never knew, though she does always look so fragile and peeky. It's one of those weird "diseases" (is it a disease or just a "condition"?) No-one seems to know much about it but it does have real symptoms she says. She's really wheezy and gets wiped out by awful headaches and very tired.

Anyway, she was talking about a spiritual healer called Louise Hay – American of course – who sounds either bonkers or amazingly brilliant. She's very determined that physical ailments are a result of things going on in the mind and that the mind and body are connected. Makes sense I'm guessing… ??!! Eg when you feel depressed (like me most of the time) your body posture changes so hence body/mind connection. Maureen says that Louise Hay has written a book explaining what physical ailments tell us about what's going on in your mind. AMAZING! So I'm going to get it from the library (you just order whatever book you want if they haven't got it already – all FREE!) and look up what dodgy hips mean. And also lower back pain because that's what I've got right now.

I'll let you know!!

***

10th November

Darling Ma

I hope it all goes according to plan tomorrow or, since you'll have been to see the good man by the time you read this, I hope it all went according to plan, and I hope to be visiting you soon in hospital! (for the right reasons of course). Anyway "my thoughts will be with you" or words to that effect. Not that you're often far away from my thoughts, actually: I often see things / hear things &c which I wish I could share with you at first hand. But I've usually forgotten them by the time I come to write! They occur to me at inopportune times!

I went to see the doc about my back last week. He sent me to see this funny little sports physiotherapist called Paulo. I think he's Spanish or maybe Italian. He waves his hands around as he speaks and told me all about the footballers, ballet dancers and swimmers he works with.

Anyway!

He made me strip off (kept my knickers on!) while he looked me up and down. My pelvis is lopsided apparently. Then I lay face down on his couch thing and he gave me a bit of (very painful) massage and shone an ultra violet light (or something like that) on my lower back – for healing apparently.

Then (get this!) he pulled my knickers down, poked at my bottom and announced that I have "flabby buttocks". What cheek! (get it?!)

He prescribed the gym and running followed by a swim to get rid of the lactic acid.

All new to me, I would have thought that my half hour walk home from the Tube station would have been enough. Obviously not! So I'm off to look for some running shoes to try out some running. Lordy! I remember how useless I was at cross country running at school. Perhaps a trot up and down Chiswick High Road and down by the River very early will be more enjoyable.

Anyway, I checked out Louise Hay on lower back which was interesting. According to her it's nothing to do with flabby buttocks but a fear of money! Whoa! That's heavy, isn't it!? Need to sort that out pdq!!! But I've decided I'll try out some morning trots all the same – firmer buttocks might be more attractive for a start!

Ms Hay also has interesting thoughts on hips and arthritis but not sure you'll want to hear it (or believe it even). I checked out tonsils too remembering my childhood habit of developing tonsillitis (until they threatened to remove my tonsils which was also interesting!!). Apparently, it's to do with frustrated creativity or not getting your own way – not sure how I managed to grow out of that!! Truly fascinating don't you think? – or just a load of twaddle?

***

10th December 1988

Darling Ma

Just checking again that you're OK about me coming back to live with you. What do you really think? I'm so afraid that you wouldn't say "no" even if you didn't want me home with you. I could quite understand if you didn't, since you're used to being by yourself now. And I do realise that I pine for you 5 times more than you do for me, since you have 4 others to pine for, while I have only one of you to concentrate my pining on! But I would not interfere with your routines one little bit.

It was not a wholly impulsive idea of mine. In fact, it has never left my thoughts since the first time I ever thought of it! And each time I visit you for the weekend I think of it again. Because the fact is that I am leading a bit of a weird existence here and am merely wallowing in self-pity and not being any use to anybody. OK, so I occasionally get a story done but my ability to write is so tightly related to my state of mind that, if I'm having a "wallowing day", I just cannot do anything. I had a severe wallowing weekend for no reason really.

[While I write I am eating a very precious plum! You would think that, having lived in London for 15 months, I would be wise to street vendors, wouldn't you? Well, to prove that I'm not: today I bought ½lb of plums for 60p – and I got 3 plums! Which is why they are precious!]

It's time for a move in my life; I've lived in London and don't regret it, but now I want to take a further step and do something useful like get a bit of enjoyment out of life and share some fun and experiences. And what better place than home with my mum and a few friends in the locale. I have a lot of love in me, mother-of-mine, and it's all being dried up. No, not dried up, but unused and bottling up so much that I could scream.

Deborah (at Maureen's party) said going back to live with your mum is a backward step and warned against it. What do you think? I know you don't like to give advice in case we do the exact opposite but I really feel I need some right now – please.

I am really enjoying work at the moment – there's no question in the foreseeable future, at least, of my changing jobs – and I've made some great friends, but none of them live in London. And altho' I'm still in touch with my friends at the BBC, they don't live in London. In fact, I have friends all over the country – my post bag is impressive! – but none of them live in London and London without a companion is a loveless place to be, and I'm fed up with visiting places by myself.

I went to Covent Garden on Sunday because I wanted to visit Jubilee craft market. I had a browse around and thought about Carol and I going there when I came to London for my interview at the BBC all those fateful months ago... Do we really decide on our actions? Or do you think they're all made for us and are meant to be? If I was meant to be doing this, why am I meant to be doing this? I think it was probably to show me that I am not such a self-sufficient, solitary, strong person as I like to make out, and to teach me the true value of Home and my mum. I have definitely learned how important my family and friends are since I've been here. I've also learned to type at supa-sonic speeds and to be accurate! I'm really pleased with my typing accuracy actually: I can type 6 page letters for Nigel without having to make any corrections!! Wow! (So that's why I read French for 3 years!)

It's now 9.20pm but there's no rush because I have to stay awake for Miami Vice at 10.10! There is a terrific clinking of glass and bottle coming from downstairs! Can you read my writing? I shan't keep your eyes much longer!

And you, marmie, how are you? I hope you haven't gone and fallen asleep over this letter! I can't wait to see you again (Friday evening!) and hope that your cold'll have gone by then and that your bones will have had some rest. I do so want you to be well again, ma!

Part Three

THE TWO CATS

By Elisabeth Henderson Clarke, 1989

Our three little rooms are now empty. I am standing on the bare floor boards in the sitting room looking around for the last time. The couple who have bought our flat are moving in today – 3.30 she said she'd be here with her husband. We aren't married but I'd known you for a very long time.

This empty little flat, like me, bears the scars of our life together. Now that that picture has been taken down, the dent in the thin walls recalls that evening you clenched your fist and punched the wall instead of me. There are clean white squares on the walls showing how the walls have been dirty and yellow through your endless smoking. The pictures and the bookcase served as masks, keeping some patches clean. You used to get out of bed in the middle of the night when I refused to make love – you were drunk often – and you'd sit in here sucking endlessly on your Marlboro cigarettes; the air is still slightly tainted with their distinctive smell.

But (I am looking at the bare floor) now that the carpet has gone, I can see the words you painted on the wooden boards: 'I LOVE YOU ALL WAYS'. I left you painting the walls while I went out shopping and when I came back, I saw your message and smiled and I can still remember that sensation of a warm surge in the pit of my stomach which meant that I was truly happy.

This has been my home. But the air in here is stale now and I am leaving, relieved.

***

I have come to stay with my mother.

'Jack's sharing a house with one of his mates,' I tell my mother as we stow all my furniture away in her loft. When we've finished, we sit cosily by the open coal fire in the sitting room and drink coffee out of mugs I remember from my childhood. But then my step-father was with us too, so the mugs hold no pleasurable memories for me. They recall days when my two sisters and I were banned from my mother's company: we must sit in the kitchen to drink our coffee. My step-father told us, 'I have things to discuss with your mother.' Through the walls we would hear him lecturing her, complaining, demanding, and we would envisage her, sitting on the floor at his feet, stroking the hand which gripped her shoulder, nodding, murmuring, comforting him.

I was relieved when my mother and step-father were divorced. My mother bought her own small house and I am staying in it for the first time. She and I are alone here with her two cats.

It's a small square room and two walls are lined, ceiling-to-floor, with books. It's getting dark but we are sitting too comfortably to get up to switch on the lamps and, besides, the coal fire gives off enough light for us to see. The corners of the room are in darkness but my mother, in her armchair by the fire, sits in a circle of orange-yellow light. She is drowsy, I see for her eyes keep closing and she struggles half-heartedly to stay awake. The two cats sleep on her lap, their warm furry bodies entwined.

I feel a warm surge in the pit of my stomach and am safe again at home.

***

My mother tells me she has a friend and they often go out together: he takes her out to dinner twice or three times a week and sometimes she cooks dinner for him here. I am glad. I was worried that she might be lonely now that she lives by herself. He is coming to dinner this evening she says to me before she leaves for work.

I spend the day reading mostly and wandering around the house. I don't want to do anything: I feel contented simply being here. Each room seems to welcome me as I step into it: there are plants and books everywhere and all is so tranquil. I am calm and completely relaxed and sing to myself. The two cats follow me and I talk to them. I tell them all about my empty flat and about Jack and me but here I cannot describe all those mixed-up emotions, the love and hate intermingled, because this house makes it seem all so long ago. Later I say, 'When's mum come home?' and the cats rub themselves softly on my ankles. I hear the garden gate swing shut and we all run to the door, the two cats and me.

***

My mother says, 'This is Mr Newman, Pippa,' and we shake hands and smile politely at each other. My mother calls him Pete.

Mr Newman is a large man: he likes eating and my mother piles his plate up high. We use a dinner set which I have never seen before; my mother has bought it especially for his use because he likes new and expensive things. Most things in my mother's home are old, though, and have been around since before I was born. But when Mr Newman comes to dinner my mother puts away the old things and brings out a new pair of black leather slippers for him and pulls the new video recorder out from behind the settee so that he can watch the old Western film he has brought with him. I am bored and get pins and needles in my foot because I am sitting awkwardly on my chair. I can feel the numbness slowly creeping upwards, to my ankle, my calf, behind my knee. Mr Newman fills the armchair he sits in and my mother is on the floor at his feet, near the new shiny black slippers. Mr Newman sips his coffee from a white cup. The cup has a gold ring around the top; I think it's a new cup. I can bear the pins and needles no longer and get up suddenly. Mr Newman still stares at the television screen but my mother turns her head to see what I'm doing. She smiles. 'Pins and needles,' I explain, screwing up my face and rubbing my ankle. 'Just going outside.' She nods and I go into the kitchen.

The air is fresher in here and my pins and needles are soon gone. I make myself a mug of coffee and now I am sitting thinking about my empty flat and about Jack and me, and I can hear Mr Newman's voice as he discusses things with my mother. The two cats rub around my ankles.

THE END

1989

It's my first evening of officially living back with Ma.

We're sitting in her small sitting room, she's knitting – she's just cast on with beautiful purple flecked wool and is making me a v-necked jumper with a collar that I chose from her collection of patterns – and I am just sitting with my feet tucked under me in the armchair, stroking her two cats who lay curled up in my lap purring gently.

There's music on. Mother loves classical music and has a huge collection of vinyl. She knows everything about classical music, all the composers, all their symphonies, all the conductors, concertos and what not. This evening we're listening to a concert on Radio 3.

It's December and cold outside. But we have the coal fire on and the room is snug and warm.

"I think you are the source of my inner problems, Ma," I say, "and you have the answers to them all too."

"Probably," she says.

"Will you help me work it all out?" I ask her.

She sighed. "You do go on so, Darling. What do you need to know?"

"Would you like a drink?" I change the subject, get to my feet and go off to the kitchen, returning with two glasses of Coca Cola. We clink glasses.

"Thank you for having me back to stay," I say.

"Cheers!" she replies.

We both take a long swig of our drinks, put our glasses down and burp in unison.

We look at each other and laugh.

"Mine was worse than yours," she says with delight.

I take another deeper swig so I can prove her wrong. "What ever would your parents think?" I say, appearing to be shocked.

"It depends how old I was," she says, laughing. "When I was a girl, I saw very little of my parents.

You have to realise that everything was different then."

"Well, we didn't really see much of you," I blurt out.

"Mmm. In a different way," she says, looking down at her knitting.

Mother still refers to Grandfather and Granny as 'Daddy' and 'Mummy'. They'd met at Cambridge where they were both reading chemistry. But Granny never worked. Women of a certain social standing didn't work in those days.

They lived in a big house called White Lodge in South West London. Mother was the youngest of twins and they had two elder sisters, my aunts Pat and Joss. The twins were apparently a mistake, Mother told me, born during the War in 1941 fifteen years after their next eldest sister, Joss.

"When I was a girl," Mother tells me, "I was made to feel that I was stupid. Twin and I (she always refers to her twin sister, Lizzie, as 'Twin') went to a public school for girls. We used to cycle there every morning from home. Mummy had been Head Girl there as was my sister Pat. But I was the dunce of the family. Everyone said.

"I remember Mummy giving me extra German lessons

because I was so useless at it. But I didn't see much of her really.

"Twin and I were looked after by Nanny. We used to do our homework in what was always called the Nursery, even when we were teenagers. Twin was always being naughty but it was always me who got into trouble. I remember once she and I were drinking lemonade and decided to have a burping competition. Of course, it was me who was burping fiercely when Nanny walked in on us and I was sent straight to bed.

"Because of rationing during and after the War, Mummy was always careful with food. We had to eat everything that was on our plate. Food was so precious. Every Saturday we would have tripe and onions for lunch. It was disgusting. And every Saturday I would have to sit there until I'd eaten it. It was loathsome! I remember one day – I was left alone in the kitchen – I poked what was on my plate down the sink plughole. It caused a terrible stench and of course I was found out."

"So why did you do the same to us, then?" I ask. "You made us sit there and eat everything on our plates even if we didn't like it. It was a form of torture, I think. No wonder we've all turned out weird about food!"

"Times were hard, Darling, just like when I was a child. If you hadn't eaten everything up, you'd have gone hungry and it was my job to make sure you didn't go hungry. And anyway," she says lamely, going back to her knitting, "It was the only way I knew. You just do what you know, don't you?"

"And so it gets passed down from one generation to the next," I say, thinking aloud.

"When I worked in that hotel before I went to Uni, remember?" I say, remembering suddenly. "I used to eat the toast that came back from the breakfasts in the dining room. I couldn't bear to throw it away as waste. So I used to eat it myself. Like 'Dustbin' did." It hadn't occurred to me before that I'd done this, some childhood habit repeated unthinkingly.

Ma smiles and carries on with her knitting silently counting the rows.

***

"I often got into trouble," Mother says one evening while we were chatting. "Mummy would say, 'Wait till your father gets home,' and when Daddy arrived home, I'd be called into his study to be talked to very sternly about how stupid I was and how I was letting the whole family down! I would just stare at my shoes while he droned on, just wishing the ground would open up.

"Daddy was disappointed in all of us really: he thought girls were a waste of space. He was horrible to Mummy too. He only married her for her money, Twin and I decided. Throughout their entire life together he was having an affair with Auntie Megan who worked at the BBC. It was quite shocking how he married Megan only months after Mummy died.

"I didn't know Mummy at all really. She was very reserved, painfully shy, I guess. Such a waste of a brilliant mind! She never worked – it wasn't the done thing in those days – but just made a comfortable home for Daddy. "The last time I saw her, when I was able to get to see her in the hospital, she made me promise not to have any more babies. I had to promise her. But the trouble was that I was pregnant with Carol at the time. She died soon afterwards, before Carol was born.

"She died of bowel cancer. Of course, she would have been ill for ages before she would have mentioned her symptoms. She would literally rather die than talk about constipation and blood in faeces or any of the things we know nowadays we have to report immediately to our GP. She was so painfully Victorian and shy.

"I'll never forget the last time I saw her. Your father didn't want me to go of course because it meant that he had to look after you all. We had no car but I managed to persuade a good neighbour friend to drive me over to see her. Her nose looked so huge on her face, I remember. She was just skin and bone.

"She would have known about Daddy's affair with Megan but in those days, divorce was not an option even though she was an incredibly wealthy woman. She would have had nothing.

"We had super holidays though, all over Europe. Daddy loved to travel especially before Twin and I were born. I remember him telling me when he was in San Francisco in the '30s. He was sitting on a wharf dangling his legs over and just contemplating how amazing it was that he was on the other side of the world from home.

"He didn't have to fight in the War because his business was apparently crucial to the war effort. They made vitreous enamel. But he did volunteer as an air raid warden. There was a rumour – Joss knew more about this – that just before the War he went to Germany and was apparently in talks with manufacturers there to supply them with vitreous enamelling processes. Not sure if that's true – but it wouldn't surprise me!

"I met a boy on a school exchange. He was Dutch and his name was Ruben. We decided we loved each other and he told me he was going to ask Daddy if we could get married. But Daddy said absolutely not and we weren't allowed to see each other or contact each other.

"Twin and I had a stupendous eighteenth birthday party at the Charing Cross Hotel in London. Lots of eligible young men were invited of course! But no-one chose me. "Twin was much more outgoing than I was. She was gorgeous. We're so unalike! You often remind me of her. She went to college to study horticulture. I was so stupid.

Granny was grooming me in domestic science. That was all I was good for.

"Then Twin met a man called Stephen and they got married in a register office. And it was Stephen who paired me up with your father not long after our 18th birthday party actually.

"Well things happened. I got pregnant, in trouble again", she smiled ruefully. "I'll never forget the moment when I plucked up courage to tell Mummy.

"Of course, I was the biggest disappointment to them. I

had wasted all my opportunities, my expensive education. They planned that I should go and live with my old Nanny in her house in Kent. When the baby was born it would be put up for adoption. Well, I refused. Your father and I got married.

"Daddy was furious and told me I would never see them again and would be disinherited. Of course, I wasn't. It was Mummy's money that she left me in her Will that bought our first house in the Fens. That meant that we never had to worry about a house ever again as we had no mortgage to pay. But I never received any of her gorgeous jewellery – they thought your father would sell it.

"I was eighteen. Your father was quite a bit older – I can't remember now how much.

"We rented a house in Surbiton.

"Your father was a very talented carpenter. But he had a lot of mental problems that I didn't know about until after we were married. He was violent. He'd been part of a South London gang in the 50s. He was lazy. He wouldn't work. After Kim was born I was worried about money. So I got your father a job as a carpenter that came with a tied cottage so at least we had a house.

"He became more and more violent. He would regularly beat me. When Louise arrived he hated her and I was worried about her with him. He was diagnosed as paranoid schizophrenic. He would go through spells of being active and good and then slump into his pathetic mode.

"No, I didn't plan to have five daughters. You somehow kept arriving. In fact, he kept me pregnant so I couldn't leave him. I had three miscarriages as well when he was particularly violent with me. He pushed me down the stairs once. I thought I was going to die.

"And then of course when you were due, we both nearly died. I'd had the other three at home really easily. But you were the difficult one. You just did not want to come out. I was in labour for 36 hours and the doctor was so worried that he drove us (you and me) to the nearest hospital which was Brackley Cottage Hospital in Northamptonshire.

"There was so much mess. We both nearly died. I was so worried what would happen to my other three darlings if I died, left to your father.

"The doctor, thank god, managed to get your father sectioned for a bit so I could recover at home with a bit of peace. And the district nurse, Nurse Henderson, was a darling blessing. That's why you have her name in yours. She came to see us every day while your father was in hospital and carried on even after he came home just to check we were safe. And our local vicar came round to see you and brought me a bunch of daffodils because it was Mother's Day. He was kind.

"In those days police wouldn't do anything when a man was violent to his wife and children. It was known as a 'domestic' that they weren't allowed to interfere with. The man was considered within his rights to do what was necessary to maintain order in his house.

"He lost his job at Waters End so I had to find him another one. It was a constant worry about money. I had to write to Mummy and Daddy to ask them for money and each time they would send me a stern lecture back with a cheque.

"I got your father a job as the carpenter at a country estate in Hertfordshire which, again, came with a tied house.

"I'd created a lovely garden at Waters End and the day before we left your father poured paraffin over all the plants so that the next people couldn't enjoy them. That was what he was like. So much anger and rage he had.

"We didn't have a car and were pretty remote at our cottage. It was on a huge country estate. I used to cycle over the fields to go shopping and would bring it home in stages, carrying a bag on either handlebar. Then I'd put the bags under a hedge and cycle back to collect two more bags. It was like a relay until I finally got all the bags home.

"But we had no money so I cobbled together the meals I could, just like Mummy had in the War I suppose. Your father would often have a fit and throw his whole plate of food at the wall in disgust.

"He would invite his friends up from London and give my clothes away. If anyone admired anything I was wearing or a picture I had from when I was a girl that I'd managed to keep hold of, he'd say "You can have it. Evelyn will give it to you." And so I had to hand over whatever it was they'd admired. I was always worried about what he'd do to you all if I didn't do what he said.

"And he smoked too, like a chimney. He would make me go to the local pub to buy him cigarettes. One evening I was there and got chatting to a man who took a shine to me. That was Jim. We used to talk every time I went to buy your father's cigarettes. We started meeting up from time to time and I managed to go away and spend an occasional weekend with him at his home, leaving you all with your father.

"I remember coming home one time. When I went into the kitchen you were all sitting on a chair each in a circle and he was standing in the middle. In that moment, he reminded me of a circus ringmaster with a whip.

"You were the only one I remember who wasn't crying but you looked terrified. I don't know what he'd threatened you with.

"Sometimes I had to leave you all with him because he was so useless. I had to do everything and I couldn't take you all with me. I had to go and get the shopping. I used to go into the woods and bring back tree branches so we could cut them up for firewood. Of course, I could only bring one branch back at a time.

"He was OK with you one at a time. Kim was his favourite and he took her with him from time to time. He also took a shine to Melanie who was so much like him with her red hair. He used to make her laugh I remember by giving her a piggy back ride upstairs to bed. I don't know why he couldn't be like that all the time!

"When Mummy died I didn't get to go to her funeral

because your father wouldn't let me. He didn't want to be left with you all. I remembered the promise Mummy had made me make to her though so I asked your father about getting sterilised. The Pill had also come out too. But your father wouldn't let me get sterilised. In those days women had to get their husband's signed consent to have any sort of contraception.

"I planned our escape. Jim was in on it. He was to come with us when we got away. Your father had a job to do at the Hall. It was a Saturday so Kim wasn't at school so he took her with him. That was the bit I didn't foresee!

"So, I had to leave her behind which was so awful. But it was the only window I could think of. Things were getting desperate and I just couldn't run the risk of getting pregnant again or whatever he might do next.

"I booked a taxi, got you altogether and off we went! It was terrible to leave darling Kim behind but at least I had you four safely out of his way.

"We stopped off at Jim's work and I told him that we were going to Daddy's house. And that was that.

"Your father couldn't look after Kim and I couldn't go back to the cottage because I didn't know what he'd do to me. So I gave Kim to Paul Rosolek. And the rest of us, as you know, moved in with Twin and Tommy for a while. Tommy hated you all and he hated us being there but them having us live with them for a while enabled us to get away from your father and start a new life."

"Who is this Paul Rosolek guy?" I ask.

She smiles and puts down her knitting. The cats

simultaneously get up, stretch and jump to the floor. They want feeding.

"I'll feed them," I say and go into the kitchen. The cats follow. I prepare their supper as they rub themselves around my ankles.

"There you go, lovelies," I tell them and they meow 'thank you' and begin to gobble up their food. I leave them eating and go back to Mother. She has fallen asleep.

***

"Paul Rosolek was my German teacher at school," Ma tells me as she continues her story one evening.

"You had male teachers at an all girls' school?" I ask.

She smiles.

"Even nunneries have male priests come to see them, Ma says. "Anyway, Mummy got to know about him through school parents' evenings and my wretched school report. I wasn't good at German but I really liked Paul. He came to White Lodge a couple of times. Twin and I had a crush on him. But - ," she pauses. Her needles stop their quiet clicking.

"What?" I ask.

She sighs. "It was me he wanted," she says and looks up at me.

"What? Your teacher fancied you?" I ask, laughing.

"He was a lovely man," she continues, ignoring me.

"But I wasn't allowed to do German the next year. Mummy taught me in the evenings after that.

"After I married your father, he turned up at White

Lodge – just passing by apparently – and Mummy gave him our address. So he showed up there at the cottage. Your father was out, thank God, and I ended up telling him everything about our situation.

"It turned out he hadn't known I'd married and had all of you. He'd come to find me to ask if I'd help with a mission, a calling he'd had if you will, to provide a safe place for children. Like a foster home, but an exclusive foster home for children from wealthy backgrounds. I wanted to go with him. It seemed a job made for me with the skills I was naturally good at. But I didn't. I couldn't."

She is quiet for a while.

"Later, though," she says, "when Kim got left behind, I found the strength to leave her with him."

She looks up at me and I go over to her and we hug, without a word.

***

One time I ask Ma why she and Lizzie hadn't spoken for all those years. She says she can't remember.

Another time I ask Ma if she'd known that Jim was a paedophile. She says she'd had no idea. I know she doesn't want to talk about it.

"Was he – you know – 'normal' in bed?" I ask.

"Yes," she says, simply, and that was that.

"Why didn't you stop Kim moving to Greece?" I ask another time. She sighs sadly.

"Because I was afraid she'd go," she says. "When Mummy and Daddy told me I wasn't to keep Kim, I reacted in a very self-destructive way by marrying your father. All my life I'd been controlled by Daddy and it was my way of rebelling, I guess. I hoped that Kim would make up her mind to stay here and not marry Christos. I didn't think it was the right thing to do to tell her how much I wanted her to stay. I didn't want her to go down the same route as I went."

***

I love our evenings together. I just sit listening to the music and watch her needles clicking, enjoying our cosy intimacy. It feels like heaven to me that, after all the turbulence and feelings of abandonment and rejection I'd experienced throughout my childhood, I can enjoy this time with just her and me.

Every now and again her attention focuses on the music, she pauses with her knitting, looks up and hums along to it. She has a beautiful voice.

"Do you think if someone makes a statement about us when we're young it's like a curse that just comes true?" I ask. "Like it makes us who we become?"

"I don't know, darling."

"It's like everyone said you were a dunce so you believed you were a dunce and didn't do the things you said you wanted to do, like be a nurse or a secretary? You're not a dunce though. You know everything about music and gardening and birds and knitting. You have a beautiful singing voice and you're interested in everything. But you call yourself a dunce. Whereas me?

I passed all my exams and have a degree but I don't know anything about music or gardening, I can't sing and I can't knit. But you once said I made you feel inferior!"

She is quiet, listening.

"I think it's a self esteem thing really, rather than about what you know. So that makes us even, we're both dunces at self-esteem!" I laugh.

"You're so clever," she says. "Sometimes you used to remind me of Daddy: the way you stared at me – you're doing it now! All critical! And you have his thin lips all pushed together."

I laugh with exasperation. "I don't look anything like Gramps," I say, "and you know it."

There is another pause as we sit with our own thoughts. "Was I really our father's child though?" I ask. "Not the child of some fling you had?"

"Darling!" she says, frowning.

"Why was I always the odd one out then?"

She sighs. "Of course, you're your father's child. But we have lots of weird family history – I guess maybe all families do. And the thing is I didn't ask questions like you're doing now so I don't know that much about what went on. You do look a little different than the others but sometimes I see resemblances with others in the family, to Twin, or to Joss. Perhaps you're a throwback," she laughs. "Joss knew everything about the family history," she says, "but of course she's gone now and I doubt it if she wrote it down.

"When I was a girl, my granny – your great granny –

lived in the house at the bottom of our garden. She'd been in bed for years – I have no idea what was wrong with her. Maybe she just took to her bed like wealthy widows did in those days.

"Joss used to go and sit with her and would listen to Granny's stories from the past.

"Daddy hated Granny of course because she could see right through him.

"I had to go and show Granny my school report every year and she would tell me how I'd come to no good.

"When I was pregnant with Kim, I went to see her because I wanted her advice. She was like a wise old crone you see.

"She'd be sitting up in bed in a huge black nightie with a shawl around her. She was a large lady. I would sit on the chair next to her. There was always a terrible smell in that room – I don't know what. Maybe it was a commode or something. No catheters in those days!

"Anyway, she was a bit like something out of a fairy tale, like the wicked witch in 'Rapunzel'. She told me she'd been waiting for me to come to her with this problem, that all my school report visits had been leading to this moment. 'You've been indulging in forbidden fruit', she said, 'just like I knew you would'.

"She told me that the child I was carrying (I hadn't actually told her I was pregnant by the way!) was already programmed by the very nature of its conception to follow my route in life. Those were the very words she used.

"All I could choose, she told me, was the route I would

take. My role in life was to nurture and protect. She also said, 'Do not trust in men to save you. They will be your ruination'."

"And you believed her?" I ask, curious.

"And she was right of course in every respect." "Because you chose to make her right?" I ask gently. "I refused to give Kim up for adoption because I loved her the instant I knew I was pregnant," Ma continues without answering my question.

"You could argue that if I loved her, I should have given her to a better home rather than the violent one she ended up in. But who's to know what goes on in other families too? And, in any case, at the time I didn't know what was in store for me or the route my life would take. So maybe it could have been a really positive route for Kim – for you all – to follow? Who knew? Anyway, enough of that! Let's watch some television."

***

"Did Granny and Grandfather ever know the truth about Daddy?" I ask Ma one evening as we sit together. "Well, true to their words, they never came to visit us after David and I got married. We wrote to each other and they knew some of the stuff that was going on. But they couldn't have even imagined the truth, I don't think.

"But then, after Mummy died, Daddy and Twin – and Twin did know the truth – they came to visit us. It was on our 25th birthday. Twin and I were twins through and through and although we've never looked like twins, it did seem we shared the same beating heart back then. "They gave me a beautiful golden calla lily.

"David showed his true self. Daddy said he'd stay and help David look after you all while Twin and I were free to go out for a birthday tea in Welwyn Garden City. Daddy would drive us there and come and collect us at the appointed hour.

"When we got back, you were all screaming the house down uncontrollably. God knows what David had been up to. He started shoving me around demanding to know why we'd been gone so long, suspecting us of plotting against him. He was paranoid you see. And all in front of Daddy.

"It was ghastly. But at least Daddy now had an idea of what was going on. He was visibly shocked I remember and told me he and Twin would help extricate me if they could.

"But then Paul had turned up on our doorstep and I was sorely tempted by his offer. He was a good friend."

"What about Jim?" I ask. "How did he fit in?"

"Jim and I were having an affair," she says.

"Bloody hell, Mother!"

"I didn't have any girlfriends. I haven't really had any since school. I don't know why. I didn't keep in touch. Probably ashamed after our expensive education. They all probably married into wealth and nobility like Pat, but I came to nothing. I would have been too embarrassed for them to know."

"They probably knew anyway," I say. "No secrets

in this world! But their versions were probably 100% worse," I laugh. "It's like when we were kids and Dad forbade us from telling anyone about anything that happened in our house, in our family. Why was everything so secretive?"

Mother picks up her knitting again.

"I don't know, darling. It's no use now anyway, raking up the past. Dad is dead and the past is gone."

"But the past lives on in us," I insist.

***

One evening as Mother is knitting, I flick through old photograph albums.

"These are amazing pictures," I say. "All from that Box Brownie you used to have." Ma chuckles. "All these photos of us. But no Kim. What happened to her? Was she with that guy all that time? She was gone for years!"
"Yes, I left her with Paul Rosolek. I couldn't get Granny's words out of my head and thought I had to try to protect her. David didn't want her anyway. So, when the dust had settled after we left, I went back to collect our stuff – as much as was left because he'd given it away or destroyed it in a rage.

"David had left Kim with your old Nurse Henderson – such a lovely, kind person. I took her to Paul Rosolek's house. He'd wanted me to live with him anyway but it would have been terribly frowned on back then. I did think hard about it.

"He'd set up a wonderful home for children like Kim:

misplaced, vulnerable. He was giving them a first-rate education. He promised me he would give Kim the very best childhood.

"I needed to protect her from the route I was taking so she didn't go the same way. I thought she'd be safe there. And she was. Except –," she pauses, looks up and smiles, "I needed her too much. I used to visit her by myself every three months or so. I couldn't help myself seeing her from time to time. She was growing up into such a lovely outgoing, beautiful, kind girl with the most amazing imagination. She would go far, I was sure.

"I fiercely didn't want her to be tarnished by my influence – my childhood baggage, Granny's curse. I thought I was keeping her safe from any of our family influences.

"But then …" She stops. "I forgot – or I chose to forget. Because I couldn't see any other way. Granny told me not to rely on a man to save me. Well, Paul Rosolek was a man for a start. Then Jim and Charlie, even Daddy. All men I relied on to save us.

"And Charlie. Well! After that stuff with Louise and everyone in the town gossiping, I decided we had to move to Scotland, as far away as we could go. But that would mean I couldn't get to see Kim. She was sixteen by then and I decided she'd be OK if she came back into our family. She was technically an adult so should have been OK, I decided."

She sighs. "But, of course, Granny was right. Kim was programmed to her fate probably before she was born. I tried to protect her, hide her away. But you cannot hide from life can you? Hopefully she's happy now with Christos and the baby over in Greece. But I do worry.

"That thing with Jaffa that time. It was like a nightmare turning real. I remember your father holding cigarettes up to my face like Jaffa did to Kim. Quite terrifying!

"Anyway. Shall we have something to eat?" she smiles and pats my hand, coming back to our present.

***

Another time, I ask Mother why none of her side of the family came to her wedding with Dad.

"Daddy disapproved of Charlie. And he was fed up with me," she says. "I took Charlie to meet with Daddy and he didn't like him. He said I was making a bad decision yet again. They'd all bailed me out so many times, they were wiping their hands of me.

"Of course, it didn't help that Charlie was an East Ender from a working-class family. So Daddy didn't approve. And of course, I know that that instinctively made me rebel.

"Daddy was very controlling with us when I was a girl. He was like a dictator really. We were always expected to do whatever he said."

"Is that why you chose Dad because he was the same?" I laugh.

"Well, I didn't know that at the time. He kept it well hidden when we first started seeing each other. He was such fun."

"I do remember that actually," I agree.

"I guess my biggest mistake was not thinking to check their backgrounds," she laughs.

"I didn't know your father's father suffered from depression after returning from the War in France. I only met him once. His mother had died. Turned out it was suicide but I didn't know that either at the time. There was a step-mother who was quite unpleasant. And David had a mental illness that I didn't know about until Louise came along. He was fine till then.

"He had these bouts that would come on apparently for no reason. He was so violent and angry, mostly to me but also to all of you and himself too. He took to sleep walking. I would catch him in the bathroom trying to cut his wrists while he was fast asleep.

"And there was me, trying to 'nurture and protect' as Granny told me to!

"And Charlie. Well, I didn't know he was beaten by his father until he shared it with us all, or that he was likely to copy that behaviour with my little treasures. And I'm terribly ashamed that I let him do it. He told me I'd spoiled you all so you didn't respect me. So maybe I thought, well, maybe you did need a bit of discipline. And he'd brought up seven children of his own, so maybe he knew better than I did.

"You know, no-one teaches us how to be a good parent, or the best ways to bring children up. You can only go on your own experiences. And, well, I hardly saw my parents. Only really for a lecture from Daddy or a lesson of some sort from Mummy.

"Twin and I just got on with growing up, working it out ourselves. There was no family discussion about sex or relationships, God forbid! And so I guess I just left you all to do the same – there were enough of you! I didn't really appreciate how much you needed me. Or maybe I did and didn't like that dependency very much. Maybe that was why I worked all those hours! How do you interpret that, Doctor?" she laughs.

"I think you had a repeating fear of not having enough money," I say, "so you tried to earn as much as you could. Just like you have a repeating fear of not having enough food which is why your cupboards are overflowing with tins!"

We both laugh. I get up to make some supper.

***

"The only time I ever really got any loving attention from Mummy was when I was very young, about ten," Mother says. "I had polio and was really ill. I was put in a bed in a room at the top of our house. I was there for weeks. Twin wasn't allowed to see me. The curtains were kept closed all the time. Mummy used to come and sit with me and read to me."

She laughs. "It was the only time I was allowed to be ill."

"Is that why you just carry on as normal now, even with the pain in your hip?" I ask her, "because you don't think you're allowed to be ill?"

"Probably," she admits. "We just have to get on with it, don't we?"

***

"What about Grandfather and his affair with Auntie Megan?" I ask her another time.

"Twin knows more about that than I do," Mother says as she starts casting off the sleeve of my jumper. "Remember she went back to live with Mummy and Daddy after she and Stephen divorced so she saw what was going on.

"They'd known each other for years even when Twin and I were children. We saw them together when we were at Kew Gardens one time. We were supposed to be at home revising otherwise I'm sure Twin would have interrupted them and said hello. They were kissing. We saw them.

"Megan was a secretary at the BBC which was why Daddy was so interested when you got your first job there. They used to go away for clandestine weekends."

"Like you and Jim?" I say.

"Can I ask you a really personal question?" I ask. "I don't know," she says. "It depends what it is." "Why have you always had a boyfriend on the go?" She looks hurt. "I haven't always."

"But your Granny told you not to look to men to save you. Maybe you just heard, 'Look to men to save you', I laugh.

"Maybe I was just having fun and not looking for them

to save me," Mother laughs back.

***

She is brushing her hair one morning out of the plait she sleeps in.

Her hair – that she'd told us she hadn't had cut since she was 21 – was down to her knees, dark brown with a distinctive blond streak over her left temple, with bits of grey now since her hip operation. She twists it up into a bun by day.

"Would you ever have your hair cut?" I ask as I sit on the edge of the bath watching her expertly put the pins in her bun to secure it.

"Dad said he'd divorce me if I had my hair cut, do you remember?" she laughs.

She looks serious suddenly.

"It was Granny again," she says. "She told me that my long hair would save me so long as I saved my hair. That's all."

"That's a bit cryptic," I say, wondering what the old crone had meant by that. "So men wouldn't save you but your hair would? Weird!"

"Yes, maybe I should have taken the other things she said more seriously," Mother says. "Hey! Do you remember that time I took you to the hairdressers and you cried and cried? You had those beautiful curls. But they were dropping out. Someone suggested to me that if you had a haircut they'd grow back. But they didn't. You were such a gorgeous fat baby with those beautiful curls."

***

That night I dream that my great granny – the old crone – dressed in a long black crepe dress has locked Mother up in Rapunzel's tower. The key to unlock the tower is lost. In the dream I know the crone is long dead but that I can find a way out of the tower. I stand at the base of the tower and call up to Ma, "Mother! Mother! Let down your long hair!" And her plait tumbles down the wall in front of me. I am only small and have short chubby legs but somehow get to the top and crawl through the open window.

Inside the room, I come face-to-face with myself, sitting in front of a mirror, snipping away at my hair with scissors, with all my dark curls scattered on the floor around me. The two cats rub themselves around my ankles.

I wake up with tears streaming down my face, soaking into my pillow.

***

One evening Ma is sewing up the jumper.

"Do you regret not taking Granny and Grandfather's advice not to marry our father?" I ask her.

"Of course not," she says brightly. "I wouldn't have my lovely girls otherwise.

"Here!" she throws me the finished jumper. I put it on. Perfect fit.

"Thank you, Marmie," I say.

Part Four

1989 – 2000

Mother had a boyfriend called Mr Wary. He was her boss at work. He was married.

He was very large and loved to eat. He had white hair and a pink face and was in his sixties. You could tell he'd been a good-looking man in his youth but he'd now turned to fat and had wobbly jowls. He turned up at Ma's house whenever he felt like it – he had a key – usually carrying a bag of sausages and some thick beef steaks. Sometimes I'd get home from my London commute to find two sausages left for me on a side plate.

I liked to poke fun at Mr Wary in a mildly insulting way.

"What colour was your hair before it went white?" I asked him.

He froze momentarily – perhaps trying to remember or, more likely, shocked at the question, as if I should know. Then he remembered to join in the joke.

"I was a blond bombshell," he said proudly. He took my face in his hands and kissed me on my lips trying to force his tongue in my mouth. I pulled away, feeling queasy. I don't think Ma saw.

He would tell Ma that he'd be round or that he'd ring at a particular time and then he didn't. I hated it that Ma would wait in for him and then sigh heavily when he didn't turn up. But then he'd turn up the next day and everything would be alright. I found that infuriating on her behalf, but I didn't say anything.

Mr Wary talked to Ma about his wife – she repeated the stories to me. His wife was suffering badly with her menopause and apparently they had to change their bed twice in the night because of her heavy bleeding.

"Why does he tell you that stuff?" I asked. "How can you bear it?"

I quickly realised that I was not really welcome back in Ma's house. She'd got used to the freedom of having none of us at home and I was in the way when it came to their sex life.

"Don't mind me," I said. "I don't mind." But she did. I knew I wasn't welcome.

But we got into a routine at last. Ma would get up early everyday to go to work with Mr Wary. She came into my bedroom at 5 am to kiss me goodbye. Then I would get up and leave early to catch the bus to the train station. Then I'd take the train to Kings Cross and the Tube to the law firm where I worked in the City.

At the end of each day I'd do the journey again in reverse.

I carried a bag that contained 'things to do on the train'. I wrote letters and read a novel. Creative writing was now completely out the window. I'd get home around 8pm, eat the offering left on the side plate and go to bed ready for the next day.

At weekends I took driving lessons and passed my

test first time.

My youngest sister Carol drove home one weekend and announced that she was going to buy a new car. So I bought her old car from her: it was a teal blue Morris Marina, 1974. I gave her £450.

Now I could leave home earlier and drive myself to the train station to catch my train. And I would be home earlier.

***

That Summer Ma finally got to have her hip replacement operation. She was 48. She had suffered terrible pain in her lower back and hip for around nine years. She couldn't get the operation on the NHS because they said she was too young. Hip replacements didn't last very long – maybe ten years. At her age she'd need several in her lifetime, they reasoned, so they needed to delay it for as long as possible. They told her she'd have to wait till she was at least 55.

She was crippled with pain. She never complained but I could see the pain in her face and the way she moved. Grandfather finally paid for her operation through his own private medical insurance. He had only recently had a knee replacement and a new heart valve at the age of eighty-nine.

And so Mother went into hospital for her operation. When I got home from work, I drove to see her. Mr Wary was there. I waited patiently for him to leave. He waited patiently for me to leave.

"How did it go?" I asked Ma.

She looked pale and thin like a sick child.

"They basically cut my leg off," she said. "I asked Mr Picker if I could see the bone they were replacing but he told me there was nothing left. He was very apologetic. I've been walking around without a hip for years."

I felt sick to my stomach imagining the pain she'd been in all this time.

"How are you feeling?" I asked.

"Oh fine," she said and smiled in her usual animated way.

I cried myself to sleep that night really appreciating the agony she'd been through the past nine years and more. Once she could demonstrate that she could climb up stairs and make herself a cup of tea, Ma was allowed to come home. But she was still in pain. The operation had not fixed the problem. The surgeon bodged the job, having left the repair so late. She was to undergo five more hip replacements – three on one leg and two on the other – and was never out of pain for the rest of her life. When she came home, I took two weeks off work and helped Ma in ways that I'd never dreamt she'd need my help with. She couldn't bend easily. So I cut her toe nails as she sat on the toilet seat, I picked things up for her,

I cooked, cleaned, did the shopping and ironed clothes. She was embarrassed to be the invalid I could tell. But I loved to look after her. We listened to music, watched television, stroked the cats and talked a lot. It was the saddest time and the best time. I had her all to myself a lot of the time except when Mr Wary came calling or a sister came to visit.

News from Greece was alarming. Kim was pregnant with her second child and having a tough time. We spoke on the phone. She rang home to speak with Ma every Sunday evening. Ma would ring her back to pick up the bill.

They were on the phone for hours while I went off to lay in the bath, the bathroom door shut, lying in the soapy steam wondering what I was doing with my life.

This time it was me who picked up the phone. She turned on the bright and cheerful lie at first out of habit until I asked her how she was.

"I'm bleeding," she said. "I think I might lose the baby. I think I might die."

"What happened?" I asked.

"I don't know. Daphne was so easy, just slipped out on the appointed day. So easy, such a happy baby. So I thought I'd have tons of babies just like Mummy. But this one! I keep bleeding. They said I need to be in hospital."

"I'll pass you over to Ma," I said. "She's in the sitting room and can't walk very well but I'll take you through."

It wasn't far from the hallway to where Ma was sitting propped up on the sofa. I gave her the phone.

"I'll make you some tea," I said to Ma as she took the phone.

"Hello Darling," I heard her say. "How are you?"

Just over three hours later I came back as she was putting the receiver down on the cradle.

"Oh dear, I'm so worried," she said. "I wish I could be with her. She never should have gone."

"What's up?" I asked.

"It seems that Christos is just like your father," Ma said. "He's violent to Kim and to Daphne. I'm worried she'll have a miscarriage."

Kim ended up spending the last two months of her pregnancy lying in a hospital bed in Greece. She wasn't allowed to move. And in the end the baby arrived in a flood of blood.

Kim told me later that she woke up covered in blood up to her neck and she had to have an emergency Caesarean to whip the baby out. They both nearly died.

But they didn't.

When I heard Kim talk about the arrival of her second daughter into the world, I thought about my own arrival.

"Do you like her?" I asked. "What do you mean?" she said.

"Well, she nearly killed you," I said. "What do you think about that?"

"It's not her," she said. "It's Christos. Half an hour after I got home from the hospital he was demanding sex even with all my stitches in over my stomach."

"Jeez!" I said. "Did you let him?"

"What else could I do? Tell him to bugger off? It's not that easy," she said. "There's Daphne. I worry about him with her."

Soon after Kim's second daughter was born, she was pregnant again. Ma was delighted but concerned.

Meanwhile, I had money in my bank and decided I wanted to see an old flame I'd met at University who now lived in California. I'd met him in the first week at Manchester during 'Freshers' Week'.

I'd gone to watch a film by myself. It was a Clint Eastwood film. The hall was packed with students. There were no chairs left.

I perched on a ledge in the dark as the film started. Suddenly a guy said, "Is there room for me?" and squeezed up next to me.

I could smell him. Spicy food? Musky?

I made a bit of space for him in the dark and could feel a hot prickling sensation begin at the base of my spine. It went all the way up my back, over my head and down my front. Prickly heat? I'd heard the term but didn't know what it meant. Very peculiar.

I ignored the guy and watched the film.

And when it ended and the lights went on, I turned to see a deeply tanned guy in jeans and a shirt with the sleeves neatly folded up above his elbows. He smiled at me. Did I enjoy the film? he was asking as I recalled the prickly heat. "Yeah, yeah, yeah" I said and headed downstairs to the bar.

A couple of days later, there was a quiet knock on my student room door which was open. I looked up and saw the same guy.

"I'm sorry," he said. "Do you have a pencil? I need to leave a note for…".

"Yeah, of course," I said, got up off my bed where I'd

been reading, and handed him a pencil.

"Thank you," he said and disappeared. Thirty seconds later he was back. He was very tall and broad chested, foreign, maybe Middle Eastern, with a gorgeous tan, not much hair, brown eyes and a beautiful wide smile. He handed me the pencil.

"We met at the film," he said.

"I remember very well," I said, recalling the prickly heat sensation.

"Would you like to go out on Friday?" he asked. "It's my birthday and we're going to Legends Nightclub in town."

"I'd love to," I said.

"Thank you," he said and walked away.

And when Friday came, he appeared at my door with two of his friends in tow. It seemed the three of them were off to Legends and Kyrell – that was his name – had invited me to go with them.

We danced. I drank Malibu and pineapple juice and we had a lovely evening.

As we walked back to our Halls, Kyrell asked me if I'd like a cup of tea.

"Another time," I said. "Thank you for a lovely evening."

And it started there: our bizarre relationship.

After Kyrell went off to work in California we kept in touch through my example by the old fashioned method of writing letters to each other since that was what I loved to do.

And so it was that I invited myself to stay with him in California and he agreed.

I waited until Ma went back to work after her hip replacement and then off I went to California. It was the most extravagant (reckless) thing I think I'd ever done. And the most fun of course.

Kyrell had taken two weeks off work to show me the sights. We had the best of times. He lived with his family – parents, sister and three brothers – just outside of Los Angeles. His family were lovely, so friendly and welcoming to this friend of Kyrell's from England.

And Kyrell was the perfect attentive lover. He'd planned out our entire holiday together. I didn't have to spend a dime and he was full of charm, attentiveness and passion.

And the weather was so fabulous I got the best tan I'd ever had, spending all my days in my bikini under the Southern Californian sun.

And then it was all over: it was time to go home.

Mother didn't recognise me at Gatwick as I came through Arrivals. I was so tanned, I looked completely different. A new me! I felt amazing!

As she drove me home, I came down from my holiday lover's high with a terrific BANG though. Kyrell was gorgeous, we had a real physical (prickly skinned) connection but he had settled in a country I kind of despised and there was no way I would have ever contemplated leaving Ma to go and live in America. It had been a wonderful fairy tale holiday but now I had to face reality. Our relationship wouldn't be going anywhere.

So I numbed myself out for a bit seeking out former flames from my pre-Uni days. I leafed through the phone book and tracked down Adam who had effectively raped me on my sixteenth birthday. He was delighted to hear me. I asked him if he'd like to meet for a drink. Yes he would, it seemed.

And so we became "fuck buddies". Whenever either of us was feeling at a loose end we'd call each other on the phone and arrange to meet for a drink or a meal and end up at his house while his mother was away, or at a friend's place while they were away. It was OK. We knew each other. It was something to do. It was fun, maybe. But it wasn't what I needed.

One day while I was on the Tube on my way to work, I noticed an advert for Date Line, a dating agency. On my way home that evening, reading one of those free magazines that was thrust into your hands as you ran down the steps to the Tube platform, I came across the same advert. When I got home, I announced to Mother that I was going to join Date Line. I wanted a proper relationship with a man. She thought it was a good idea. And so I joined Date Line. I was sent a list of the names and addresses of six men who appeared to match who I was looking for. I crafted a letter to each, posted them and sat back and waited just as I used to sit back and wait for the response to the short stories I posted out to magazines on my list.

I had three letters back and passed them to Ma for her

views.

"This is the only one who can spell," she said, passing me the letter I'd received from a guy called Robert Grayson. There was a photo enclosed too showing a blond guy in his late 20s/early 30s wearing shorts and a t-shirt, leaning back against a car in the sunshine with shades on. He looked quite nice.

In his letter he told me he'd been married twice, had two daughters by his first wife and was mad about cars and lived in a local town which was about an hour away. I wrote back and told him I was a graduate from Manchester University and worked at a law firm in the City. I loved books, theatre and socialising. I'd split up from my boyfriend and was looking to meet someone new, round about my age or a little older as men took longer to mature.

I posted the letter and waited.

He wrote back. I wrote back. He wrote back. Finally, I gave him our phone number and he rang me.

It was fascinating chatting on the phone with someone I'd never met but who had opened up his feelings, dreams and desires just through handwritten letters.

We arranged to meet in a bar in Knebworth on his way back from dropping his girls with their mother. I felt really excited!

I got out of my Morris Marina to see him leaning over a silver Ford Escort 1.4 GL, car key dangling from his finger. He was tall and slim with blond hair and a face etched in lines. He was wearing light jeans, a white shirt and a black leather jacket.

"There you are," he said and nodded at my car. "Someone had to," he laughed.

"What?" I didn't understand.

"Morris Marina!" he said. "Someone had to buy one."

I laughed back. "I bought it off my sister," I told him. "She'd never had any problems with it apparently but it's cost me a small fortune ever since I bought it. I think it's because she ran over a cat in it. Bad luck!"

We walked into the pub. I felt like I knew this guy, I guess because we'd been sharing bits of our lives through our letters over the last few months. I felt immediately comfortable with him. He had a gentle mocking way about him which I liked.

We talked about his kids who were aged 8 and 12. His wife had run off with another guy and left the kids behind. He was devoted to them. But his wife came back while his mum was looking after them and snatched them back. The Court had given them joint custody: he had them every other weekend and on Tuesday nights.

It turned out he'd just walked out on his second wife who he'd married very soon after his divorce from wife number one really, he now realised, to have stability for his kids to come and stay with. She'd had her own house. But it hadn't been a good move and he walked out a day after their first wedding anniversary.

He'd taken his life into his own hands, bought a new build 2-bed flat, decorated it out bachelor style (as he called it) and now just wanted to meet someone new.

He was from an old mining village in the North East and had gone from school to work as a Blue Coat at Butlins on the south east coast. That was where he'd met his first wife-to-be. He'd got her pregnant and they married – far too young he said. He was nineteen.

"Gosh, same age as my mum when she had her first child," I said.

His wife's parents lived in Hertford and they lived with them to start with before they got a council house.

"We lived in Hertfordshire for a while," I said, "in a house on a country estate."

"I think I rescued a car from there," he said, "a Ferrari. We had to get it out of a ditch and recover it. I remember the nettles."

Rob was obsessed with cars and now worked at a garage in Bedford as a crash repairer.

"Why a crash repairer?" I asked.

"I remember when I was a nipper, probably around four or five. My Grandda had a crash in his car. And then it came back from the garage all repaired. It fascinated me. I wanted to be able to do that for a car," he said.

"Like a car healer?" I said.

"Yes, exactly. It was like magic." He smiled.

As we chatted, we realised we had so much in common, so many similar patterns in our lives. I told him how my mum had escaped from my dad with her girls. It turned out his mum had also escaped from his dad with her three boys. The big difference was that his mum had remarried a lovely gentle guy who helped bring the boys up as if they were his own, not like our Dad who had beaten and bullied us into submission and treated as slave labour.

"Not like mine," I told him. "He was a brute who treated us like slaves. He loved my mum but hated us. Trouble was he couldn't have her without her girls. He vented all his anger out on us. He was like a massive scar on my life."

"Why did your mum let him do that?" my companion asked.

I looked up at him.

"I have asked her that question," I said. "I think my mum has been oppressed by men all her life, starting with her own father. It's like she's this really strong woman who brought us up despite the odds and would do anything for us, but then she's completely submissive when it comes to men. It's like she just lets them do whatever they want – like she's powerless."

"What about you?" Rob asked.

I didn't answer. I got up to find the Ladies.

It turned out this guy also liked Status Quo just like me and had the same box set as me. This was the first guy I'd ever met who shared my love of the band. It was a good sign I decided.

He loved '70s music. "I wasn't even born then," I said. We looked at each other and laughed.

"Do you like running?" I asked.

"Er – no," he said.

"Ah well, that's something I have to carry on doing by myself then," I smiled.

We arranged to meet again on the following Sunday.

Ma was curious to hear more about Rob. What did he do? How old was he? What were his shoes like? "His shoes?"

"Yes, you can always tell a man by his shoes."

"You never told me that before," I laughed. Actually, he had lovely shoes: black leather lace ups and black socks, I noticed, not white fluffies like a lot of my early boy friends had worn.

The following Sunday we met at a Pizza Hut in Stevenage. It was very crowded but we found a table for two and resumed our conversation. I told him all about my work at the law firm, about my previous job at the BBC, about University.

He told me about his school in the North East where teaching had been very poor. He'd left at 16 with 2 'O' Levels. The only option for most male school leavers in the area was to work in the mines which he had no intention of doing. So he'd gone off to Butlins.

"Sounds like running off to the Circus," I said.

"Something like that," he said.

We'd been talking so much for over an hour that we'd forgotten we hadn't placed our order. A waitress appeared and asked if we'd like to see the dessert menu. We looked at each other and burst out laughing.

"We haven't had our first course yet," we both said in unison.

***

Rob's mum was coming down to stay with him the next weekend when he had his kids. It was his birthday on the Saturday. He asked if I'd like to meet up with them. He thought they'd be going to explore the local shopping centre

"How about I meet you there for lunch?" I said, feeling quite honoured and excited to be invited to meet his family.

I was excited and nervous to meet with his mum (or 'mam' as he called her) and his kids. I took ages deciding what to wear knowing that first impressions would be very important. I wanted them to like me, I wanted Rob to be proud of me. But at last I decided to wear the clothes I liked and felt comfortable in: leggings, boots and a long thick jumper just like everyone was wearing then.

As I walked into the restaurant I could see Rob looking nervously around for me. He was sitting in a booth with his mum and two beautiful blond girls. They were so pretty. They all looked pleased to see me and started chattering as if they knew all about me.

"Dad says you drive a Morris Marina," the eldest child said. She was the spitting image of her dad. Her face made me wonder how Rob's first wife must feel seeing her cuckolded husband's face in her eldest child every day.

"Yes, I do," I said, smiling. "I love my car. But your dad doesn't approve," I laughed.

We ordered our lunch. It was Rob's birthday and I'd bought him a card with a picture of a Ford Capri on the front. "My favourite car," he said. "How did you know? I had a gorgeous Paris Blue Capri before I got the Escort. But I decided I'm too old for Capris now so I got rid of it."

Rob's mam told me Rob had said I worked in the City. "I do," I said. "I'm only a secretary, though, nothing fancy."

"Do you have your own office?" she asked. "Our Pat has her own office. She has to wear tights to work. No bare legs. I think that's right. I don't think it looks good to be at work with bare legs. It gives the wrong impression I think."

Rob's mam worked with women ex-offenders in a rehabilitation centre in Hartlepool.

"Are you coming back with us to Dad's?" the youngest girl asked. "We're going to make Dad a birthday tea. Grandma's brought everything from Marks & Spencer's." Rob laughed. Marks & Spencer was his mam's favourite shop. He said people called him Mark Spencer when he was a kid because the label was in all his clothes.

"No, I have to get home," I said. "My mum will be expecting me."

Becki looked disappointed. "Will you come again?" she asked.

"I hope so," I said, "if I'm invited."

***

Rob invited me to a club where he'd been in the habit of going on a Sunday evening with his mate Tim, when they'd both been on the look out for women.

I togged myself up to the nines in my favourite dress. It was emerald green, tight fitting with a high split up the leg. I decided on bare legs since I had a nice tan.

Tim looked me up and down and said, "You must be Bess. Rob has told me a lot about you."

Rob and Tim worked together and were best mates. At thirty years old, Tim was completely bald and hilariously funny. It was like sitting drinking with a couple of comedians.

The club was a place for pulling. It was hilarious. There were a lot of middle aged men with white suits and gold medallions standing around in a circle while women danced together in the centre. It was amusing to watch, but uneasily so – I knew I'd been a part of that before.

When the slow music started, Rob asked me to dance and we did. He pulled me close to him, the first time we'd touched! All around the dance floor we were being casually eye-balled by the white suits who hadn't yet chosen their prey.

"They're all jealous of me," Rob said in my ear as I breathed in his gorgeous scent.

We left Tim chatting up a red-headed girl and drove on to Rob's flat, me following his Escort in my Morris Marina.

He proudly showed me around. The place was spotless. It had a large sitting room, kitchen, two bedrooms and a bathroom. The smaller bedroom had bunk beds for his girls and lots of their stuff was strewn around.

He made us coffee and put on the Phil Collins record I'd bought for his birthday.

"Can I borrow your phone?" I asked. "I need to call my mum and tell her I'll be later than I said."

"How old are you?" he joked.

"It's not that. It's just that she'd be worried," I said. I told Ma I was at Rob's flat and would be late home.

"Just be careful," she said.

We sat on his sofa for a while before he finally held out his hand to me. I looked down and gave him mine.

"Contact!" he said and bent to kiss me. And then he led me into his bedroom. We finally made love.

Afterwards, he made toast and jam with more coffee and we sat in bed eating it and then made love again.

It was after two in the morning when I finally got back to Ma's house. And I'd have to be up in three hours' time to get ready for the Monday morning commute to catch my train to London. It occurred to me that if I'd stayed at Rob's I could walk to the station and catch the train from his, taking about an hour off my travel time.

More and more I stayed overnight at Rob's flat. He drove me to the station in the morning and I caught the train to London. In the evening I walked back to his flat. He would share one of his ready meals for one with me, we'd make love and curl up and watch telly or listen to music.

On Fridays, though, I always went home to Mother's. Mr Wary would invariably be there and there would be two sausages on a side plate for me. I'd do my clothes washing, clean and tidy Ma's house and we'd go out somewhere. Sometimes Mr Wary took us out for a meal. Normally, though, Ma and I would just go out for a drive to see the rhododendrons at Sandringham or to visit a stately home and gardens or for a trip to the seaside.

Ma still suffered from pain in her hips and walked a bit lopsided but she never complained. Sometimes she worked in her garden while I sat inside writing. Occasionally sister Melanie would come up to see us with her man and her puppy. Or sister Louise would come up with her husband Pete. My sister Carol had gone to live in France with the Frenchman she'd met while working at a posh hotel.

Ma would give me food parcels to take back to Rob's on Sunday afternoons with lots of fruit and vegetables. I started taking over the preparation of our evening meals.

And so we got into this rhythm.

"Why don't you ever stay here at the weekends?" Rob asked. "The kids think you don't like them."

"Of course I do. But they want to spend time with you," I said. "And I want to spend some time with my mum."

The truth was that I needed my own space and there wasn't any in Rob's flat though it was extremely convenient in the week for reducing my travel time – and the cost of my train season ticket. When it came to renew my ticket I shaved off £1,000 in train fares by beginning my journey from Rob's.

Mother hadn't met Rob yet. One evening she rang me

at Rob's. Rob answered the phone and passed the receiver to me. "It's your mam," he said.

"Hello Darling. It's only me. Gosh! Doesn't he have a dreadful accent?" she said cheerfully. "When does he have his girls next?"

"Next weekend."

"I thought so. I wondered whether Rob would like to bring his girls our for a picnic at Stamford. The Battle Proms is on next weekend and the weather forecast is amazing."

"Hold on," I said and asked Rob if he'd like to go. He said yes.

"That's good," Ma said. "I'll get tickets."

The following Saturday Mother and I packed up an enormous picnic and set off for Stamford where we met up with Rob and his two girls. They took an immediate liking to Ma and chatted happily with her as we chose a spot on the grass and spread out our blankets, cushions and picnic. They'd never been on a picnic before and their eyes were huge as they looked at all the good things to eat that we'd prepared.

Rob was shy with Ma. This was the first time they'd met and I was really keen for them to like each other.

The band played while the sun went down, we munched on our picnic, lay back on the cushions wrapped up in blankets as it got cooler. And then, when it was dark, the evening finished with a truly spectacular firework display. "Thank you for our lovely picnic," the girls said politely to Ma as we began to pack up all our stuff.

"Yes, thank you," Rob said. "It's lovely to meet you at last."

As Ma and I drove home, she said, "What lovely girls. They're so well behaved. Whatever happened to their marriage, Rob and his wife did a good job with those children. But he doesn't have a lot to say for himself, does he? I think you could do so much better, Darling."

"Do you have to go so soon?" Ma asked as I began packing up my stuff the next morning ready to go back to Rob's flat.

Most of my clothes were at his flat now so at least I didn't have to work out which clothes I needed for the week ahead at work. I just took back the clothes I'd washed at Ma's house plus the bag of fruit and vegetables she'd put together for us.

"I thought we might go for a drive out for lunch." She looked wistful and I felt a pang of guilt.

"Well, Rob wants me to spend some time with him and the girls before he takes them back home this evening," I said. "He says they think I don't like them because I'm never there when they are."

"And I'm wondering whether you like me," she said.

"Oh Ma!" I said and gave her a hug. "It's difficult. I feel a bit torn. I love coming here – to see you and stay in your lovely little house. You give me space that I don't have at the flat. But Rob can get moody and then he picks an argument… ." I tailed off.

"Just like Charlie used to with me," Ma observed.

"What? Do you think I've landed on a man similar to

Dad?" I asked, suddenly wondering if I had.

"Why not?" she said. "Melanie has."

Sure enough, just as Mother had married a man twenty years older than her, so had my sister Melanie. He was deeply critical of everyone and everything too, just as Dad had been.

"We just have to see if Rob suspects me of having affairs just as Dad did you," I laughed.

"Why would we choose a partner who resembled our fathers when the fathers were abusive? Do you think you've gone after men just like your father?" I asked Ma.

"It's strange that Rob and I both share the same story of our births – how you and I both nearly died when you were having me and Rob and his mum both nearly died when he was born. His mum had to have a hysterectomy and was in hospital for ages afterwards and Rob was looked after by his Nan. Weird patterns don't you think?"

She shrugged. "You think too much, darling." She kissed me goodbye and waved me off at the front gate of the house which I thought of as my sacred space.

Later that evening as Rob drove us back from dropping the kids off he was very quiet.

"Are you OK?" I asked.

"Yep."

"The girls seemed to enjoy last night."

"They talked about the picnic all day," he smiled. "They told Mam all about it over the phone when she rang."

"Brilliant!" I said, really pleased. "My mum really

liked your kids. She said they were so well behaved which is something coming from her. We were all really badly behaved apparently when we were kids."

When we got back to his flat, though, he was still quiet and moody.

"What's up?" I finally demanded, fed up with the tense atmosphere I had no idea why he was producing.

"I hate to say this, Bessie." He stared into his coffee. Then looked up. "Are you having an affair?"

"What?" I said.

"I thought so! That's why you're over at your mam's every weekend. You're having an affair with someone over there, some old flame."

"Of course I'm not!" I shouted, exasperated.

"See! You're all defensive," he said.

I slammed out of the room, put on my running gear and went out for a run. When I got back he looked a bit ashamed.

"I'm sorry," he said. "It's just that since Lorraine did what she did, I find it hard to trust. And I don't really understand what you see in me."

"Just because she had an affair, it doesn't mean to say that all women are unfaithful," I said.

"I don't really blame her in a way," he said. "We were so poor when we first got together. I worked all day at the garage and then in the evening I stayed behind to do private work. I bought old bangers, restored them and sold them privately to make some more money. And Lorraine did evening bar work where she met that bloke.

I don't blame her. I was never there. I just wanted to earn money so we could buy a house. And we did! I'm the only one in our family to buy a house – the other two have always only rented. But I wanted more. I don't care what people say about Maggie Thatcher. It was because of her that I was inspired to work hard so I could buy us a house and nice things. We sold that first house for a fortune and bought a massive place in Stevenage. But then, Lorraine had that affair and destroyed our family.

"You're gorgeous," he said. "You're beautiful and so kind and so sexy. I don't know what you see in me."

"Maybe I'm just attracted to a fellow human being damaged at birth by his mother," I laughed. "I love you," I said and took his hand. "That's all you need to know."

The next day when I got home, the flat was empty.

He'd been home and left a note: 'Gone to work on Dave's MGA. Home around 7.30.'

I went for a run, had a shower, rang Mother and finally started making dinner ready for 7.30.

7.30 came and went. I put the meal in the oven to keep warm. 8.00 went by, 8.30.

He came in at 9, black from head to toe and stinking.

"Filler," he said. "Dave rang me and told me he'd bought an MGA banger. I went round to have a look. He asked if I could restore it for him. I started and got a bit carried away," he looked sheepish but happy. "You don't mind, do you? If I do some work in the evenings?"

"Of course not," I said. "I'm not sure what dinner will be like now though."

And so every evening I let myself into Rob's flat while he worked on Dave's MGA, went for a run, had a shower, rang Mother, read a book for a bit and cooked a meal, not knowing what time he'd be in. It was usually around 9.00 when he got in stinking of filler and covered in oil and dust.

Apparently he'd given me the space I wanted.

And then it happened that Lorraine began to ring on a Friday evening to say that the girls wouldn't be able to come and stay that weekend. Rob was distraught.

"Why?" I asked. He looked a bit uncomfortable.

"I think she's jealous of you," he said. "Last time they were up, you were over at your Mam's, they were saying how they'd been telling their mam about you and how happy I was."

"She can't stop them from coming. There's a Court Order." I said.

I took advice from a friend at work and wrote a letter to the Court on Rob's behalf. The kids returned to their weekend visits.

Next, Lorraine applied to the Court to have Rob's maintenance increased, citing the fact that I was living with him so his income had increased.

"What? So I have to contribute to the maintenance for your kids?" I said incredulous. "I don't live here anyway. I live with my mum."

"I think the kids have seen your clothes in the wardrobe," he said, miserably.

***

Rob began to complain about pains in his panel beating elbow. He took days off sick to rest it. As it got worse, I suggested he should go to his GP to get referred to a specialist.

"You need an X-ray," I said. He was referred to the hospital.

Apparently, the nature of the work Rob did was causing an inflammation in his elbow. He might have to give it up. "But you love your work," I said. "What else would you do?"

As Lorraine became more and more aggressive in blocking the kids from coming to visit Rob, his elbow became more and more painful and he began to turn nasty. He was depressed. He was off work, he wouldn't speak with me and when I tried to coax him to talk about what was bothering him he would snap and snarl and start an argument. He took to lying on the sofa watching crappy TV.

I secretly consulted my Louise Hay book on the true meaning of physical ailments. Elbow problems were about having to accept a change of direction which was a bit cryptic I thought.

***

One day while I was at work, I got a phone call from our Post Room. Apparently, there was a parcel for me. I went down to the basement.

"Parcel for Carl Bird?" I smiled.

"It's for you," the head of Deliveries grinned, pointing to a vase of twelve red roses.

"What?!" I said completely taken aback. No-one had ever sent me flowers in my whole life! Maybe it was a romantic gesture from Rob apologising for being horrible.

There was a note attached: 'Lots of love Kyrell XXX' and it was handwritten. Kyrell was here?

"Where is the guy who brought these?" I asked Daryl. He shrugged.

"Just left them for you and went."

I took the flowers and returned to my desk feeling a bit freaked out. I put the vase on the filing cabinet next to my desk and looked at them. The phone rang.

"Hello!" It was Kyrell.

I could hardly believe the emotions that went running through my whole body as I heard his voice: lust at the sound of his familiar voice and the memories associated with it, anger that he should just turn up like this, shame if Rob found out about the roses and what conclusions he'd jump to, joy at being sent red roses…

"Hello?" he said again. "Are you there?"

"Kyrell!" I said. "Where are you? How are you here?"

"They gave us a plane ticket to wherever we wanted to go," he said. He worked for McDonnell Douglas. "It's been a record year. They gave us this as a bonus. I decided to come and see you."

"What? Me? Why?"

"I need to see you so much," he said.

"What the fuck?" I thought I'd thought but I'd actually said it out loud. The voices around me stopped to listen. "Look, I can't talk. I'm at work," I said into the phone.

"When can I see you?" he asked.

"Um. The weekend? Where are you staying? I'm working on Sunday. I can see you at lunchtime at 12 midday." I put the phone down.

I felt confused and outraged. How dare he? Just come waltzing back like this when I was trying to get on with my life. When I'd found someone, a proper mate at last who I could settle down with? But, then, Rob was not the best mate. My mum disapproved of him, he had so much baggage. He was damaged goods. So was I. What right had Kyrell to come back into my life? But then my old lustful self kicked in. Rob thought I was having an affair. What if I did have an affair?

"Who are the flowers from?" my boss asked.

"Too long a story," I said.

I drove back to Mother's house at the end of the day.

I told her the what had happened.

"Well?" she asked. "What are you going to do?"

"I'm meeting him for lunch on Sunday," I said. "I have to go to work – Carl has a big job on."

I went into work on Sunday. 12 o'clock passed. 1 o'clock, 2 o'clock.

Then, at 3.30 I got a phone call from Reception. "Hello," he said. "I'm sorry. The traffic was awful."

"Look," I said. "I can't come down. I've got work to do." I put the phone down and went back to work.

That evening when I got home, Rob was in his usual depressed mood.

"Shall we go out for a drink?" I asked.

"No, I can't be bothered," he said.

I went for a run.

The next day Rob got a letter inviting him in for an operation on his elbow. He was 35. He would never work on cars for a living again but would have to choose a new direction.

***

I drove to the hospital to pick Rob up after his operation. He was wearing a plaster cast on his arm.

"What did they do?" I said.

"They sawed off the medial epicondyle," he said. "Where your funny bone is," he added. We actually laughed.

"That's not funny," I said. "What's that supposed to do?"

"They reckon the muscles or tendons or something in my elbow are so big that they were rubbing on that bone and that's what was causing the pain," he explained. "So by cutting off that knobbly bit, it leaves more room for the muscles. It makes sense I suppose," he added seeing my look of disbelief.

"And how long do you need to keep that on?" I asked pointing at the plaster cast.

"A month, they said."

"Are you allowed to drive?"

"No."

"What about the kids?"

"Lorraine will have to bring them up," he said.

But she didn't. I heard him pleading with her on the phone. When he hung up he refused to tell me what was going on.

Half an hour later the phone rang. I answered it. It was Lorraine. I'd never spoken with her before in the three years I'd known Rob.

"Rob is in the bath," I lied. "What can I do for you?"

"Mona left some shoes at your flat," she said. "I wondered if Rob could bring them down."

"He can't drive, as you know," I said. "But I'd be really happy to drive down and collect the kids on Friday after school."

"Over my dead body. I'm not having my kids in your car, you witch," she said.

I actually did that thing of taking the phone receiver away from my ear to stare at it. What did she say?

"What did you say?" I asked, returning the receiver to my ear.

Silence.

"You don't even know me," I said.

"I'm sorry," she said. "But you don't know what it's like."

"What what's like?" I asked.

"Having kids."

"How do you know? As I said, you don't know anything about me."

"Rob is a very selfish man," she said. "You need to know that. Do you know that… ?" and she began to give me examples of how selfish Rob had been to her, but I'd stopped listening.

"Funny that," I said. "He's told me so much about you and him but he's never tried to do a character assassination on you."

"Maybe he's changed," she said. "Maybe you bring out the best in him."

"All I know is that he adores his kids and you've got no right to stop him from seeing them just because you're jealous of me."

I put the receiver down. I turned round to see Rob standing in the doorway leaning against the door frame. He didn't say anything, just turned round and left the room. I heard him open the fridge door and snap open a can of lager.

The next week Rob received a letter summonsing him to Court. Lorraine wanted more money from him as maintenance for the kids based on the fact that I was apparently living with him.

After six weeks off work, he'd been sacked by his employer as incapable of doing the job he'd been employed to do. He was spiralling into depression. He didn't want to do anything, wouldn't speak with me or, if he did, it was to provoke an argument.

The day of the Court case arrived.

"What happened?" I asked when I got in from work.

Rob smiled for the first time in ages.

"I have to pay her 5p a month," he said.

"What?"

"She turned up in a flashy new car which I just happened to mention to the Judge. I told him I'm unemployed. And the Judge said I had to pay 5p a month and she has to pay costs. As we walked out I handed her 20p and said, "Here y'are, 4 months in advance." He laughed.

I went home to Mother's at the weekend. We had a lovely time, so relaxed and happy after the atmosphere in the flat with Rob. I cooked dinner on Saturday evening and we sat down to eat it while watching Morse on television,

While we were eating Ma said, "Um. Kim is coming home. She's leaving Christos. I've told her she can come to live here. You'll have to leave, I'm afraid."

"What?" I put my knife and fork down. "They're all coming here?"

"Yes darling."

"But where will I go?" I said.

"You've got Rob," she said.

"No I haven't. I can't live there with him. I want to be with you."

"But you do live with him, Darling. It's time you went," she said and carried on eating.

I finished my meal in silence. I felt sick.

When we'd both finished I took the plates into the kitchen, went upstairs to the bathroom and vomited my whole dinner into the toilet.

When I got back to Rob's flat the next day, he was out. I unpacked my stuff and walked around the flat. There was no space. I just couldn't live here with him and his moods.

At work the next day I went out to lunch with a friend. "Why don't you get a flat in London?" she asked when I told her my problem.

"It's too expensive," I said. "I've tried it before."

"You might be surprised," she said.

I picked up a copy of the evening paper and flicked through it on my commute home. There was a flat going in Muswell Hill for just £350 a month. I rang the number the next day and arranged to meet the landlord after work.

***

I walked from the Tube station to the address the landlord had given me.

It was a beautiful evening and the trees along the roadside were thick with blossom. It looked a lovely area. There was a Sainsbury's opposite the Tube station I noticed.

The address was a huge detached house that had been carved up into flats. The one available right now was at the front of the house on the ground floor.

The front door was open and the landlord was waiting for me in the wide hallway.

"I've come about the flat," I said.

He nodded and unlocked the door to the flat. It was really a bedsit: an enormous room with a high ceiling and tall windows looking out to the road. There was a wardrobe and a double bed. Two doors led off the main room: one to small bathroom with a toilet thick with lime scale, the other to a tiny kitchen. There was a faint whiff of gas. The tap in the sink dripped every ten seconds or so.

"Three months deposit" the landlord said, "and a month's notice to leave. You get the deposit back if you leave it in good order."

"Did the last tenant get his deposit back?" I laughed.

He ignored my remark.

"I've got someone else interested," he said.

"OK. I'll take it," I told him, wondering where I'd find the money for the deposit.

When I got home Rob was watching television. I went to kiss him and he turned his head away.

"Would you like something to eat?" I said.

"Nope," he said.

"What's up?"

"Nowt," he said.

"Why don't you talk to me?" I said.

"Oh shut up. I'm watching this," he said and turned the telly up.

I changed into my running gear and went off for a run.

Later that evening I said, "I'm leaving you, Rob. I can't bear it like this anymore."

"Go on then," he said.

***

Grandfather had died in January that year. In his Will he'd left £1,000 to each of his grandchildren. I'd also been given the desk from the study in his house together with the Captain's chair that went with it. Probate hadn't completed yet but I asked Ma if she would lend me the £1,000 that was due to me so I could use it for the deposit on the bedsit in Muswell Hill. She agreed. She also agreed to help me move all my stuff from her house down to London if I would arrange a rental van.

I knew that Rob hadn't believed me when I'd said I was leaving him.

"I'm moving out in a couple of weeks," I told him.

"What?" He looked up from the television he was glued to now non-stop. "Where're you going?"

"I told you I've got a bedsit in Muswell Hill," I said.

"But. I thought you were just saying that." He was silent. "Look," he said eventually, "if you think I'm going to beg you to stay, I'm not."

"I love you," I said, "but I can't live with you like this."

I kissed him on his head and went off to bed.

***

The next weekend was the May bank holiday and Ma was going away for the weekend with Mr Wary. I'd been collecting boxes for a while and spent the long weekend packing up all my stuff that had just continued to grow in volume since I'd left University.

I was taping up a box with brown parcel tape when the news was announced that Ayrton Senna had died at

Imola. I knew that Rob would be devastated. I rang him. He was in tears.

As soon as I'd finished packing up all my stuff into bags and boxes ready for my move the next weekend, I drove back to his flat. He was devastated at the Formula 1 racing carnage of that weekend. Roland Ratzenberger had died the day before and Rubens Barrichello had also had a serious crash. Rob was very down.

"Let's get out of here and go for drink," I suggested and he agreed.

We sat opposite each other in the bar with our drinks between us. I reached over and took his hand.

"I don't want to leave you, Robbie. I love you. But I can't live with you with all this crap going on. And Ma has kicked me out of her house because Kim and her kids are moving into her house next Sunday. So I have to be out by then."

He nodded, not saying anything.

"You can have my car – sell it, whatever. I won't need a car in London. And I'll write. And you can come and see me if you like. Alright?" I gave him my new address.

And then I left him.

***

Ma drove me down to North London and helped me empty the van I'd rented.

"Do you want to stay for a coffee?" I asked her.

"Uh, no," she said looking around. "I need to get back. Make sure you make your bed up first."

We hugged silently and then she was gone.

I sat on the bed feeling empty and abandoned.

I made the bed. I emptied some boxes. I scrubbed out the kitchen. I scrubbed out the bathroom – the lime scale didn't shift.

I put my books in my bookcases. I hung my clothes in the wardrobe.

I needed to speak with someone. There was a communal payphone in the hallway outside my door. I rang my sister Melanie.

"Hello," she said. I could hear lots of voices in the background.

"Sounds like you're having a party," I said.

"Yes, everyone's here," she said. "Ma picked Kim and co up from the airport in the van you hired and they've all come over here for dinner. Lou and Pete are here too. They all send their love." I put the phone down.

I was livid. I had been kicked out and they were all celebrating.

***

My new journey to work was very straightforward: short walk to the Tube station, straight through on the Northern Line to the City.

"How was your journey?" my boss asked. "You must have had a lie-in! Will I be getting an invitation to your house warming party?"

I looked at him. "You'd be very welcome to visit. But… it's a dump, but the journey was only 45 minutes which was great."

I bought some heavy duty lime scale remover from the local DIY shop and squirted the whole bottle around my toilet bowl.

There was a letter waiting for me from Rob. I remembered the letters he used to write to me when we joined Dateline before we'd ever met. But now his tone was of a beaten man. He was so sorry for having pushed me away, he wrote. He missed me like crazy. He wanted me back.

I made myself a cup of coffee and carried on emptying my boxes. Finally, I turned my attention to Grandfather's desk that was now mine.

It was a beautiful piece of furniture and I felt very honoured to have it as my own. It was dark oak with a faded dark green leather top. It had nine drawers all of which were stuffed full. There were hundreds of black and white photos all dated with the location or event on the reverse, mostly from the 1930s. There were rulers, geometry sets, ink pens still in their boxes, aged lined notebooks some with Grandfather's distinctive handwriting. Most of the stuff was junk that whoever had cleared Grandfather's study had not felt able to bring themselves to chuck away.

The phone in the hallway rang. I went out to answer it. It was my sister Louise. She never rang me so I was curious to find out the reason for her phone call.

"Were you at the party yesterday then?" I asked.

"Bessie," she said. "We all think you should pull

yourself together." I put the phone down and went back into my room. The phone began ringing again. I ignored it and went back to the contents of my desk.

And then I found a pack of letters held together with an elastic band. They were from Mother addressed to my Granny and Grandfather, her parents, mostly dated 1964.

The last letter, though, was dated 15th August 1966 shortly after Granny had died of cancer and a day after Mother and her twin's 25th birthday. Ma wrote...

'My Dearest Daddy, It was marvellous to see you and Lizzie down here yesterday. Thank you very much for your present, and the delightful card. I can only apologise for my outre marie, and hope he did not do too much brain-washing while we were out.

I had not the courage yesterday to tell you of the further addition which I am expecting at Christmas; although I believe you suspected it already. I cannot excuse myself by any explanations, although Lizzie knows the circumstances. I can only say it is the utmost in irresponsibility.

I really feel that I cannot go on living with David any longer. The situation is quite intolerable but he just does not understand this when I try to talk to him. He knows I would leave him if I had the place to go to. And this is where the greatest problem lies. My friend, Mr Rosolek, is considering buying a house and has asked me if I will go to it with the children, and act as his housekeeper. Of course I would be very foolish not to consider this seriously, but I wonder what the outcome would be when

David found out.

Mr Rosolek is devoted to the children, and I know that our future would be completely assured domestically, financially and morally. However, I have to find accommodation for between two and three months until David has resigned himself to the situation, and Mr Rosolek has found his house.

I feel so helpless, all the more so because of the coming baby; but I must get away from David before something far worse than last Saturday's fight takes place, and before I am so mentally exhausted that I give up.

There is plenty more to say, but all along the same lines, so I will leave it. I am looking forward greatly to seeing you on Wednesday – and wonder if you will have any suggestions, as to how this may be resolved.

With much love and thanks for everything,

Evelyn'

I wrote back to Rob. I told him all the things I hadn't been able to say to him before for fear of him flaring up into a rage. I told him how unhappy I'd been, how useless I felt at not being able to help with the situation with Lorraine and his kids, how sorry I was about all the stuff he'd had to endure and now unable to work in the job he loved to do, but how bored I was that he wouldn't do anything other than watch crappy TV. I told him we were two depressed people who shouldn't be together. But that I loved him still and cared deeply about him. We shared similar stories handed down from our mothers – we'd both nearly killed our mothers at birth and felt rejected by them as a result.

It was for the best, I wrote, that we should be apart for a while but see how it went. I ended up by inviting him to our work's Summer Ball in a couple of weeks and he could stay over if he liked and make a weekend of it.

He wrote back to say he would love to come and see me.

I ordered a black tie suit for him from Moss Bros and met him at Kings Cross on the Friday evening. He squeezed me tight to him when we met on the platform.

"I've missed you," he said. He was tearful.

I babbled on. We were on my ground now. I took him back to our office where he changed his suit in the gents. He came out looking very dapper and gorgeous.

"I look like a bouncer," he laughed.

I stashed his bag under my desk and changed into my party gear which was a long gold lacey sheath dress that I'd bought from Freemans Catalogue. I had gold slingbacks and a gold coloured clutch bag to match.

"You look gorgeous," he said, "super sexy."

We walked hand in hand towards the Royal Artilleries grounds where our ball was to take place in a specially erected marquee.

It was a hot summer's evening and it felt so good to be reunited with Rob like this. He must have been feeling the same. As we approached the venue, Rob turned to me, got down on one knee in the middle of the road and asked me to marry him!

I smiled happily. "No," I said. "I don't want to get

married." But it was the most romantic thing he'd ever done and I was impressed.

We had a fabulous evening. I felt very proud of my man and introduced him to everyone we bumped into.

It was gone 1.00 in the morning when we finally climbed into a taxi to drive to my bedsit. I unlocked my door and let Rob in. I heard him suck in his breath. He burst into tears.

"What's up?" I said.

"Is this it? This is where you live? It's terrible," he said. "I can't believe you left my lovely flat to move here. You must have really hated me."

He sat on the bed crying loudly and gasping.

I sat down beside him and put my arms around him.

"Ma kicked me out of her house to make room for Kim. That's why I had to move here. I couldn't live with you while you were like you were. This was all I could afford. And anyway," I said, standing up. "I think I've made this place quite nice. You should have seen it when I arrived."

The place was now spotlessly clean for a start. All around the high walls I'd hung up the posters Ma had bought me from every West End opera, ballet and musical we'd been to together over the last five years. I had my beautiful desk with the Captain's chair surrounded by my bookshelves. And I'd finally got the toilet clean.

***

Mother never rang me now. It was her birthday coming

up in August. I thought hard about a present to send her. I decided to buy her tickets to see Phantom of the Opera. It was a musical we'd both wanted to see but had never got round to. It would be lovely to see it together and to spend some time with her.

So I sent her two tickets in her birthday card.

The day came and went. It suddenly dawned on me either that she couldn't get to London or she'd gone to the theatre with Kim.

And then she rang. It was so lovely to hear her voice. I chatted excitedly for a bit about what I'd been up to, my promotion at work and the wonderful patisserie just round the corner.

"Bessie," she said at last. "I shouldn't have to ask for this. But I need the money I lent you for your rent. I know you've had Gramps' £1,000 and I need it back."

Silence.

"Hello?" she said.

"I'm here," I said. "But I'm not giving you the money. I've decided. I've lost you. I'll keep the money instead." I could hear her shock.

"How did you get on at the Phantom of the Opera?" I asked sarcastically. "D'you know? I was tempted to ring the theatre to say there was a bomb planted so you'd all have to evacuate." I was red hot with rage and could feel my blood pounding in my head as I poured it out.

"I don't understand you," she said.

"I never want to speak with you again," I said and put the phone down.

POSKI

By Elisabeth Henderson Clarke

It was the last straw. I could feel rage and frustration amassing suddenly and boiling in my gut. I opened my mouth to answer her.

"Are you there, Jessie?"

Like an old fashioned whistling kettle on the boil, I suddenly shrieked, "I never want to see you again!" and slammed down the telephone receiver.

I was trembling as I went back into the sitting room, but the relief was enormous. I flopped onto the sofa, reached for a cigarette, lighting it with hands that felt strangely weak, and breathed in the smoke noisily. I brought my knees up to my chin and hugged them.

Chas was looking at me. "You OK, Jess?" he asked. "Was that your mum?"

I nodded. She had rung to thank me for the two theatre tickets I had sent as a Christmas present, for Swan Lake which we had both wanted to see again. It was a wonderful performance, she said. She had taken Claire, my eldest sister, whom I loathed. But she was supposed to have asked me to go.

"There is – so – much – I wanted to say to her," I said, feeling deflated and trying not to cry. I could feel my face crumpling with the effort. My throat was hot. "I needed her to tell me things, to explain the past, why

I'm like this – why I feel so... so..." Involuntarily, I was smoothing the scars on my wrists. I looked across at my husband who was stroking his cat – his cat because it would have nothing to do with me and would hiss if I ever tried to stroke her (Chas said she was jealous of me) – and sitting back comfortably on the sofa, his blond rug of hair tousled and boyish, his tanned, attractive face contented with its lot but those lovely green eyes looking concerned at me.

It never ceased to amaze me that this wonderful man should love me, as he did, so uncomplicatedly, so unconditionally. "I love you," I said. He was 6'5" and my tower of strength. I adored him.

"I love you too," he said as he held out his hand offering a hug. From the security of the circle his arm gave me, I became calm again.

"I won't be able to talk to her again now," I sighed. "I've really blown it."

The cat had run off with an indignant hiss and now Chas was stroking my long hair. "You could write to her," he said.

"No," I was weary but suddenly determined, "I'll ring her tomorrow. I can't leave it like this."

***

I stood in the hallway and listened to the phone ringing on the other end. My mother is often in the garden so I held on to give her time to get back into the house. I let myself slide down the wall until I was squatting on my heels.

Prrr-prrr, prrr-prrr. The noise from the other end was like a cat purring and I could imagine Poski, my mum's black cat, sitting by the phone purring contentedly, knowing that I was trying to speak to my mother and knowing that she was not there. Prrr-prrr, prrr-prrr. I listened until the phone went dead and then decided that Chas was right as usual, I should write to her.

I poured a whisky, added ice and went to my study.

I sipped the chilled whisky and smoked cigarettes for a while before I began to write. I used my best writing paper and the gold-nibbed fountain pen Chas had given me for Christmas.

The alcohol was quickly in my brain and I wrote to my mother straight from the poison that was in me, my pen moving swiftly over the smooth thick whiteness of the page, everything I needed to explain to her. I felt she had always been jealous of Chas, a successful photographer, good looking, always at ease with himself. But, by letting me talk and accepting what I have to say, and loving me despite what I say, I wrote, without doubt, Chas saved my life. At any rate, it was he who had wrapped my lacerated wrists in towels and driven me to A & E that night. And now, after all the counselling and group therapy sessions, I am still on sick leave. I can feel the shadow of a block in my healing and I know the only person who can explain and dispel that block is you, mother. But you won't listen. You won't let me talk about those things.

I gulped at the whisky, stubbed out a cigarette. I was becoming filled with self-pity and self-loathing as the depressive action of the alcohol settled into my mind.

My pen moved on.

I unburdened responsibility for my life and past actions from my own shoulders onto the paper, blaming it all on my mother. And finally, having filled four A4 pages both sides, I told her (and each word seemed to sting at the wounds on my wrists) that I now realised she didn't love me – probably didn't even like me, and I could manage without her.

I didn't re-read the letters; I knew what I had written. I wanted her to read this and feel the hurt a little. I folded the letter carefully as my drunken fingers could manage and sealed it into an envelope. I put it on the telephone table and would post it later.

Meanwhile I went upstairs, crawled under the duvet and was instantly asleep.

***

When I woke, the room was dark. My mind struggled for a moment to remember where I was and how I had come to be there. And then I felt a stab of remorse as the cold knowledge that I had done something very wrong crept into my mind. The letter.

I switched on the bedside lamp. It was six o'clock. I heard the front door shut.

"Chas!" I called.

I couldn't send the letter. I had written too much. My mother mustn't read it. I threw back the quilt and ran out to the hallway, the heel of my hand to my head. It seemed a band of steel had been tightly fastened around my head while I slept. I staggered a bit but reached the bottom of the stairs. I trod on the cat's tail; it hissed and shot away. The hall light was on. The cat crouched under the telephone table, its tail swishing slightly. I ignored it.

A note beside the telephone read, "J. Just popped out to catch the first post. Love you. C."

I stood, staring at that note, my hand clutching my head, feeling the nausea churn in my stomach. I rushed to the bathroom.

***

Afterwards, I sipped at a mug of coffee without tasting its contents. The first post went from the post office in the town centre and Chas would have driven to get there. I couldn't stop him from sending the letter. I had stamped it first class and so mother would read it tomorrow. Out of anger and haste, I had sparked off a relentless chain of events. I was now helplessly unable to prevent my mother from reading the venom I had written and I now knew I did not want to hurt her. The only thing I could do was ring her and warn her about the letter and ask her to destroy it without reading it.

I rang her number. The cat purred down the line again. Nobody answered. I was still standing there, hypnotised by that gentle purring when Chas came in the front door. He smiled and raised his eyebrows at the phone.

"'S OK," I said and put the receiver down. "I was ringing mum, but she's not in." We kissed. "I'll try once more," I said and redialled. "You caught the post then?" I asked. Chas stooped to pet his cat, still in hiding beneath the table.

His pause made me hope – perhaps he hadn't got to the post office.

"Oh yes," he said, still crouching over the cat, rubbing her belly as she stretched and rolled. "All posted." My heart sank.

My mother's voice was in my ear. "Hi," I said. I noticed white paper beneath the cat. She was rolling on it. "Jessica?" my mum asked. "Is that you?"

"Uh – yes. Um. Mum, I – um." I giggled nervously, bending down to pull my envelope from beneath the cat where it must have fallen and she had lain on it. The cat hissed. "What's that?" Chas asked and we both stood, each holding one end of the envelope.

"Yes darling?" my mum was saying. "If it's about last night, I know. We all lash out at times and say things we don't mean..." I looked at Chas. He was puzzled.

There was a new purring on the phone. "It's Poski," my mum's voice said happily. "Can you hear her?"

THE END

Rob and I became very close again. Every other fortnight I would catch the train after work on a Friday and travel up to see him. He planned things for us to do, places to go, we had amazing sex and loved every moment of being together.

And then once every two months or so he would catch the train to London on a Friday evening and spend the weekend with me. And we explored the city together, walking for miles.

One Friday evening, he suggested we should get up really early the next day and he would take me to Scarborough, the seaside place up north where he used to spend his school summer holidays as a kid. I said yes. We left his flat at 5 am and arrived at the North Yorkshire seaside town three hours later. It was a beautiful hot sunny day.

We walked down to the beach and I was blown away. The sea was gently lapping in and out with a sighing sound like someone breathing contentedly. The sun sparkled off the sea as we walked along the water's edge hand in hand in silence. The castle on the cliff top added poetry to the scene.

I fell in love again. It was peaceful, calming, exhilarating.

***

I decided I'd like to move back to live with Rob. We were in love again and I missed him. He'd begun a new career as a vehicle damage assessor – changing direction as he had to though still working with his beloved motorcars.

We lay in bed one morning at his flat. I asked him if he'd let me come back.

"Of course!" he said.

"One caveat though," I said. "I need a room of my own. So you need to turn the kids' old room into my study."

"Of course," he said again.

The radio was on as we lay there, and the song playing was 'I want you back' sung by the boy band, Take That. Rob sang along to the lyrics which he appeared to know well. I stared at him and laughed. "You know all the words!"

"I sing it all the time," he said, smiling. "I've been hoping you'd come back for good."

And so, practically a year to the day that I'd moved out, I moved back. And now I had a room of my own.

***

I never heard from any of my family and I didn't reach out to them. It was better that way, I told myself. I was safe and no buttons were pushed.

I was thirty and felt deliciously content for what seemed like the first time in my life.

I asked Rob if he would marry me. "Of course," he said.

We kept it quiet. We decided not to tell our families. We told very few people, just our closest friends.

We got married at the local Register Office with twenty

or so friends watching. Then we went next door to a hotel where we drank Champagne and took lots of photos. It was a beautiful sunny autumnal day full of love and it felt all the better to have no family there to worry about what they thought.

Six weeks later I had a telephone call from my sister Melanie.

"I thought you should know that Ma's in hospital."

"What?" I froze. I could feel my heart pounding. "What's happened?"

"She's got Bell's Palsy. It's like a stroke."

"Oh my God. Is she OK?"

"I don't know. You might want to call her." She gave me the hospital number to ring.

I rang the number straight away and was passed to Mother.

"Hello Darling," she said. Her voice was tired and small and a bit slurry.

"Oh Ma! What's happened?"

"I'm fine," she said. "I was just doing too much and getting all worked up with Kim and the children."

"They did this to you?" I asked.

She didn't reply.

"How long will you be in hospital?"

"I don't know. They say a few days' rest. I have shingles in my mouth. And this. They're keeping an eye on me. My eye's a bit weird and I look rather peculiar." Her words were quite slurry. It was hard to hear them.

"I've been thinking, darling," she said slowly. "When

I'm better, perhaps I could come and see you down in Muswell Hill? I'd like that."

I felt a pang of guilt.

"I don't live there anymore."

"Oh," she said, surprised. "Where are you?"

"I moved back with Rob."

***

At Christmas time, my sister Carol invited us over to her place in France. One day while she and I were washing up after our meal, she suddenly grabbed my left hand and stared at my wedding band. "You're married!" she said accusingly. "You never told us!"

And so the secret was out.

***

Six months after we were married, I discovered that I was pregnant. I noticed my breasts had become hard and tender and I had spasms of nausea throughout the day. I instinctively knew I was expecting.

I bought a pregnancy testing kit from Boots which confirmed my gut feeling.

I had to laugh inwardly when I recalled all the unprotected sex I'd taken risks with in my promiscuous teenage years. And then I get married and poof! Pregnant! I did not want a child. When I was a girl I had always assumed that I'd get married and have babies. But the thought of the responsibility of motherhood for me now appalled me. I would be a terrible mother, passing on all the crap that had been handed down to me to another poor human being to endure. No way would I let myself do that.

So I went off to my GP who was herself heavily pregnant, told her I was pregnant and asked if I could have a termination.

"Actually," I said, "can I get sterilised too? I don't want the risk of getting pregnant again."

She referred me to a gynaecologist at the local hospital for a second opinion.

He stood at a lectern in his office while I sat opposite him.

"I prefer to stand," he said. "I get problems with my back sitting down too long." (Fear of money, I thought, smiling to myself.)

"This is a big decision you're making," he told me. "So I have to ask you some questions before I can agree to do the procedure you're requesting." He tapped the side of his head. "I need to be clear that you're of sound mind," he explained smiling.

"You don't have children," he told me, reading the notes he'd been sent by my GP.

"Not everyone wants children," I told him. "My husband has his own kids from a previous marriage. He doesn't want anymore."

"What about you?"

"Well, I don't feel the need to pass on my programming to other human beings," I told him. "I had a shit childhood and all sorts of head trash that I'm still dealing with."

"But you might change your mind once you've dealt with that," he smiled again.

I shook my head. "I'm too selfish. I've seen how difficult it is bringing up children. I don't want it."

"What if your marriage were to end? These things happen as you know. You might find a new partner who wanted children."

"He'd have to find someone else then," I said adamantly.

"OK," he said and scribbled on his notes. "I believe you. Maybe more people would benefit from thinking like you. We'll do it. But I'll just clip your Fallopian Tubes rather than cut them – just in case," he smiled again and we shook hands.

I didn't have to tell Mother but I rang her all the same to tell her I was pregnant.

"Oh, darling!" was her immediate response, her voice tender and sounding delighted.

"I'm not keeping it though. In fact, I'm going to be sterilised to make sure it doesn't happen again. You have enough grandchildren anyway." Mother now had eight grandchildren from four of her girls.

***

Immediately after my fallopian tubes were clipped to prevent my eggs from travelling down into my womb, Rob took me away for a week to what had become our favourite destination: Scarborough.

We had a glorious time. The weather was red hot,

everything looked beautiful and I wore floaty summer dresses.

One particularly idyllic morning, we walked barefoot on the beach along the water's edge. I said to Rob, "Why don't we live here? We love it so much. It feels so good. We could move far away from everyone."

I looked at him and he looked at me.

"Do you know what?" he said, "When I was a nipper about this high," he put his hand down to the level of his knee, "I used to play on this beach and wish that I could stay here for ever."

"What? Building sandcastles for the rest of your life?" I said.

"Something like that," he laughed.

"What do you think then?"

"I've been waiting for you to suggest that." He hugged me to him.

***

I heard through the grapevine that my sister Kim had moved out of Mother's house. It turned out that one of her friends who lived a few streets away from Ma had won the National Lottery. She'd bought a flashy new house on the outskirts of the town and offered her old house to Kim.

I could hardly believe it! But it was true. How come these things always just landed in her lap?

Ma rang me and asked if she could come to see us.

"Of course," I said.

She'd never been to our home. I hadn't seen her for so long.

"Can I bring someone with me?"

"Who's that?" I asked.

"I've met someone very nice and I'd like you to meet him too," she said.

It was Paul Rosolek.

***

They came for dinner.

When I opened our door, Ma was standing there with Paul Rosolek. He was tall and held himself straight-backed, dressed smart casually in grey chino trousers and a dark green polo shirt.

He shook my hand with both of his and promptly took his shoes off and put on other shoes he'd been carrying.

"You don't need to," I said.

"Of course I do. I always wear indoor shoes indoors and outdoor shoes outdoors."

I looked at his indoor shoes which looked like outdoor shoes to me. I wondered what Ma thought of that but, when I turned around, I saw she'd also replaced her shoes with a pair of slippers she'd brought with her. I looked at Rob and we smiled.

We had a pleasant conversation over the dinner I'd made. Mother looked well and I told her so. Her hair was up in her timeless bun, though it was now completely silver. She was wearing a dress I'd never seen though I hadn't actually seen her for years. I'd only really known her to wear her work overalls and her gardening trousers and sloppy jumper, occasionally she wore a smart dress when we went to visit Grandfather when he was alive. She was clearly making an effort with her new man.

It turned out that Paul Rosolek had kept in touch with Ma all these years. He'd sold his business and retired. When he heard that Kim had moved to live with Ma he made plans to relocate to their town. He'd bought a plot of land and had a bungalow built directly opposite Kim's new home.

"How's your hip?" I asked.

"Which one?" Ma asked.

Apparently she'd now had three replacement operations on both hips.

"They're not good," she said, "but hey-ho. There could be worse things."

As I emptied the wine bottle in our glasses, Ma said, "Paul has something to ask you."

Rob and I both looked at Paul expectantly.

"Um, yes," he said, dabbing at his mouth with his serviette. "Um." He took Ma's hand. "I would like to marry your mother and she said I needed to ask your permission."

I stared at them both. I think my mouth fell open.

"Well, of course, if that's what you want," I said.

"I've always been very fond of your mother," Paul said, patting her leg. "I've sold my business and have a good pension and I'd like your mother to share my new home with me, just as she failed to share my home with me all those years ago." He laughed. "It's got a big empty garden too that I know your mother is itching to get her hands into."

Ma smiled. "Oh, Paul!" she said.

I found myself just staring at them.

Rob cleared his throat and I looked at him.

"This calls for celebration," he said. "Shall we open another bottle of wine?"

Paul's eyes lit up. "Oh, that would be very nice," he said. "Your mother is driving us home."

"Not for me. But thank you," Ma said looking directly at me.

"You must come for tea some time," Paul said.

"Yes, that would be nice," I said and started clearing the table.

After they'd left and Rob and I were alone, I said, "Do you know? That was spooky! It just brought back a picture in my memory of Dad – my step father – asking us all how we felt about him marrying Mother. And she stood there saying, "Oh, Charlie." And look what happened after that. Maybe this one will be better. She's known him since she was a teenager after all. Third time lucky!"

"Well, you're my third wife and I think I'm very lucky," Rob said giving me a hug.

Part Five

In 2007 we moved far away from my family to start our new life in Yorkshire.

For Rob it was like a coming home. For me it was the realisation of a dream, proof that we can do whatever we want if we want it enough. I'd moved on at last.

I got to run on the beach every morning watching the sunrise over the sea. We explored all the bays along the North Yorkshire coastline and the Moors with our Ordnance Survey maps. I worked from home during the day and wrote stories in the evening. It was my perfect life.

"But you'll be so far away from us all," my sister Melanie said as I told her that our house sale and purchase were about to complete.

"So," I said. "You never come to see us now. What difference will it make?"

Mother rang me from time to time but she was often abroad now.

Paul loved to travel in Europe and they went for long motoring holidays throughout Italy and France. At Christmas time he took her away to spend the holiday period with aged relatives in Sussex. Ma seemed hardly to be at home to have a chat over the phone but it sounded like she was living a comfortable lifestyle with opportunities she'd never had in her whole adult life which I knew had been devoted to the struggle of looking after her girls and then Kim and Kim's children. So I was pleased for her.

Exactly one year after we moved to Yorkshire, Rob found out about a special classic car event that was happening in our old home town in Cambridgeshire. We decided to go back South and make a weekend of it. I mentioned our plans to my sister Melanie who suggested we should have a family get together while Rob and I were in the area. Ma was away that weekend though. And Carol was in France and not able to get to England at such short notice.

And so it was, for the first time in years, Kim, Louise, Melanie and I met to have dinner together. Rob was also there as the token male.

Of course we argued and bickered about the food and any other thing. It was as if all the adult years peeled back and we were sitting at the tea table again in our old house in the Fens.

Finally, Kim interrupted the arguing to say, "By the way, I have some news. I'm getting married. I thought I should tell you." She said, staring pointedly at me because of course I hadn't told any of them about my wedding.

"We'll come," I said at once.

"Yes, I'll come," Louise said. "I'll come," Melanie said.

"No children," Kim said, "except my own. There are only twenty-five places so no kids allowed."

"I won't come then," Melanie said, "if my three can't come."

And so the bickering resumed.

***

Rob and I drove down to Kim's wedding.

She wore a beautiful blue satin dress and looked gorgeous. She was 49 years old.

I couldn't help myself and tears dripped from my eyes as I watched her being married. She looked up at me, saw the tears and did a double take, frowning.

Her new husband, Steve, had apparently been an on/off lover ever since her divorce from Christos. They'd split up because he was very controlling and possessive just as Christos had been, just as our stepfather had been and just as our father had been.

Afterwards, as we sat around in her garden, drinking Champagne and laughing, I asked her quietly, "So what changed? Why did you marry him when you kicked him out before?"

"Isn't that what you did with Rob?" she asked. "I heard you split up and then went and got married."

"What do you mean?" I asked. "You mean we're all repeating each other's stories?"

She just looked at me with her beautiful grey eyes. Two years later she would be divorced again. Six years later she would be dead.

***

Our new house was very old and had lots of rooms. I had bought it because it reminded me of my childhood home in the Fens. This time, though, there were just two of us. Rob could be upstairs and I'd be in the kitchen and we couldn't hear each other if one of us called out.

Sometimes I'd be at the kitchen sink and feel Mother behind me. I would stand there recalling when I was a little girl and Mother would be at the sink. I was only small and would gently squeeze in between her arms and put my hands with hers in the hot soapy water. I remembered how safe I felt there with her arms around me.

One time I felt Mother gently touch me between my shoulder blades. I spun round but of course she wasn't really there.

She rang one day and asked if she and Paul could come and visit.

"Of course!" I said. "We'd love you to."

I cleaned the house from top to bottom. I made up their bed. I planned a walking route to show off our beautiful town. I planned our meals and bought the ingredients. They were due to arrive for lunch. They turned up at 4pm.

I rang Ma on her mobile. "Where are you?"

"We're just crossing the bridge," she said.

"The bridge? What bridge?"

"The Humber. Paul wanted to come the scenic route and then we stopped off for lunch and then had a snooze in the car… He likes to have a midday nap."

"You were supposed to be here for lunch," I snapped.

"I know but Paul doesn't like getting up early. And – uh – well, he wants to stop off and… then he was tired and..." she tailed off awkwardly.

"You're still two hours away," I said. "Don't you want to see us?"

"Don't be like that, darling," she said. "Paul likes things done his way and that's that."

When they finally arrived, I could see that Ma was really tired.

"I'll make you a cup of tea," I said. "Plus we have Yorkshire tea loaf I bought especially for you."

She ate it ravenously.

"Let me show you the house. And you can see what Rob has been up to."

I took them both around each room pointing out all the work that Rob had done to repair, restore and improve our home.

"It feels just like the very first house we bought, do you remember?" Ma said and squeezed my hand.

"Without the beatings," I said.

I could tell she loved the house just as I did. We ended up back in the kitchen. Rob and Paul were down in the cellar.

"Come here," Ma said. And we hugged, a wonderful, wordless long hug.

"I love this place, darling," she finally said. "I'm so proud of you." She was quiet. Then she said, "I'm so sorry I've treated you so shabbily. Please forgive me. I love you, I've always loved you, you were such a funny little thing, so shy but so clever."

With my chin resting on her shoulder, I let tears roll out

of my eyes down my cheeks. And we hugged like that for ages while we listened to our men chatting in the cellar and our breath going in and out.

Finally, I said, "I love you Ma. I've always loved you. And I forgave you years ago. Please forgive me too."

She took my face in her hands and smiled into my eyes, just as you would if you loved someone. "There's never been anything to forgive. I'm your mum," she said.

***

I had a call out of the blue from Lizzy, my aunt and my mum's twin sister. She and her husband Tommy were coming up to North Yorkshire for a week and could they stay with us on their last night? Of course! I loved having people visit us and was tremendously excited that Lizzy and Tommy wanted to come.

It had been glorious warm blue sky weather the whole week of their holiday. But as so happens after a hot day at the seaside, the day they were due to arrive dawned with thick fog. It wasn't just a thin 'sea fret' hanging around the beach, but the whole town was cloaked in a dense fog. We wouldn't be able to show off our beautiful town to my aunt and uncle.

They arrived at lunch time and we showed them quickly around our house before sitting down to lunch. We ended up sitting there for the rest of the day.

I had never had a proper conversation with Mother's twin sister beyond a perfunctory chat at family parties (which she rarely attended). And because Mother and she had not spoken to each other for years while I was growing up, we had hardly ever seen her.

I knew very little about either Lizzy or Tommy except what Ma had told us. But I liked them very much. They seemed not to care what people thought. Lizzy was outspoken and swore (I had never heard Mother swear). She wore jeans (Mother had never owned a pair of jeans) and tied her hair back in a scarf. She didn't look anything like Mother, her twin: she was much taller and had completely different facial features.

It had been said that I took after Lizzy but I didn't think so. We both had brown eyes which no-one else in our family had, but that was about it. I guess because I didn't look like anyone else in my family, and neither did Lizzy from her generation, it was easy to conclude then that we were similar misfits that stood out, she unapologetically so, and I who had a feeling of separateness but was desperate to belong.

They told me the story of how they'd met at Cambridge Horticultural College in the 1960s.

Tommy was still a handsome man. He was short and broad shouldered with thinning hair swept back, and deeply tanned from his life outside. He had a lovely wide smile.

Lizzy had been briefly married to a man called Stephen who was a friend of David, my father. Stephen had introduced Mother to David when ma was eighteen.

Lizzy had also quickly become pregnant. "Sex and birth control were NOT discussed when I was a girl,"

Lizzy said. “We just went like lambs to the slaughter. Your mother chose to keep Kim which I’m delighted she did. But I never wanted brats so I got rid of mine.”

“Wow!” I said, impressed that she’d pulled that off in those days. I didn’t ask for details though.

“I very quickly realised Stephen was no good – not like your mother with David – so I left him. Then I met Tommy at College. We both loved the same things and we had a dream of owning a smallholding with lots of animals, growing our own food, that sort of thing.

“We found this wonderful cottage with all this land next to a disused airfield and bought it immediately. “After Mummy died, Daddy and I went to visit you all at your cottage on the country estate. Of course, I told her about the house and the next thing was that she asked if she could come and live with us with all of you because she needed to leave David.

“I couldn’t say no. I knew something about the way he treated you all. And then, there you all were on our doorstep. It was literally the first week Tommy and I moved into our new place together. We were young and in love. Neither of us could abide brats and so you can imagine it was not a happy time.”

Lizzy showed us a scar around her throat which I had never noticed.

“I was seriously stressed and developed very bad complications with my thyroid. In the end they did an emergency operation and whipped it all out.”

I stared at the scar, thinking about the spiritualist,

Louise Hay on her interpretation of thyroid issues that went hand in hand with my own childhood history of tonsillitis. It looked like she'd had her throat cut; I guess she had. It reminded me also of the Bell's Palsy Ma developed when Kim and her kids landed on her.

"Tommy completely lost it," Lizzy continued, "and said it was him or Evelyn. It was a terrible situation to be in so Tommy disappeared and went to travel around Spain. He said he'd come back when you all left. Finally Evelyn found a place and you all disappeared and Tommy came home again."

"Like the song," I said.

Lizzy stared at me.

"Ah!" Tommy got it, "When Johnny comes marching home! Right! The American Civil War song." He laughed. "It was a civil war I guess."

"Is that why you and Mother didn't speak all those years?" I asked.

Lizzy looked puzzled. "Don't you know?"

"Know what?"

"We didn't fall out about you all coming to the house," Lizzy said. "It was a tough time but once you were all gone, we were fine again. We used to speak on the phone a lot. Your mother kept lots of animals just like we did and was always ringing for advice. She gave them all to us when you moved to a smaller garden."

"I asked Mother why you two didn't speak and she said she couldn't remember," I said. "She said it was probably something really stupid."

“Evelyn tells lies,” Lizzy said. “That was the reason. I’d had enough of it especially since we’d done so much to help her leave David.

“Jim came to see us to tell us that Evelyn was having an affair. He was distraught. So I asked Evelyn. I said, Jim says you’re having an affair. Are you? She denied it. And the next thing we hear is that she’s chucked Jim out and moved Charlie in. So I called her out. And I told her I would never help her again.”

“Did she say why she’d chucked Jim out?” I asked. It was on the tip of my tongue to tell Lizzy that Jim was a paedophile, but I thought of the entire can of worms that would open and decided to keep quiet. She didn’t need to know now.

“That’s why none of us went to Evelyn’s wedding to Charlie. Because she lied after everything we’d all done to help her and get her away from David. Jim was a good man and really cared about you all, a lot. It was obvious.”

“Evelyn never told you the reason we didn’t speak all those years because she was probably ashamed. She’s always used people. But we get on fine now, In fact, she and Paul are coming to visit us in the Summer,” she said.

“But your mother tells lies and I know that is true!”

“Wow! I never knew that story.” I thought for a moment. She used people to help protect us, she’d thought. She’d do anything to try to protect us, and never told anyone. “Kim uses people like that too. That’s why she and I don’t speak,” I said.

“Ah, Kim’s a wonderful girl!” Tommy said. “Such fun,

so amusing."

That's the side she wants you to see, I thought to myself. Inside I was wondering about Ma's lies. Had she lied to me with all those stories she'd shared?

***

Whenever Ma rang I always asked when she was coming to stay with us next. She made excuses. It seemed Paul kept them busy most weekends and there was no time available to come up.

Finally, though, she asked if they could visit. They'd be up on Friday afternoon and could they stay until Monday and leave after breakfast?

I booked theatre tickets for Friday evening.

They arrived late because Paul had left late. He didn't seem very happy. He asked if he could have a snooze before dinner. "OK, but just forty minutes," I said. "We need to leave time to eat and time to walk to the theatre."

We chatted with Ma while Paul slept.

She told us how Paul hadn't wanted to come. "After all we've been through, he doesn't like any of my girls," she said, "and always finds reasons not to let me spend time with any of you. I'm sorry darling."

"Can you get him up?" I asked. "We need to eat something. You must be starving."

We got to the theatre literally five minutes before the performance started.

Rob dug his elbow in my side as we sat and watched the play. It was hilarious and there was a lot of guffawing going on in the audience. Paul was fast asleep with his chin on his chest.

"Did you enjoy the play?" I asked Paul. He'd woken up just as we all started clapping as the cast made their bows.

"I think I fell asleep," he said.

We went to the pub on the way home and he perked up a bit. He and Rob got talking about motorsport while Ma and I had our own conversation.

"Are you OK?" I asked her.

"I'm not feeling all that clever actually," She said. "And he's being really horrible to me."

"Shall we get you home?" Paul leaned over and patted Ma's hand interrupting us.

The next morning Ma came downstairs to join us at the breakfast table.

"What would you like for breakfast?" I asked her.

"I'd better wait for Paul." She said.

"Coffee? Tea?" I asked.

"No darling. I'd better wait," she said. "We have this everyday at home. He just will not get up. He'd lie in bed all day if I wasn't there. He'll never get out of bed before nine."

He finally appeared and sat down.

"I'll make you some toast," I said and pushed the bread down into the toaster.

I poured orange juice and made mugs of tea and sat down again. After a while, as we carried on chatting, Paul loaded his knife with butter.

"Oh!" he said, looking at his empty plate. "No toast!"

"Sorry Paul," I laughed. "I forgot it!" I fished the toast out of the toaster and passed it to him. I caught Rob's eye and we both laughed.

We drove to a nearby bay and walked for a bit on the beach. It was a beautiful hot sunny day. But Ma was struggling a bit and said she didn't feel well. This was not like her at all.

"Let's go home and have some lunch on the way," I suggested.

"Would you like a snooze?" I asked Ma when we got home.

"I think I would actually," she said looking a little relieved. I was a bit worried. This wasn't like her at all.

Paul piped up, "I think I'll join you," he said and they both disappeared upstairs to bed.

"I cannot believe that man," I said to Rob as we sat in the garden. "I've waited my whole life to meet him like he's some sort of superstar and all he does is sleep! I don't know why he agreed to come. He clearly doesn't want to be here. I don't know why she puts up with him."

"It's the way she is," Rob observed. "I sort of think she likes being a servant."

"I don't so. I think it's a pattern she does, but she's not happy with him, I know."

We sat in the sun, waiting for our guests to reappear. It was 6 o'clock when they did and Paul announced that they really needed to be getting home.

I didn't argue. I was glad in a way.

It was the last time they came to visit us.

Part Six

Mother rang me to tell me she had cancer.

"Right," she said. "I have something to tell you." I sat down immediately, feeling a huge cloud of foreboding filling my chest. I think she'd been rehearsing her speech, she was so matter-of-fact and determined to give it to me straight.

"I have cancer."

Silence.

"How do you know?" I finally said.

"Because I've had the blood tests and a scan."

"Why did you have the blood tests and the scan?" I asked.

"I wasn't feeling well. You know that. I was terribly constipated which is not normal. I remembered Mummy with her constipation and how she was too embarrassed to tell anyone and it turned out to be terminal cancer. So I went to my GP except he wasn't there. Thank goodness because he's useless. There was a locum, a lovely lady who I felt completely at ease with and able to talk to. She sent me off for blood tests and they showed I was terribly anaemic as usual and unusually high CA 125. It's ovarian cancer."

"Oh Ma," I said. "Can they do anything?"

"I'm to have some chemotherapy," Ma said. "And then I'll have a hysterectomy." She sounded completely emotionless.

"Oh Ma!" I said. We were silent.

"Has it spread?" I asked at last. "How long have you had it?"

"It hasn't spread," she said. I knew she was lying.

I dropped everything, told my boss I needed to take some days off to go and visit my mum and drove down to see her.

Paul was quite pleasant. "I'll leave you girls together," he said, put his hat on and went out for a walk.

Ma and I hugged, a long silent hug. I could feel her heart beating. It seemed impossible that she could be ill.

"Are you in pain?" I asked.

"No, not at all. It seems so ridiculous that I'm ill. Really, I feel absolutely fine. I can't really believe this is happening."

The door opened. Kim walked in.

"Hi Bessie," she said breezily as if it hadn't been four years since we'd seen each other last. "I thought that must be your car." Her house was directly across the road from Mother's house and they always knew each other's comings and goings.

Mother disappeared to the loo.

Kim said, "Don't let her make you think it's not serious. It's everywhere – in her pancreas, her liver. Of course, Paul is in complete Catholic denial. He won't accept there's anything wrong and refuses to let her talk about it. He's a fucking useless bastard I tell you. He hates me you know. After me living with him all those years and being his star pupil, now he hates me. Because

I tell him the truth. I don't care! Mummy comes out to meet me in the road outside after dark to tell me what he's been up to. She doesn't feel able to tell him how she feels to his face. So she tells me. D'you know what? They've offered her high powered chemo but she's decided only to have a single shot so that he's not inconvenienced!"

When she finally paused for breath, I said, "Are you sure that's why? Maybe she doesn't want her hair to fall out. Isn't that what happens when you have chemo?" I said. An image of Mother's granny came to mind sitting in her black nightie gravely warning Mother to save her hair.

Kim babbled on.

I was trying to process what she was saying when Ma came back into the room.

"What are you two talking about?" she laughed. "I could feel my ears burning!"

"I was only telling Bessie what she needs to know," Kim said. "Would you like a cup of tea?"

We were sitting drinking tea when Paul's face suddenly appeared at the window.

"I'd better go," Kim said "or he'll only have a go at you," she told Ma. "I'll call you later. Bye Bessie." She pecked my cheek and was gone. Like a whirlwind.

"Will you stay for lunch?" Ma said. "I can offer you some soup and a sandwich."

"That would be lovely," I said. "Let me help."

"No, no, you sit and talk with Paul. I'll make it," she said and went off to the kitchen.

"Your mother will be fine," Paul said cheerfully. "I've never known a more determined woman. And she has you five girls to keep her going."

***

Mother had her hysterectomy operation. Paul rang us. He sounded so excited.

"I've just come from your mother," he said. "She told me I needed to ring you all and you are first on my list. The operation was a complete success. The surgeon is delighted. It's all out," he told me. "I'm skipping with delight."

"Ah, that's amazing. Thank you so much for letting us know, Paul." I felt so happy.

"Let's go for a drink," I told Rob and we went out to our local. We raised a glass to Mother and I said, "Thank you God!"

***

Six months later, I had a phone call from Mother.

"It's bad news," she said. "It's Kim. She has cancer. And it's terminal."

"What?!" I couldn't believe what she'd said.

"You'd better ring her," Ma said.

"I cannot believe this," I said. "Does she have to copy absolutely every fucking thing in your life?"

"Don't swear!" Mother said.

"I'm sorry. I'm in shock. I'll call her," and put the phone down.

I hadn't really had a proper conversation with my eldest sister for longer than I could remember, certainly since I blamed her for having to leave Mother's house back in 1994. So it had been at least twenty years since I'd spoken with her in any meaningful way.

I rang her. She didn't actually recognise my voice at first. She thought I was Carol.

"No, it's Bessie," I said.

"No, it's not. She wouldn't ring me."

"It is. I've heard you're ill. What is it?"

So she gave me a blow by blow account of how she'd seen blood in her poo while using a portaloo on a day out at Sandringham. She'd reported it to her GP who'd referred her to the hospital. They hadn't hung about. She told me how the young registrar had broken down in tears to tell her she had cancer of the colon which had spread to her liver. She told me how she had called her kids in to the consultation room and ordered him to tell them the facts so that she wouldn't have to and how they'd all huddled together weeping.

My sister loved to tell a story. I didn't know how much of this was embellished but it was tough news all the same. They'd sent her to Addenbrookes in Cambridge where they had a specialist department. They said they could remove the cancer from her liver and the liver would regenerate. But then the scan images came back.

"It was like your polka dot bikini, Bessie," she said. "All these black dots on both sides. They said it's too far gone. They can't operate. They predict I have six months to live. Can you imagine? I've been in a really bad place."

The tears were silently streaming down my cheeks as she told me the story. She was her old breathy excited self but I knew from old that it was the front she showed everyone. Maybe it was the only way she knew to be now, she'd performed for so many years.

***

I felt completely helpless, being so far away from Mother and my sister, And I knew only what they were prepared to tell me.

Mother's CA 125 levels were up again. And now both she and Kim were having chemotherapy together in the same chemo centre. Paul insisted on accompanying Ma and Ma went with Kim.

Kim resisted every chemo session she had. She was on a very intensive six month course apparently to give her time to get her affairs in order. Each session Mother described reminded me of our childhood visits to the dentist when I'd imagined Kim jamming herself into the doorway and Mother having to prise her fingers away from the door frame. It sounded terrifying and the side effects even more so.

Mother's life saving hair came off in one go.

My sister Louise rang me and told me how she was helping Mother to plait her hair one evening and the entire plait fell off her head, leaving just straggly bits of hair clinging to her scalp.

"Oh my God!" I said, remembering the old crone's

words. I felt sick.

"What did Ma say?"

"Nothing. Well, she said 'That's that then' I think." Louise laughed nervously.

I felt quite guilty for feeling so healthy but decided to do something with my health.

"I've decided to run a marathon," I announced.

Everyone was amazed. I'd always declared that I would never run a marathon despite my regular jogs

I wasn't actually intending to run a whole marathon now but a marathon in two halves. And I would do it for charity. I asked Mother and Kim to choose a charity I should run for. They came up with Macmillan Cancer Support.

And so I began my training. I set my goals high. What if we could raise £2,000?

I booked myself onto the half marathon race that was taking place at a place not far from where Mother and Kim lived so they'd be able to come and watch me cross the finish line. Then three weeks later I was booked onto the Great Scottish Run in Glasgow.

I began my training and I started the fundraising. Kim rang me.

"I'd like you and I to have a weekend away," she announced.

I'd been thinking the same thing. It felt like we had so much to catch up on and explain to each other.

"What do you like doing?" she asked.

"How about a spa retreat?" I said.

"Leave it with me," she said.

She booked us a weekend spa retreat at a lovely spa hotel in Sheffield. She would get the train and I would meet her in my car and drive us to our spa hotel.

It had only been a few weeks since I saw her last but the change in her health was horrible. She'd completed her six months of chemotherapy and had the catheter removed from her collar bone area.

"I can go swimming now," she smiled. "I couldn't get wet before."

But she didn't feel like it. She insisted I go in the pool. While I splashed quietly around she sat in a chair by the side and dozed.

"Are you in pain?" I asked that evening.

"A bit," she said.

"Don't they give you anything?" I said. "You're not supposed to suffer. You don't have to suffer these days. There's morphine."

"Really?" she didn't seem to know.

After dinner which she didn't eat, we went to our room and started to talk.

"Why didn't we talk all these years?" she asked. She genuinely didn't seem to know.

I told her about how her return to England had meant that I'd had to move out from Ma's house, how I couldn't live with Rob at that time and had moved to a bedsit in London where I'd nearly had a mental breakdown.

She told me the story of Christos and how violent and abusive he'd been to her and their kids. She'd taken it on the chin to protect them.

"Don't you see?" I asked, "how you've copied Ma's story?"

"I know, I know" she said. "Don't you think I've worked that out?"

"But why? I asked. "Why would you want that for yourself?

"It's not that I've done it consciously."

"I know. It's some deep-seated programming. Life, eh? It's a mystery how it works."

"I don't know what you think," I said, "but I believe that cancer's caused by repressed feelings. You know, all the stuff we were not allowed to let out: anger, resentment, all that stuff we were never allowed to express.

She nodded. "I do believe that. I'm certain mine came on the year I got married to Steve. I should never have done that – I knew he was a controlling bastard. The Macmillan Centre sent me off for some reflexology to clear out emotional garbage. I cried non-stop for two whole days afterwards. It was awful but a blessing to let go of all that. I told Mummy she should give it a try but you imagine what she said to that."

"I've got something to show you. I thought you might be interested so I brought them with me. But first I'm going to order a glass of wine. Do you want anything to drink?"

"Umm, I fancy a glass of bitter shandy."

I laughed. "That's what Ma drinks when she's out with Paul," I said and rang room service for our drinks.

I handed Kim the pack of letters I'd found years before in Grandfather's desk when I'd first taken possession of it, letters Mother had written to her parents, our grandparents, in 1964 when she had just three baby girls.

I painted my toe nails and sipped my wine while Kim read the letters.

"What a fabulous piece of history," she said finally as she put the last letter back in its ancient envelope.

"I'm so sorry we lost touch with each other," I told her and gently hugged her.

"Oh Darling," she smiled and rubbed her nose into my neck. "It's a long time since we were at Beauties. We had such fun there."

"Will you go there tonight?" I asked smiling, "For old times' sake?"

"Do you know?" she said. "I think I might."

***

The first of my two half marathons was just a month later.

Rob and I had booked overnight accommodation in a pub near to the race. We popped in to see Kim on our way there. She didn't look well at all and would give a little gasp every now and again and clutch her side. She leaned against the door.

"I hope you never have to go through this," she said.

All my family turned up for the race and some old friends too. I was very moved. We had already raised £3,500 and I was determined to run a great time.

Kim was finding it difficult to walk now so they'd

brought a folding chair for her and she positioned herself at the start line which would also be the finish line.

It was a lovely warm day and I was excited and nervous.

I finished the race and was elated.

As I was catching my breath, Kim appeared. She'd clearly summoned all her energy to walk over and threw her arms around me.

"Thank you, thank you," she sobbed into my neck. "I'm so grateful for all that you've done for us."

We stood there hugging wordlessly until other people began jostling in to say well done.

It was Kim's 55th birthday on the day after the race. I rang her and texted but she didn't reply. It turned out she'd fallen over in the night on her way to the loo and had decided to spend her birthday in bed.

She passed away exactly a week later. I had a dream and she whispered into my ear, 'I'm letting go of you now' and I pedalled off on my bicycle.

I read a poem for her at her funeral.

A week later Rob and I took a train up to Glasgow so I could complete the second of my two half marathons. This was the Great Scottish Run.

I imagined Kim cheering me on and gave it all I had. I ran a great race and took four whole minutes off my time in the first race.

When all the fundraising was completed and added up, it turned out we'd raised £4,200 for Macmillan.

NatWest Bank kindly gave me one of those big charity

cheques.

I drove down South to meet Mother and Kim's youngest daughter at the Macmillan Cancer Centre at King's Lynn Hospital. Together, we three generations of women from the same family held the cheque as we posed for the Press photograph.

"You look gorgeous." I said to my niece. Interestingly, she wore the same look of long legs, short skirt and high heels as I had used to flaunt at her age. Where had she picked that up from? Her mother had never dressed like that.

As I drove home again, I imagined a huge family dressing up cupboard with thousands of drawers stretching back over time where each new young member would help themselves to personality traits, characteristics and states of mind that had been placed there by previous generations. The thing was, I mused, if we made our selections unconsciously as children, it would take a lot of effort and self-awareness to identify whichever bits we later found we didn't really want and put them back to start afresh.

***

Following Kim's death. I spoke more frequently with Ma on the phone.

I was very aware that she'd lost her main confidante. Her cancer had returned but I never knew whether she was telling me the whole story. I knew she lied. She always said she was fine. She was certainly always very positive. She would complete a chemotherapy round, bravely enduring the debilitating side effects. There would be a pause where she and Paul would head off for a holiday. Then the results would show a lowering of the cancer levels. There would be another pause. Then more tests. The levels would be up and her oncologist would select a new drug for her to try.

Then the day came when there were no more drugs left for her to try.

She'd tried everything available that her body could withstand. There were some she'd tried where the side effects were immediately so vicious that she'd had to quit straight away.

"You're so brave," I told her.

"No, I'm not," she said. "There's no other way to be, is there?"

"How do you feel?" I asked her.

"I don't feel anything," she said. "Except I can't believe this is happening to me."

"You must miss Kim so much," I said.

"I do," she said. "But I've still got all of you."

"Do you ever see her?"

"What? Like a ghost?" she asked.

"Yes."

She was quiet. Then she said, "I saw her in a dream. It was so vivid. She was wearing a beautiful blue dress with blue satin pumps. And she said, 'I'm so sorry'. That was it."

"The dress she wore when she came back to us," I said,

"or on her wedding day."

***

I drove down to see Mother one weekend in early January. She had just got back from an appointment with her oncologist.

She and I stood at the sink in her kitchen with the window sill filled with huge dark blood red cyclamen.

"Well?" I asked.

"There's nothing left I can take," she said. "So. What now?"

"Nothing." She shrugged. Dr Daley actually gave me a hug which I took to mean bad news. I asked her how long. They're not supposed to say. But she said four months."

We hugged.

"Let's make it six," I said, sniffling.

"None of that," she said, frowning at my tears.

She looked out of the window. "There's so much to do in the garden. Lots of tidying up I need to get on with."

"How's Paul been?" I asked.

"Oh, you know, useless," she said. "He won't accept the verdict but he'll have to, sooner or later."

After that, I made the 300 mile round journey practically every weekend to visit Mother, either just for a few hours or I stayed overnight, sleeping in my sister's old house across the road which was now owned by my niece.

One weekend I was there with my sisters Louise and Melanie. Paul went out for a walk.

“I need to talk to you all,” Mother said. “This here,” she poked a folder on the floor under the table with her foot. “Can you pick that up?” She flicked through it. “This,” she said, pointing to a form which read DNR across the top. “If anything happens, I DO NOT want...” she tailed off, unable to say the words.

“Now I have a prescription that needs collecting. Will one of you collect it please?” she asked.

“We’ll all go,” we said.

When we handed over the prescription, the Pharmacist lent near to us and said gently, “Who is this for?”

“Our mum,” we said.

“It’s end of life care,” he said and handed us over an enormous bag. We walked back to Mother’s house in silence, each with our own thoughts.

***

Each time I saw her she was more and more frail and less and less able to do anything.

One day in March I arrived after 10 o’clock and she’d only just got up. Paul had actually laid out the breakfast things for the first time.

Mother sat and poured herself a bowl of Rice Krispies.

She sat looking at her hands.

“I can’t,” she said. “I’m going to sit on the sofa.” And so she and I sat there holding hands.

Occasionally we’d speak, reminisce, make a joke, laugh.

“I wonder how much time I have left,” she said. I was

quiet.

Then she said, "Would you speak at my funeral, Darling?"

"Oh Ma," I said. "Of course. I'd be honoured."

They had a lot of clocks throughout the house. We listened to them chiming at their different times. Mother had copied Grandfather who had deliberately set each of his many clocks a minute or so apart so the house was full of different chimes for five minutes at a time.

"Do we have to copy what our parents do?" I asked.

"I think we get to choose," she replied.

"Really?" I wasn't so sure.

"Everything's a choice," she smiled and squeezed my hand.

"I've left you the grandfather clock," she said. "I hope you want it. Then you can get to choose whether you match it up with other clocks or deliberately set them to chime out of sync. Which will you do?"

I thought for a bit.

"I'd better keep the family tradition," I said, "and copy you and Grandfather."

"When I was a girl," she said after a while, "Daddy used to go round the house every Sunday evening sorting out all the clocks. I used to hide under his desk."

"Wow! That's the desk in my study at home," I said. "I can't believe you were so small you could hide under that."

***

I was away for work at a three day conference in Telford, staying at a hotel. From there I planned to go and pop in to see Mother.

On my arrival on the first evening, I bought a bunch of daffodil buds to brighten my hotel room. I put them in a glass of water.

The next evening, after the day's conference, I sat in my room writing up notes. It was completely quiet as I scribbled away.

And then I heard a soft crack. I spun round in my chair to see that one of the daffodil buds had opened while I'd been writing. Amazing! I thought. I'd actually heard a daffodil bud opening! I immediately wanted to share that experience with Mother.

My phone rang. It was my sister Melanie. Ma had been taken to the Macmillan Centre. She'd fallen out of bed. They'd decided she couldn't stay at home. Paul wasn't physically able to look after her. A bed was ready for her.

"I'll be there tomorrow," I said. "I'll leave the conference at the morning break."

I got to the Centre at 5.30, having stopped off to buy Mother a bunch of daffodil buds.

"You look much better," I told her. She smiled.

"It's because I'm where I'm meant to be," she said. "No more resisting." I took her hand.

I told her the story of the daffodil buds which delighted her.

"Do you remember?" she said. "Well, you won't remember of course. The vicar brought me daffodils on the day that you were born. It was Mother's Day."

"I do remember," I said, "because you told me."

And then we sat together until the nurses chucked me out at 8.30.

"I'll be back tomorrow morning," I said and kissed her goodnight.

In the morning I saw I'd had a text message from her in the early hours: 'I waited and listened,' the text read, 'then POP! It opened.' There was a photo attached of the opened daffodil bud.

I went to sit with her again. I saw she was wearing a fresh nightie. She hadn't had a good night. She'd been sick, she said.

She began to cough a bit as we sat together chatting occasionally.

"Don't listen to me. I'm just talking nonsense," she said.

"No. 'Nonsense' is Edward Lear. 'The Owl and the Pussycat'."

She began to sing the nursery rhyme word perfect.

"I love you, Ma," I said.

"I love you too," she said.

Then she said, "Can I ask you? Will you have good memories of me?"

Tears splashed down my nose. "Of course, Ma" I said and bent my forehead to her hand.

Other people started to arrive: Paul, my sisters, nieces and nephews.

Her coughing got worse and worse as we sat with her.

Until suddenly, violently, she fell forward and began vomiting.

The nurses came rushing with hospital top hat bowls. She filled bowl after bowl, eight bowls. It was black blood.

I stood beside her in shock as the nurses helped her.

She was growling like a tiger. And then silent. She was gone.

Later, as I was driving home I tried to make sense of what we'd witnessed. Ma had had a catastrophic bleed that it turned out the medical team had anticipated due to signs they'd noticed (which she'd kept quiet about). Such a bleed is not uncommon in cancer patients.

But it suddenly came to me that the bleed was Mother metaphorically vomiting up all of the years of bottled up anger and shame and resentment, all the unspoken rage that she'd not felt able to express during her life due to her early upbringing.

Then, once she'd purged herself, she was ready to go.

I felt so proud of her and filled with love.

Epilogue

Mother had a huge wardrobe she'd taken from house to house. It ended up in the house she shared with Paul. It had an enormous drawer at the bottom where she'd saved all the memorabilia from our very early childhoods – school reports, cards we'd each made for her, school exercise books, old letters, memories of our camping holidays and so on.

After she passed away, I emptied the contents of the drawer and took them home to look through.

Among the contents was a paper bag neatly folded over.

When I looked inside, I found her plaited hair. She'd saved it after it had fallen out. The strangest thing was that it was dark brown – not silver as it had been when it fell out – with a distinctive band of gold.

THE END